D1071084

Dear Reader,

I have very much enjoyed writing this segment featuring another side of Aunt Edie. I'm a huge movie buff and had a grand time researching movies from Edie's time. I'm so glad you've joined us in getting to know Anne and her family, as well as Blue Hill.

Much like Ben and Ryan, I had a childhood "fort" where I could sneak off to read and write in my diary. Because I had such wonderful memories of my own special place, I was thrilled to take part in helping the boys build a place of their own.

I hope you enjoy reading about Anne's latest adventures...and learning about Aunt Edie's secret past...as much as I enjoyed writing about them!

Blessings,

Robin Caroll

writing as Emily Thomas

Secrets of the Blue Hill Library

Nowhere to Be Found
Shadows of the Past
Unlocking the Truth
Theft and Thanksgiving
The Christmas Key
Off the Shelf
Gone in a Flash
All Sewn Up
If Walls Could Talk
The Rightful Owner
Cracking the Code
The Valentine Visitor
Without a Trace
Stagestruck
All that Glitters
Lights! Camera! Action!

Lights! Camera! Action!

Secrets of the
BLUE HILL LIBRARY

EMILY THOMAS

Guideposts

New York

Lights! Camera! Action!

CHAPTER ONE

G race Hawkins, if you don't hurry up, I'm going to dinner
without you." But Anne Gibson smiled at her friend as she
pushed her glasses back up the bridge of her nose. She and Grace
had been planning their night out for several days, and Anne was
happy Saturday had finally come.

"I'm hurrying. I just need to send Wendy an e-mail to confirm
the placement for the Winter Wonderland ad in the paper." Grace,
editor of the *Blue Hill Gazette*, shot Anne a mischievous grin. "You
know Wendy will be all over me if I don't."

"True," Anne said with a nod. Anne loved her friend, Wendy
Pyle, but understood all too well what Grace meant. Wendy was
always taking charge and heading up something or other in
Blue Hill. How she found the time to be such a good wife to her
coach-husband while raising their seven children, not to mention
being such a voracious reader, Anne would never know. Somehow,
Wendy did it all and made it look easy. Anne was always a little in
awe of her, to be honest.

Tonight, Anne was extremely grateful to Wendy, who had
graciously agreed to watch Anne's kids so she could have a
grown-up dinner alone with Grace.

A siren wailed outside on Main Street. Grace and Anne
both froze and turned to look out the window, as if that would

bring about immediate understanding. After all, Blue Hill, Pennsylvania, was a tight-knit town.

"Turn up the scanner, please," Grace said as she moved from behind her desk.

Anne leaned and turned the knob on the box in the corner.

"All available law enforcement personnel report to 228 Main to assist the fire department as needed, especially with the theater evacuation." The female's voice booming from the police scanner sent chills down Anne's spine.

"228 Main. Is that the movie theater?" Anne asked Grace.

On her feet, Grace snatched her coat and scarf from the stand in the corner of her office. "Next door, I think. It's definitely over there on the east end of Main."

Anne wasn't sure what was going on, but she grabbed her coat from the back of the chair she'd been sitting on while waiting for Grace.

"By the theater there are some warehouses and a couple of consignment shops." Grace grabbed her notebook and car keys. "I need to cover this for the paper."

"I'm going with you," Anne said, leaving no room for argument.

Grace shrugged. "Suit yourself. Come on." She led the way out of the paper's office. Like some of the other businesses lining Main Street, the *Blue Hill Gazette* was housed in charming Victorian architecture. Less than four steps from the curb, the two-story, red-paint dwelling had a quaint covered porch for the first floor, with the triangular gable just above the front door.

Anne hurried to keep up, barely clicking her seat belt as Grace fired up the engine and slipped her car into gear.

"I can't recall the last big fire in Blue Hill," Grace said as she pulled to the side of the street to let another fire engine pass.

"I've not really heard of any since I moved back," Anne said. Moving back to Blue Hill had been a hard decision but one she was glad she'd made.

Anne had grown up in Blue Hill, playing in the very house she now lived in with her children, Ben and Liddie, and that also served as the town's library, a loving legacy left from her beloved great-aunt Edie.

Her great-aunt Edie had moved into the house in Blue Hill with Edie's parents after they'd sold their family farm. When Anne's great-grandparents grew frail with age, Edie reset her life to stay put in Blue Hill so she could care for her parents. They'd left Edie the house in their will, and Aunt Edie had left it to Anne…with the stipulation that a portion of the house be used as a library for the town of Blue Hill.

Anne had gone to New York City more than a decade and a half ago, following the career path Aunt Edie had encouraged her to take—the career path in library science that had allowed Anne to follow her dream and feed her love of reading. It was there that she'd met Eric, an editor at a big publishing house. That he was a dozen years her senior hadn't stopped Anne from falling in love and marrying the man of her dreams. They'd welcomed two beautiful children into their lives—Ben and Liddie—before a sudden heart attack had claimed Eric's life. That was over three years ago.

Now Anne was back in Blue Hill, following Aunt Edie's bequest to turn her old house into a library. And Anne was perfectly content with her new life.

Well, except for the pangs of romantic loneliness that hit every now and again, but Anne wasn't in a position to even consider romance right now.

Especially not when Grace parked the car behind the police barricade, consisting of an old sawhorse, with two officers helping moviegoers out of harm's way. People were spilling out from the old theater as firefighters moved around them. An ambulance's back doors were open, and EMTs assisted some of the people coming from the theater. Fire hoses littered the ground like angry snakes.

The fire trucks were parked just behind the barricade, their strobing lights casting odd shadows against the winter skyline. Reddish orange flames stole out of second-story windows of a wood building, curling and dancing toward the setting sun.

The burning stench polluted the air as smoke hung heavy down Main Street. Police continued to move people from the theater to safety beyond the barricade.

Anne stared up at the fire devouring the building beside the theater. "What business is that?" she asked Grace as she reached to help an elderly couple around the sawhorses.

"It's one of the empty storefronts, right?" Grace both confirmed and asked the uniformed police officer standing guard behind the sawhorse.

He glanced at Grace, his expression not changing. "You know I can't comment on that, Ms. Hawkins."

Grace let out a loud and heavy sigh. "Come on, it's not like I can't see it for myself and then go look it up at the courthouse." She waved toward the fire hissing as the firefighters shot it with streams of water from their hoses.

The moviegoers crowded around the barricade, their gazes fixed on the fire. Anne couldn't help but wonder if they stared grateful they had escaped the fiery monster claiming at least one building.

"Theater is all clear, Chief," one of the firefighters hollered.

The police officer moved the sawhorses closer together and flashed a weak smile at Grace. "The building on fire isn't an active business but is a warehouse. Storage. No one was inside, and it seems everyone's been evacuated out of the theater," he said.

"It's spreading! Hit the top of the theater with a couple of streams," one of the firefighters yelled out.

Anne's hand absentmindedly covered her mouth as she widened her eyes at the horror unfolding in front of her. As if the fire were bending and spreading its arms, it covered the roof of the movie theater, smothering the worn slate roof in its flickering flames. The water shot from the hoses and sizzled against the hungry fire but wasn't enough to stop the blaze from engulfing the roof of the theater.

On many occasions, she and the kids had enjoyed a weekend matinee at the theater. They'd laughed together, cried together, and gone on amazing journeys into the magic of movies as a family. Would that all be over now?

Grace, too, sucked in air and took a step backward, staring up at the flames. Firefighters continued to battle against the spreading fire, but their efforts seemed to be in vain.

The early evening breeze changed direction, blowing over the rolling hills lining the little town. The wind seemed to pick up speed as it rushed down Blue Hill, named so because of the fields of bluebells surrounding it during late spring. But not this time of year. The trees standing guard around the library perched atop

Blue Hill resembled gnarled old men with their bare limbs spread like arms opened to the heavens.

People filled the street, evacuated moviegoers who couldn't get to their automobiles to leave. Cars parked haphazardly along the curbs on both sides of the street by people who'd followed the fire trucks, police cars, or ambulances, their headlamps splitting the night almost as eerily as the yellow glow from the fire. The flashing lights from the fire trucks still spun against the darkness. So many people. So much action. Confusion and chaos seemed to descend upon the east end of town.

"We've got to stop this fire from spreading!" one of the firefighters hollered.

"More water. We need to douse it more!" another one yelled back.

Anne stood rooted to the curb. She gripped Grace's arm and silently prayed.

More police cruisers with sirens screeching shuddered to a stop alongside the barricade. Uniformed officers spread out along the street and side streets, their mere presence somewhat calming the crowd.

"What can we do to help?" a man behind Anne and Grace asked one of the officers.

"Just stay back. Stay out of the way."

Everyone seemed entranced as the firefighters continued to work. Many of the onlookers in the street pulled scarves over their nose and mouth. Anne's throat burned, but she couldn't make herself move. Apparently, neither could Grace, who held her notebook and pen tightly. Anne could see Grace's scrawling script all over the page.

"I think the offshoots are contained. Let's get the main out for good," the fire chief yelled to a group of his crew.

Sure enough, the theater's fire seemed to have been put out. On the remains of the warehouse, the flames were tamer. Not as bright. Not as high. Only a few licked outside the barrier of what remained of the outer wall.

"They'll have it out soon," Grace said, leaning close to Anne's ear to be heard.

Anne nodded as a car whipped up as close to the barricade as possible without hitting all the people filling the street. A middle-aged man flung open the driver's door and stumbled out. His thinning gray hair stuck out in tufts as he headed straight for the barricade, not even taking the time to close his car door.

"I'm sorry, sir," the uniformed policeman began, "you'll have to stay behind the line."

"Let me pass." The man charged onward.

The officer grabbed his arm. "Sir, I'm afraid you'll have to remain on the other side of the barricade."

"But that's my theater." The man twisted away from the policeman's grasp and rushed past the sawhorse. "I have to get to my theater."

One of the other officers stepped in the man's path and stopped him. "Sir, you have to wait here. The theater's been totally evacuated. You need to let the firefighters do their job."

"But that's my theater." The man's voice was so desolate, it nearly broke Anne's heart. She moved closer to him, as if her proximity could offer this stranger some comfort, which was just silly, but that's how she felt.

Grace moved closer to the man. "Mr. Rollings?"

The man turned, facing her. "Yes?"

"I'm Grace Hawkins with the *Gazette*, remember? I met you at the theater's fund-raiser a couple of years ago," she said, moving even closer. Grace nodded in the direction of the theater. "I'm so sorry, but I think they put out the fire that reached your theater."

"I hope so." Mr. Rollings faced the fire again. The light sources threw illumination on his concerned expression.

"I think the fire started in the building next door," Grace said, stepping alongside the theater owner.

Instinctively, Anne moved on his other side.

He glanced back at the fire, which was now growing dimmer. Firefighters had moved closer, their hoses blasting streams of water into the warehouse at varying angles. "It would appear so, I guess."

"Do you know that storefront? What it is? A warehouse now? Who owns it?" Grace asked.

He nodded. "That's Marcus Kombs's place."

Grace wrote on her notebook. "What does he use the building for?"

Mr. Rollings shrugged, but his focus stayed clearly on his property. "Storage, I guess. He used to run a video and game-room place and used part of the building for storage, but the store went out of business years ago and he just kept it as a warehouse."

Anne stared at the building as Grace wrote. The firefighters moved about, and several of the hoses had already been cut off. No more flames were visible.

"Sir," the police officer said to Mr. Rollings, "if you'll come this way, the fire chief would like to talk to you." He glanced at Grace before taking the theater owner's arm and walking him past the barricade. "Our investigators would like to ask you a few questions as well."

Grace smiled. "And thus the investigation begins." She pocketed her notebook and smiled at Anne. "Some girls' night out, huh?"

Anne shook her head as they headed back toward Grace's car. They weren't in any hurry as there were so many cars blocking their exit. "I'm glad nobody was hurt. It could've been so much worse."

Smoke still hung low, clogging what was normally clean, crisp Pennsylvania air. People moved toward their vehicles, everyone seeming to talk at once.

The ambulance crawled from behind the barricade, then eased down Main Street.

"Well, its lights aren't on, so that must mean no one is being transported to the hospital. That's a good sign," Anne said to Grace, leaning against the hood of the car.

"I think so." Grace tapped on her smartphone as they waited for the people to get into the cars around them.

"What are you doing?" Anne asked.

"Pulling up an Internet search on Marcus Kombs," Grace answered.

Anne shook her head. Her friend would come up with not only an informative article for the paper on tonight's fire, but would intrigue the skeptical reader as well.

"Hey, Grace," a lady called out as she passed by. "Guess we'll get all the facts in the next edition of the paper, eh?"

"Working on it, Molly," Grace answered.

"Did you hear that the fire chief said he thought the fire might've been set?" a man joining them asked Grace.

Grace pushed off the hood of the car. "The chief said that?"

The man nodded. "Heard him call for the arson investigator."

Grace shot off toward the barricaded area.

Anne rushed to keep up. "Surely that's standard procedure, right?" she asked Grace.

"I don't know. That's what I intend to find out." Grace walked past where the sawhorses once stood.

Several police officers directed cars to Main Street from the theater's parking lot. Grace walked right on past two officers, stepping carefully over hoses and debris. Anne picked her way a bit slower.

"Anne!" a distinct woman's voice rose above the cacophony of voices, the hissing of dying embers, and equipment sounds.

She stopped following Grace and turned toward the voice. "Hi, Yvette." She smiled at the two little girls clutching their mother's hand. "Hi, Cindy. Hi, Becca," she said to Liddie's best friends, planting a wider smile in place so as to not frighten them more than they obviously were, judging by their wide eyes and pale faces.

"I figured you must be here since we saw Ben with Ryan and Coach Pyle's son," Yvette said.

What? Ben wasn't here...he was with... "You say you saw Ben here?" Anne asked, struggling to keep her voice and tone even, though her heart was pounding as if she'd just run a marathon.

Yvette scrunched her eyebrows. "Well, I can't be sure, but I thought it was Ben. With Ryan Slater and Coach Pyle's boy. Christian."

Yes, those three were often together. But they shouldn't have been here. Ben should have been home with Wendy. But since Christian, Wendy's son, was mentioned…it was entirely possible the boys were here.

Anne reached for her cell phone, then remembered it was in her purse back in Grace's car. Suddenly, waves of nausea rolled over her.

One of the uniformed officers, Joselyn "Josie" Bolling stood nearby and clearly overheard their conversation as she approached Yvette and Anne. Josie and Anne had gone to school together, although Josie was a couple of years behind Anne. "Is your son lost, Anne?" she asked. "I know Officer Banks is questioning a few teenagers who weren't in the theater, hoping to find someone who saw something."

Anne shook her head. "Ben isn't a teenager. He's nine. He's only nine."

Yvette laid a hand on Anne's shoulder. "You know, I might be wrong. Maybe it wasn't Ben I saw," she said. "I mean, is he supposed to be here?" The lift in her question was like a knife in Anne's heart.

She wasn't sure where her child was. What kind of mother did that make her?

Josie held up her hand. "Anne, is Ben supposed to be here?"

Anne shook her head. "Wendy is babysitting Ben and Liddie at the library. Wendy Pyle."

"I thought I saw Ben and Ryan with Christian Pyle," Yvette interjected. "Maybe Coach Pyle brought the boys to the movies or something?"

Possible, but Wendy would have said something to Anne. Surely she would have.

"When did you see the boys?" Josie asked Yvette. "And where?"

"Before the fire. I mean, there were no sirens or anything," Yvette said with a shrug. "We'd been at the consignment shop just down there." She pointed at a storefront across the street from the now smoldering remains of the warehouse beside the theater. "We'd just exited and were about to head back to our car in the theater's parking lot — we'd seen an earlier show — and I saw three boys running back in the direction of town." Yvette shook her head. "I could have sworn it was Ben, Ryan, and Christian Pyle, but I could be wrong."

"And this was before the fire?" Josie asked.

Yvette nodded. "But not too long before. I noticed the boys, then started to take the girls across the street, but Becca dropped our bag and spilled some of the costume jewelry we'd bought. We had enough time to pick everything off the sidewalk and stick it back in the bag and start walking toward the parking lot. And that's when the fire alarm sounded in the warehouse, and seconds later the fire truck came."

"So you saw the boys running off just minutes before the fire alarm went off?" Josie asked.

Yvette nodded.

Anne's mouth filled with a metallic taste. She could almost see the thoughts rushing through Josie's mind.

Becca's eyes were really big against her Kewpie face. "I didn't mean to drop my necklaces, but the bag was kinda heavy."

"It's okay, sweetie. If you hadn't, we might have been in the fire truck's way." Yvette hugged her daughters close to her legs. "We better get going. I think the girls have had enough excitement for one day, and it looks like the parking lot has cleared out."

Josie nodded, but Anne still couldn't find her voice. Had Ben been here?

"I'll be praying I was mistaken," Yvette whispered to Anne, then took the girls and headed off down the street.

Grace joined Anne. "Sorry I left you, and I'm even sorrier to tell you I've got to cancel dinner. I need to work up the front-page copy."

Anne nodded, still numb. "I need my cell from your car. I need to call Wendy."

Grace frowned at Anne, looked at Josie, then back at Anne. "What's wrong?"

"Someone thought they saw Ben with two friends running away from here just before the fire broke out," Anne replied.

"Ben?" Grace asked. "But he's at the library. With Wendy."

"Yvette Jacobs thought she saw Ben and Ryan and Christian."

Grace puckered her lips. "Well, I can't imagine why they'd be here, but maybe there's a reason. Did you call Wendy?"

"My cell's in your car."

"Let's go. You can call Wendy on the way," Grace said, already taking long strides, leading the way back to her car.

"T–Thanks," Anne told Josie, then turned and followed Grace. It took her several steps to catch up.

"Do you think Wendy let the boys go out? I mean, it's not like they couldn't go outside and play, right?" Grace asked as she unlocked the car doors by clicking her key remote.

Anne slipped into the front seat and dug around in her purse for her cell phone. "It's a bit of a hike for them to come from Bluebell Lane on foot." Especially when it was already dark out. Ben knew Anne's rules, even if Wendy had said they could go out and play. She quickly dialed her home number.

"I'm sure everything's okay." Grace turned the car around and headed the short distance back to the *Gazette*.

"Yeah." But Anne gripped the phone tighter as the first ring sounded.

Then the second ring.

The third.

Anne's breath caught in her chest. What had happened?

"Hello," Wendy said, almost out of breath.

"Wendy?"

"Hey, Anne. Sorry, we were outside letting the kids race Hershey in the backyard."

"Ben?"

"Yes, he's the only one who beat the dog, but Liddie and I are pretty sure Hershey let him win." The laughter filled Wendy's voice and warmed Anne's heart. Ben was at home. Safe. Yvette must have been mistaken after all.

Relief finally released Anne's tongue. "Grace has to work, so I'll be heading home soon."

"Oh, because of the fire." Wendy made a *tsk* sound over the phone. "That's so sad. Is it out now?"

"Yes." Anne took off her seat belt and got out of the car. "Is it all over the news?" She hoped Liddie hadn't seen it or she might be frightened. The five-year-old might be rambunctious, but she was tenderhearted and very caring and gentle.

"Oh, I don't know. We haven't been watching. We've been outside. Liddie and Emily were chasing Ben and Hershey." Emily was Wendy's eight-year-old daughter, whom Liddie practically idolized.

Anne waved at Grace, who waved back before stepping across the *Gazette's* threshold. "Then how did you know about the fire?" Anne asked Wendy as she slipped behind the wheel of her own car.

"Why, Ben told me."

Anne's heart plummeted to her toes.

CHAPTER TWO

Thanks again, Wendy," Anne said as she waved from the back door of the living space over the library in the old house. "Bye, Emily."

"Not a problem. Happy to try again when you and Grace can set a good day." Wendy ducked behind the wheel of her minivan and slammed the door shut.

Anne waited, watching Wendy back out of the drive. Her headlights lit the area of Anne's home, and Anne let out a contented sigh as she paused at the door.

Blue Hill, Pennsylvania, was a charming town pushed against rolling hills that spread out toward the majestic mountains in the western part of the state. The town's landscape captured attention, especially during the fall when foliage was brightest. Autumn brought pumpkin patches bursting with the orange gourds that drew in more tourists to the area. Even now, with the lingering scent of smoke seasoning the air, Blue Hill was a beautiful place to live.

Shutting and locking the door, Anne headed to Liddie's room. Her daughter, with her caramel hair with hints of blonde, looking more and more like Eric with every passing day, sat on her bed with three of her favorite Barbie dolls. She smiled as Anne entered. "Hi, Mommy. Did you have fun tonight?"

Anne sat on the edge of the bed and ran her fingers through Liddie's bangs. "I missed you," Anne said.

"We played in the backyard. Wendy pushed me in the tire swing. I went really, really high." Liddie's brown eyes widened with excitement.

"You did? I told you not to go too high. It scares me," Anne said, mussing Liddie's hair as she teased.

"I didn't go too too high, Mommy." Liddie grinned and snuggled against Anne. "And then we raced Hershey up and down by the picnic table. I didn't beat him, but Ben did, but Emily said Hershey might have let him win."

"Sounds like fun." Anne kissed the top of Liddie's head and caught a whiff of little girl sweat and outside. "And you smell like you need a bath and your hair washed." She stood and put her hands on her hips. "Grab your pajamas. I'll start your bath for you."

Anne pulled up the stopper in the tub and turned on the water. After setting the temperature, she pulled the handheld showerhead down for Liddie to reach easily. Although Liddie was only five, she was already exerting her independent streak in wanting to do things for herself. She did pretty well shampooing her hair, but it would be some time before she would be able to do the final rinsing.

"I'm gonna wear my princess pajamas," Liddie announced as she marched into the bathroom.

"That sounds lovely, honey." Anne turned off the water and checked the temperature a final time. "I'll be back to help you rinse. Make sure you scrub your scalp."

"Okay, Mommy."

Anne waited until Liddie sat safely in the bathtub before cracking the door and heading across the hall to Ben's room.

Ben sat on his bed with its tartan plaid bedspread, a Spider-Man comic book spread open across his lap. The lamp on the nightstand next to his bed glowed, casting a welcoming hue across the boyish room that was painted in shades of blue and brown with a navy area rug. A picture of Eric holding Ben as a baby sat beside the lamp. Ben looked up as Anne entered. "Hi, Mom."

She missed the days when he had called her *Mommy* instead of Mom…when he would snuggle against her as she read him a bedtime story…when he would wait for her to lead him in prayers…when he wasn't possibly out after dark with his friends in an area where a fire broke out.

"Ben, I need to ask you something," Anne said, leaning against his bedroom doorframe. She needed to stay close enough that she could hear Liddie in the bath, which wasn't hard since Liddie had the habit of singing loudly as she bathed.

"Sure." Ben set Spider-Man onto the bed and drew his knees up to his chest. "What?"

"While I was gone, did you leave here?"

Ben stared at her with hazel eyes that were almost identical to her own. "What do you mean?"

"Ben, you know what I'm asking." Anne returned his stare. "Did you leave here tonight?"

Ben shook his head. "I didn't."

Anne pressed her lips together and crossed her arms over her chest.

From the bathroom, Liddie continued to sing songs she'd learned in Sunday school. Her voice carried across the hall.

"Then how did you know about the fire?"

He shrugged. "Ryan told me."

So Yvette must've seen Ryan and some other boys and just mistook one of them for Ben. Anne let out a slow breath. "He was there?"

Ben threw her a confused look. "No. He heard it on the radio and called me."

Yvette must have been mistaken all around. But still...Ryan was only ten, hardly an age where a fire was important enough to warrant a phone call. "Why would Ryan call you about that?"

"Because we've hung out around there a couple of times. It's not too far from the park," Ben said.

"Jesus loves me, this I know," Liddie sang.

"Why would you hang out around there?" Anne asked Ben.

He shrugged. "I dunno. We've played ninja in the building next to the theater. It's usually empty."

"...tells me so," Liddie continued to sing.

"Why wouldn't you just play in the park?"

Ben sighed loudly and rolled his eyes. "Because we need a *place*, Mom. A hangout, you know?"

No, she didn't know, but she understood the need for a special space. But an abandoned warehouse? Empty or not, that wasn't safe. "Isn't there somewhere else you can play? Someplace inside?"

Ben shook his head. "Not where we can run without getting hollered at."

A flicker of guilt danced in Anne's chest. She recalled the many times she'd told Ben and Liddie to "keep it down" because they were above the library. She didn't think she'd raised her voice, but maybe the kids perceived it that way.

"They are weak, but He is strong," Liddie sang.

An idea hit. "Why don't you build a tree house out back? You could probably get Ryan and Alex to help you," she said.

Alex Ochs had been her best friend before they were high school sweethearts. When she'd accepted Aunt Edie's bequest and returned to Blue Hill, she'd hired Alex as the contractor for the library renovations. Over the past several months, they'd reestablished their strong, friendly connection. There were times lately when Anne wondered if maybe she might have some stronger feelings toward Alex, but she always brushed off the thoughts. He was a good friend to her, and his nephew, whom he'd been raising since his sister and her husband had died in an accident, had become Ben's best friend.

Alex and Ryan lived close enough to work together on a project like a tree house—just down the hill and right off the road. And Alex *did* own a construction business.

Ben's eyes went wide and the excitement lit up his entire face. "Really? Can we, Mom?" He nearly jumped on the bed. "Do you think Alex would be okay with that? I mean, Ryan and I can do all the work."

"*Mooommmmmmyyyy*, I'm ready for rinsing," Liddie called out.

"Just a minute, sweetie," Anne yelled back. To Ben, she smiled and said, "I don't see why not." The more she thought about it, the more it seemed like a great idea. "I think it could be very fun for you boys. Something to do together." And something to keep them safely on her property.

Ben jumped to his feet. "I have to call Ryan."

Anne laughed. "You should probably ask Alex, too, before you get too far along."

"Mommy!" Liddie called again.

"Coming." Anne flashed her son a quick smile before moving across the hall to the bathroom.

Ben looked as happy as when he'd made the softball team. And that made Anne happy.

* * *

"Where did you get the idea for the boys to build a tree house?" Alex asked Anne as they walked out of Blue Hill Community Church together. They shook Reverend Tom's hand and exchanged pleasantries, then moved on outside.

Anne shrugged and smiled, lifting her hand to shield her eyes from the February sun. "Well, Ben said they needed a place where they weren't hushed." She laughed as Alex led her out the front door under the beautiful stained glass window. Anne glanced over her shoulder to make sure Liddie was still coming along with Cindy and Becca. She waved at Anne as she skipped along with her friends just as Ben and Ryan rushed by.

The midday sun caught the reds and blues of the stained glass, causing them to shimmer and glisten. The raw beauty of the setting never failed to steal Anne's breath, and she paused a moment to take it all in.

Anne had grown up in this very church. The original church bell still hung above the steeple. Countless vacation Bible school weeks, Sunday school sessions, when they made crafts out of trash items, accepting Jesus as her Lord and Savior and the whole church praying with and over her...the memories of the church wrapped around her like a welcoming warm shawl, just as they did every single time she stood in awe of the red brick building that had been constructed back in the late 1800s.

The church still spoke to her heart and soul.

"Ryan is beyond excited about building a tree house with Ben," Alex said, pulling Anne back into the present. "He must have asked me a million questions last night." He pointed at the boys sitting on the tailgate of Alex's truck, their heads bent as Liddie stooped to pick up a dried leaf from the ground.

Alex put a gentle hand under her elbow to gently lead her toward their vehicles parked side by side, a gesture he'd done many times over, but this time...

This time Anne actually noticed the warmth of his touch. A subtle difference, just a minor shift in her perception...no, that wasn't right. Not perception. Awareness. Just a subtle difference of her awareness of Alex's presence. His closeness. With the breeze stirring the air, she could detect the spiciness of his cologne.

"Mr. Ochs!" a man called out.

Both Alex and Anne turned to find a man rushing to them. Anne recognized him from the fire last night.

He shoved his hand out to Alex. "Mr. Ochs, I'm Patrick Rollings. I own the movie theater."

Alex kept his hand under Anne's elbow and shook with his other. "I'm so sorry about the fire. Was there much damage to your place?"

"That's what I'd like to discuss with you. I've spoken with my insurance agent, and an adjuster will be by in the morning to look over the property. He advised me to have my own contractor there as well, preferably the one who would be doing the repairs. I'd like you to be the one." Patrick shook his head. "I'd like to hire you to be my contractor."

Anne shifted slightly but didn't move out of Alex's grasp. As he spoke about the damage and tomorrow with Patrick, she took the opportunity to really study Alex, not as a regular friend but as a man.

Alex stood a little over six feet, with hair the color of light milk chocolate. He had the bluest eyes Anne had ever seen, and they sparkled when he teased. Always had. From working outside, he was not only tan, but also extremely muscular. She'd always found him handsome, ever since they'd been high school sweethearts before she went off to college and broke his heart. Time had made him even more attractive. Maybe it was the way he cared for Ryan, or the way he was always willing to step in and help her and the kids—or anyone who asked, for that matter.

"Wow, that's pretty awesome, don't you think?" Alex asked, turning back to her.

It took Anne a moment to realize Patrick Rollings had left and she stood alone with Alex in the parking lot. "Um—um, what?" she stammered.

Alex dropped his hand from her elbow and snapped his fingers in front of her face. "Earth to Anne, come in Anne," he said, then laughed. "Where'd you go?"

Heat burned her cheeks, and she dropped her gaze and shook her head at the same time. "I was just thinking, I guess. I don't really know," she said. Anne looked at him. "So you're going to do the repairs on the theater?"

He put his hand under her elbow and led her toward their vehicles, where the kids were hanging out. "Not just the repairs. Patrick has thought about renovating the theater for some time now but hasn't for one reason or another."

Anne recalled reading that in an article Grace had run in the paper. Patrick Rollings had been quoted saying as much, but Anne never thought Alex would be the one hired for the job. How awesome for Alex.

"Now that he has to have the repairs done anyway, he wants to go ahead with renovating the whole thing," Alex continued. "A total renovation, much like we did for the library." His face reflected as much excitement as Ben's had last night when Anne suggested the building of a tree house. Speaking of the tree house…

"Alex," Anne said, "with the new job, will you have time to help the boys with the tree house?"

The excitement slid off Alex's face. "I want to help them, you know I do, but this is work."

She shook her head. "I understand. Work has to come first. The project can wait." But the boys would be so disappointed. Then again, maybe not. "I have an idea."

"What?" Alex asked.

"Why don't you let the boys take on all the planning? They can look up house plans in books in the library, make a supply list, and try to earn a little money to go toward the building supplies. It'll be good for them to take control of the project, and by allowing them to do that, it'll buy you some time to work on the theater," Anne said. As she shared her idea out loud, her own excitement grew. "Plus, it will also give the temperatures more time to warm up for when the boys are outside working."

"That's a great idea, Anne." Alex's voice was as smooth as a chocolate shake, and the way he said her name was almost a caress.

She couldn't tell whether it was pride or Alex's attention that brought the blush burning her cheeks, but Anne couldn't hide the smile. "Let's tell the boys. I bet they'll be excited." Anne led the way to the back of the truck, grabbing Liddie as she faced Ben and Ryan.

"Uncle Alex, Ben and I were thinking we could build the tree house on the other side of the tree that already has the big tire swing. We could—"

"Ryan," Alex said, effectively interrupting his eager nephew, "Anne and I were talking, and she's come up with a great idea about the tree house."

Both Ben and Ryan's faces fell. Anne pinched her lips together to stop from laughing out loud. She could only imagine what they feared she would say. She was almost tempted to talk about the gallon of pink paint leftover from the church's garage sale, but she was afraid they'd cry. "Since this is to be your special space, I thought maybe you'd like to be project managers."

Now they both looked confused.

"What's a project manager?" Liddie asked, saving the boys from having to admit they didn't have a clue either.

"A project manager oversees the entire project from start to finish," Anne explained. She smiled at Ben and Ryan. "That means you'd have to find the blueprints, the plans, for a suitable tree house. You'll have to make a list of all the needed materials, after you measure the space, of course. You'd have to find out the cost of the materials, figure out how much it will cost to build the tree house, and think of some ideas to help pay for the materials. A project manager makes all those decisions."

Ben and Ryan looked at each other, their expressions unreadable.

"You would be in total control so you would get exactly what you want," Anne explained further.

"Can I be a project manager, Mommy?" Liddie asked.

"No, honey. Not this time," Anne answered but hugged her daughter against her legs.

"Isn't that a great idea?" Alex asked. "You would get to make all the decisions on everything."

"We have to pay for it ourselves?" Ryan asked.

Now Anne did laugh. So that's what they were worried about. "Well," she said, "I wouldn't expect you two to pay for everything by yourselves, of course, but I think you both could come up with some suggestions on how to make some money to at least help. Don't you?"

Ben nodded, and after a heartbeat of a moment, Ryan did too. "We'd really get to make all the decisions, Mom?"

Ah, there was the kicker. She nodded slowly. "Within reason, of course. Once you boys decide on a plan, you'll need to run the blueprint by Alex to make sure it's buildable on the space we have. After that, you'll start with the measuring and budgeting and so forth."

Ben grinned. "Can we start today? Now?"

Anne laughed.

"Sorry, boys. Not today," Alex said. "My parents are just back from a mission trip, and Ryan and I are going to their place for lunch." He glanced at his watch. "And we're already late."

"Come on, kids." Anne motioned Ben down from the back of Alex's truck. Disappointment lined every curve of his precious little face. She winked at Alex. "Why don't you let Ryan come home from school with Ben tomorrow? They can do their homework, then start looking for tree house plans."

Ben's smile flashed back into place. So did Ryan's as the boy jumped from the tailgate. "Please, Uncle Alex?"

"Sure. Why not?" Alex shut the tailgate.

Anne clicked the button on her remote to open her car doors. "Ben, help your sister into her booster seat, please."

"Thanks, Anne," Alex said. "I appreciate it. How about I grab a pizza and bring it over when I pick him up as a thank you? We can eat dinner, and the boys can tell us both about what they found out."

"Sounds like a plan." Anne got behind the wheel of her car and gave a little wave to Alex as he backed his truck out of the parking space.

"Mom, thanks for letting us do a tree house," Ben said.

"You're welcome." Keeping him close and safe, that made everything worth it. That's all she ever wanted for her kids—for them to be happy and safe.

CHAPTER THREE

"Mommy, Mommy. We're having a hair-age day at school, and I have to bring pictures and stuff of my ant people," Liddie announced as she hopped into the backseat of the car and secured her booster's seat belt.

"What?" Anne asked as she looked for Ben and Ryan in the throngs of kids spilling out of the Blue Hill Elementary School, a tall, three-story brick building. It was seventy years old, recently remodeled, and was previously home to the high school. Anne had made a lot of memories in that building.

"I have to find pictures and stuff of like Aunt Edie."

Now it made sense. "Ah, you mean a Heritage Day and you need items of your ancestors," Anne said, smiling as she waved at Ben and Ryan sprinting toward the car.

"That's what I said," Liddie replied in the factual tone she used with her dolls.

Anne didn't have time to answer before Ben swung the door open behind Anne and slipped into the middle beside Liddie, Ryan squeezing in beside him and shutting the door. Both boys put on their seat belts as Anne started the car and eased into the flow of other parents picking up their children. "How was school, boys?" she asked.

"Long and boring," Ryan answered.

Anne grinned. Alex had told her Ryan was struggling a bit in English, which surprised Anne since he was such a big reader. "Probably only because you were excited about coming to the library to start looking for a tree house design, right?"

Ryan nodded.

Anne smiled. "Do you boys have a lot of homework?"

"None!" Ben's face was lit up like on Christmas morning. "Mr. Layton said we did so great in class that we deserved a homework-free night."

"Well, that was sure nice of him," Anne said.

"So we can start looking for a plan as soon as we get there," Ryan said. There was no mistaking his excitement.

"How was lunch at your grandparents' yesterday?" she asked. Alex's parents were missionaries and out of the country for the better part of the year, but when they were in town, they tried to spend as much time with Ryan as possible.

"Fine. I told my grandpa about the tree house and us being project managers and all. He asked me to help him stack some firewood, and he paid me five bucks," Ryan announced proudly. "So I'm already starting on making money to help buy all the stuff for the tree house."

"That's great," Anne said, steering the car onto Bluebell Lane toward home.

"Mom, I want to be able to make more money than just my allowance," Ben said.

"Then come up with a list of things you see needing to be done around the house or library and we'll discuss it, okay?"

He grinned at her in the rearview mirror, then bent his head beside Ryan, and the boys began whispering.

"Can we look for some Aunt Edie stuff when we get home, Mommy?" Liddie asked.

Anne nodded. Both Remi and Bella, the Miller twins, were working today. "Sure. Maybe we can find some stuff up in the attic," she answered as she pulled around the library to where she parked her car.

The boys jumped from the car while Anne moved to help Liddie. "Boys," she called after them, "there are graham crackers and apples with peanut butter on the counter for you. Pour some milk to go with them."

"I love graham crackers, Mommy."

Anne bent and kissed the tip of Liddie's nose as she shut the car door and took her daughter's hand and headed toward the back stairs that led to their private entrance.

She barely had time to stow her purse and pour Liddie's glass of milk before Ryan and Ben were finished with their snack and ready to start looking for tree house plans in the library.

"Liddie, I'm going to get the boys started, then I'll come back and we'll go search the attic for some items for your Heritage Day, okay?"

"Okay, Mommy," Liddie said as she dunked a peanut-butter-covered graham cracker into her milk.

The boys led the way downstairs to the library. They were already in deep discussion with the Miller twins when Anne crossed the floor.

"Aren't they excited?" Remi asked, smiling wide. She was the older of the girls by a full three minutes and stood an inch taller than Anne's five-foot-seven-inches. Remi's brown hair wove into a fishbone style that was as thick as a three-ply rope. Her eyes were as deep brown as Liddie's, and as unguarded.

"So where do we start, boys?" Bella asked Ben and Ryan. Bella was shorter than her sister by at least six inches or so, and her hair was much lighter than Remi's and hung in loose, wavy curls down past her shoulders. Her eyes were as blue as Alex's but much more intense.

Both boys began talking at once.

"*Shh*, boys. Keep it down," Anne said, then stopped herself as guilt popped up in her chest. "Girls, the boys are going to be full project managers on the tree house project, so they're responsible for doing the research themselves." She looked pointedly at Ben before turning back to Remi and Bella. "It's okay for you to help them find books of blueprints or show them how to search specifics online, but they need to do the actual work." This would teach them how to see a project through from start to finish, and keep them busy and out of trouble while working on something they truly wanted to do. Good life lessons all around, Anne figured.

"Yes, ma'am," Bella said, giving Anne a military salute with a smile that revealed perfectly white, perfectly straight teeth.

"Good. Then I'm off to slay the attic," Anne said.

"What are you doing up there?" Remi asked.

"Liddie has a heritage project and needs some pictures and items of her ancestors. There's plenty of stuff of Aunt Edie's up there for us to discover."

Remi nodded. "Holler if you get lost in that abyss."

Anne laughed. "I will. Holler if the boys get unruly," she said as she headed back to Liddie.

Liddie was wiping away her milk moustache when Anne returned. "I finished my snack. Can we go to the attic now, Mommy?"

"Let's clean up the kitchen first," Anne replied.

Within minutes, the dirty dishes were in the dishwasher and the counter wiped down. Anne put her hands on her hips. "Okay, Miss Liddie, what exactly are you supposed to have for this Heritage Day?"

"I have a paper that 'splains," Liddie said, reaching into her backpack.

"It's *explains*, sweetie," Anne automatically corrected.

"Here," Liddie said, handing her a sheet of paper, "here is the explaining."

Anne let it slide because it was cute. She scanned the project outline. Seemed easy enough. Two items from an ancestor, at least one photograph or a copy of a photo of that ancestor, and to fill out the provided family connection chart that the student would color. Not too difficult. Anne set the paper on the counter. "Okay, let's do this." She led the way into the attic, making sure Liddie was careful in her steps.

Once in the attic, Liddie was everywhere: looking in drawers of old cabinets, pulling out old books and albums from shelves, and opening trunks. Anne rushed to keep up with her daughter, finally kneeling beside Liddie as they pored through one of the old trunks Anne had never been through. As they carefully removed yellowed papers and magazines, Anne found a movie lobby placard. She slowly lifted it from the trunk and held it up for a better view.

It was about eleven by fourteen inches, in colors prominent back in the early 1950s, and depicted a movie titled *Summer Swoon*.

Anne turned it over to see if there was any indication on the back as to why Aunt Edie would keep this. Nothing. She turned back to the front to look at the picture. A handsome-for-that-time man, obviously a B or C actor since Anne didn't recognize him, stood in bathing trunks on a beach. A gaggle of teenage girls clustered in bunches behind him. The movie title was in ridiculous curly red script at the bottom of the picture.

"Look, Mommy, here's another one," Liddie said as she reached back into the trunk.

"Hang on, sweetie." Anne set the lobby placard gently on the attic floor, then pulled a movie poster from the trunk.

The movie poster was about twenty-seven by forty-one inches and depicted the same movie.

Why had Aunt Edie kept these? They must have meant something to her. Maybe she'd gone to see this movie on her first date. Still, it didn't explain her having the lobby placard and movie poster. Those things were hard to come by.

"Mommy, look," Liddie said, pointing into the trunk again.

Anne did, and found a yellow-edged script titled *Summer Swoon*. *What?*

Carefully, Anne flipped through the old screenplay until she found a highlighted part. Shifting so she could see better in stronger light, Anne read:

Betty, looking all doe-eyed: Isn't he dreamy?
Carol makes a face: I saw him first.

Betty frowns, then sticks her tongue out at Carol.

Sandra approaches, flipping her scarf over her shoulder: But I have a date with him.

-Scene fades-

The two lines of Betty's were highlighted. Out beside the instruction to frown and stick out her tongue, written in Aunt Edie's recognizable scrawl was, *Narrow eyes when doing this and shake head. More emphasis for the camera.*

Did this mean…?

"What is it, Mommy?" Liddie asked.

"I'm not sure, sweetie." Anne lifted the movie poster and stared at the cast listing at the bottom. Sure enough, *Edie Summers* was listed as one of the "Swooning Girls." Anne looked at the picture again…yes, there, just to the left of the man was Aunt Edie.

"Mommy, what is it?" Liddie asked again.

"Aunt Edie was apparently in this movie," Anne said, gathering up the movie poster, lobby placard, and script.

Liddie's eyes went wide. "She was a movie star?"

Anne laughed as she stood. "I wouldn't call her a star, sweetheart, but she was definitely in a movie." Anne had never known. Then again, there was an awful lot about Aunt Edie that Anne had apparently never known.

"Can I take that poster? For my project?" Liddie asked, hopping from foot to foot.

Anne shut the trunk and led the way from the attic, careful not to bend the movie items they'd found. "Copies, most definitely."

She helped Liddie back into the living area of the house. "I'll go make the copies in the library. I need to check on the boys anyway."

"Can I play Barbies?" Liddie asked.

"Sure," Anne said, planting a quick kiss on her daughter's cheek. "I'll be in the library if you need me."

She waited until Liddie had skipped to her bedroom before heading downstairs. The boys weren't in sight as she approached the front area. "Where are Ben and Ryan?" she asked Remi.

"Bella's got them set up in a corner of the Nonfiction Room. They've found several books already."

"Enough to keep them looking for a while," Bella added as she joined them. She nodded at Anne's load. "Whatcha got there?"

"Apparently, my aunt Edie was in a movie," Anne replied as she spread the items out on the work table. She showed the girls the script and pointed out her aunt in the picture.

"Wow, that's really cool," Remi said.

Anne smiled. The teenager sounded as impressed as Liddie had. "It's yet another facet of my aunt's life that I'm just now finding out about."

Edie Summers had been quite the woman. Anne was beginning to believe she was the Most Interesting Deceased Woman in the World—a true renaissance woman with wide-ranging interests and skills that ranged from one end of the spectrum to the other, in no particular order. Anne had vivid, wonderful memories of spending time with her aunt, here in this very house, but there had never been any mention of her being in any movie. She'd have to ask Mildred Farley about this. Mildred was Aunt Edie's very best friend.

Anne sat behind the computer terminal and opened the Internet browser. She typed in the pertinent information, then let the search begin. Remi and Bella crowded around her.

"Here," Anne said, clicking on one of the result pages.

A full listing of the movie details loaded. Anne read out loud, "*Summer Swoon*, a summer beach movie starring Rory Carson debuted May 1950 with a very limited distribution run. The movie quickly played out at the theaters, replaced quickly with *Annie Get Your Gun*, starring Betty Hutton and Howard Keel."

"I've heard of *Annie Get Your Gun*," Remi said.

Anne smiled and continued reading, "*Summer Swoon* cast several unknown actresses to portray the girls swooning over the hero, Rory Carson. Most never went on to play in any other movies, such as Joy Walters, Rosemary Thomas, Sarah Leeker, Frances Downside, Edie Summers, and Kate Orchard."

"Wow, her name is even listed," Bella gushed.

Even Anne had to admit that was pretty cool. She printed the article, then turned back to the lobby placard and movie poster. "Remi, would you please carefully make copies of those for Liddie's project? I'll have to consider what to do with the originals, but I certainly don't want them buried again in a trunk up in the attic."

"Oh, of course not," Remi said as she moved the items to the oversized copier.

The door to the library whooshed open. Bella turned. "Oh, hi, Officer Banks. How're you? I've missed seeing Mia at the kids' Story Time lately."

"She's into dance these days and spending her Saturdays taking ballet."

Anne smiled at her old friend from high school. Michael Banks was broad-shouldered, large, and foreboding—great features to have in law enforcement, Anne would suppose. He had dark, curly hair that didn't quite hide his growing bald spot, but he had really soft and kind blue eyes that beseeched people to trust him.

"Hey, Michael. What brings you to my neck of the woods?" Anne greeted him.

"I'm actually doing some follow-up on reports about the fire Saturday night."

"Oh. Right. Yes, I was there. Come on, let's head back to the kitchen area to talk," she said, leading the way to the back of the library.

Michael followed, sitting opposite her at the little dinette table.

"Would you like some water or coffee?" she asked.

He shook his head. "I appreciate it, but I have a lot of stops to make."

Translation, he needed to ask his questions and move on. "Okay. Well, I was there with Grace. We'd heard the sirens, turned up the scanner, then Grace said she needed to cover the fire for the paper. She and I got in her car and headed—"

"So Ben was with you?" Michael asked.

Anne wrinkled her nose and shook her head. "No, Ben was here with Wendy and her daughter, Emily. Wendy was watching Ben and Liddie so I could have dinner with Grace."

He flipped through pages in his little notebook. "I'm sorry. One of our officers had noted a report that someone saw Ben, Ryan, and Christian running from the site before the fire broke out."

Josie Bolling had to have reported what Yvette thought she saw. "That's incorrect," Anne said. "Ben wasn't there and neither was Ryan Slater. Ben was here with Wendy the whole time. He heard about the fire from Ryan, who heard it on the radio and called Ben to tell him."

Michael frowned. "Are you sure, Anne? I mean, I know boys sometimes sneak off. Jen and I had a go of it when Jed hit his tweens and then again with Tim."

Anne forced herself not to be offended. "You can ask them yourself. Both boys are here."

"May I speak with them?" he asked.

Anne nodded. "Let me ask one of the girls to get them." She quickly found Bella and asked her to send Ben and Ryan back to the kitchen area, then returned. "Bella's getting them," she told Michael.

"Thanks, Anne. I mean no disrespect, you understand."

"I know. You're just doing your job."

Ben rounded the corner into the kitchen, Ryan at his heels. "What is it, Mom? We're really into this one book's plans."

"You remember Officer Banks, right?" Anne asked, gesturing to Michael.

"Yes." Ben smiled at Michael. "Hi."

"Boys," Michael said, "I'd like to ask you a couple of questions about the fire."

Ben's stare shot to Anne. She winked at him. "It's okay."

"There's a warehouse next to the theater. Do you boys know anything about it?" Michael asked, his voice soft and unaccusing.

Ben nodded. "We sometimes go in and play there."

"But only when it's empty," Ryan added.

"Who?" Michael asked.

"Me and Ryan and Christian Pyle and sometimes Zachary Baker," Ben said.

"But Zach not all the time because he gets in trouble a lot," Ryan contributed, nodding.

"How do you get in there?" Michael asked.

"The door doesn't lock so good," Ryan said.

"Were either of you there Saturday?" asked Michael.

Both boys shook their heads.

"I was here with Mrs. Pyle. She was babysitting me and Liddie while Mom was out," Ben said.

"I was at home with Uncle Alex. He was watching basketball on TV, and I was in my room listening to the radio," said Ryan. "A newsbreak came on about the fire, and that's how I found out. I called Ben to tell him."

"I see," Michael said, jotting notes in his notebook. "What about Christian or Zachary…do either of you know if either one of them was by the warehouse on Saturday?"

Again, both boys shook their heads.

"Have either of you ever seen anybody else around the warehouse?" Michael asked. "Besides you two and Christian and Zachary?"

Ben and Ryan stared at each other.

Anne recognized that look. "What?" she asked.

Ben lifted a single shoulder in a casual shrug. "A man sleeps in there sometimes."

Anne swallowed the gasp and gripped her hands together in her lap, under the table. It was dangerous enough for him to be playing in an empty warehouse…but a man sleeping there?

Michael shot Anne a warning look before asking, "How do you know?"

"If we go early on a Saturday, we can sometimes see him still sleeping on the floor. He covers up with old newspapers," Ryan said.

"And we saw him going in one Friday night when we were playing in the park, almost at dark, right before Mom said it was time to go," Ben added.

Anne's mouth was dry. Why had Ben never mentioned this to her before?

"Do you know who the man is?" Michael asked.

Both boys shook their heads.

"Okay. Well, thank you, boys," Michael said.

Ben looked at Anne. "Can we go back to our table now?"

Anne nodded, and Ben and Ryan beat a hasty retreat. Anne stood as Michael did. "I didn't know anything about a man," she said.

"I could tell. I'm sure you've spoken to Ben about not going into any building, empty or otherwise, right?"

"Of course. As soon as I found out. That's why I told the boys they could build a tree house here. That's what they're working on now, finding tree house plans," she said, leading him back through the library.

"Good idea." He tapped his notebook. "I'd better get going. Lots more reports to follow up on."

Anne remembered hearing about possible arson. "Do they know what started the fire yet?"

"Initial reports show a possible accelerant used, but follow-up tests aren't in yet. The owner, Marcus Kombs, is out of town, but his wife believes there was nothing in the warehouse that could have started the fire."

If Ben and his friends had been there when the fire started...

"Thanks, Anne," Michael said, heading to the door.

"Sure. Tell Jen I said hello. Bye." Anne stared off into space.

It was obvious that Ben wouldn't just up and volunteer information. Anne made a mental note that she would begin to ask him point-blank for information about what he was doing. To think of the danger he could have been in sent shivers down her spine.

She would protect her kids at all costs.

CHAPTER FOUR

Anne's cell phone rang as soon as she pulled into her drive on Tuesday afternoon. She put the car in park, then reached for the phone from the console. She recognized Alex's number and smiled. "Hi, Alex," she said as she pressed the phone to her ear.

"Hi, Anne. I hate to bother you, but I need a favor." The stress was evident in the cracking of his voice.

"Of course. What?" she said without hesitation. She would do anything for a friend, but especially Alex, who had done so much for her and the kids since she'd moved back home. Ben and Liddie raced up the back stairs.

The afternoon had become overcast, with temperatures dropping into the high twenties. Forecast predicted a slight chance of snow late tonight into the early morning hours. Anne would have to remember to ask Ben to bring firewood up onto the side porch by Hershey's bed.

Alex continued. "You know how we were supposed to start work in the morning at the theater?"

"Right." Alex had told her that the insurance adjuster had already gotten back in touch with Patrick and he'd hired Alex to start the renovations.

"Well, I sent one of my workers to the theater to make sure our initial deliveries had all been received so we'd be ready to start work in the morning. I just got a call from Buddy and he says the site's been vandalized."

"Oh no." Anne's hand covered her mouth.

"He says it's not too bad, but I need to be there. I've called Patrick and he's going to meet me there so we can call the police, if needed, but I really don't want to drag Ryan out in this cold weather for goodness knows how long."

"Oh, I totally understand. So you need me to watch Ryan?"

"Would you mind? I hate to ask, especially since you just watched him for me yesterday," Alex said.

"Don't be silly. He and Ben are diving into the whole project-manager thing. They can do their homework together, since Ben told me he has math and social studies, then work on the project. Do you need me to come get him?"

"I'm actually about to head over to the site. Would you mind terribly picking him up from there?"

"Of course not. I'll grab Ben and Liddie, and we'll head that way shortly." Anne started for the stairs.

"Thanks, Anne. I really appreciate it," Alex said before hanging up.

Anne smiled as she climbed the stairs and opened the back door. "Ben! Liddie! Come on. Put your coats on. We're going to pick up Ryan from Alex's work site."

Ben was in the living room in a flash. "Ryan's coming over?" he asked, all but bouncing up and down.

"Yes," Anne said with a chuckle. "So get your coat on. It's getting even colder outside."

"Do I have to go, Mommy?" Liddie asked, already wearing her flannel pajamas and fuzzy bunny slippers.

"Yes, you have to go. What do you think, silly, you could stay here by yourself?" Anne teased.

"Remi's at the library. She could watch me," Liddie answered.

"No, ma'am. Remi is hard at work in the library. She doesn't have time to be your babysitter right now. And tell me, why are you wearing your pajamas?" Anne asked.

"Because I was cold and they're comfy."

"You haven't had a bath yet. Go take them off. And put the clothes you wore today back on. Don't go dirtying up another set," Anne said, grabbing her gloves from the counter. Just from the time she'd left to pick up the kids until now, the wind had picked up, making it seem colder and more biting.

Ben returned, wearing his coat and hat.

"When we get back and you walk Hershey, will you please bring up some firewood and put it on the porch? I think we're going to need a fire tonight," Anne said.

"Is that considered an extra chore?" he asked.

"It's considered helping keep yourself warm," she said but smiled to soften her tone. "But if you bring some up to the back porch landing, I might be able to scrounge up a few dollars for you."

"Thanks, Mom. Can I wait in the car? Liddie takes forever."

"Sure, go ahead. I'll go hurry her up," Anne said, carrying Liddie's coat to her room.

"I'm almost done, Mommy," Liddie said. She put her last boot on and held out her arms for her coat. "See?"

Anne helped her with the coat, then they descended the stairs together. After Liddie was secured in her booster seat, Anne headed the car toward the theater.

"When we get there, I want you two to stay in the car. Do you understand?" Anne asked as she turned onto Main Street. "I'll leave the car running and the heater on so you'll stay warm."

"Okay," Liddie answered.

"Why can't I come with you?" Ben asked.

"Because it's a construction site, and I don't want you in the way or getting hurt," Anne said. She pulled into the theater's parking lot and parked beside Alex's Ford truck. "You two stay in the backseat, understand?"

"Okay, Mom," Ben said.

Anne nodded, then got out of the car. A heavy gust of wind pushed against her, creeping down the back of her collar and seeping into her bones. She ducked her head and walked faster.

Alex and Ryan met her at the front of the theater. "I really appreciate this, Anne," Alex said.

"I told you I didn't mind." She smiled at Ryan. "You can go ahead out to the car, honey. Ben's crazy excited to see you."

"Bye, Uncle Alex," Ryan said, hoisting his backpack on his shoulder and sprinting to the car.

Anne turned to Alex. "How bad is it?"

"Look." Alex led her to the main entry.

She could see little damage from the fire but realized that was mainly on the top of the building. But the vandalism she had no problem finding. Across the main wall, where there were glass holders for movie posters, someone had taken paint and just randomly streaked the walls. No rhyme or reason to the slaps of paint. Not like graffiti, just more of a...mess.

"Oh, Alex," she whispered.

"Yeah. Just that, and a can of paint knocked all over the carpet in one of the hallways. Nothing unfixable or even costly, just more of a hassle," he said.

"Do you think it's kids? Has Patrick seen it?"

"Patrick just left, and yes, he thinks kids are the culprit. Another reason I'm really thankful you agreed to take Ryan."

Anne nodded. "Have the police been here yet to file a report?"

Alex shook his head. "Patrick didn't want to call the police. Not just for this petty business."

"But it's still vandalism of his property," Anne argued.

"I know, but he didn't want to report it. Not after the fire — and that's still an open investigation."

"I suppose, but I still think it should be reported."

Alex smiled. "We don't get to make that call."

"True," she said. "Well, I better get back to the kids."

"I'll pick Ryan up on my way home. I shouldn't be too much longer. I just have to wait for Buddy to get back with the replacement paint, then I'll run by my office. A lady recently put in an application for me for work-site clean-up jobs. I'd like to see if she could start on this tomorrow morning," Alex said, pointing at the paint smears over the wall and glass cases.

"Take your time. I'll make sure they do their homework, then they'll stay engrossed in their tree house project." Anne hurried to the car and shut the door behind her. "Everybody have your seat belts on?"

"Yes," all three kids answered.

"Then we're off," she said, backing the car out of the parking spot.

It took only a few minutes to reach the library from the theater, but when Anne stepped to follow the kids inside, it was as if the temperature had dropped another several degrees. "Ben," she called, "you need to let Hershey out to run. Please remember to bring up some firewood to the porch."

"Okay, Mom." Ben and Ryan ducked inside the house, dumped their backpacks, then rushed out toward the porch run for Hershey.

The chocolate Labrador retriever jumped around the boys in circles as they ran toward the woodpile. Anne knew to keep the big woodpile far enough away from the house so as to not draw termites to the building, but it was close enough that Ben could carry several loads to the porch. With Ryan's help, she'd have plenty of wood for the week.

Anne went inside and checked the cash in her wallet. Good. She had two five-dollar bills, one for each of the boys for their work.

"Mommy, can we have pizza again for supper?" Liddie asked.

"No, you may not. I have vegetable soup in the Crock-Pot for supper," Anne answered.

Liddie's bottom lip pushed out. "I don't like soup."

"Yes, you do. I even have the wafer crackers you like," Anne said.

Liddie smiled. "I do like them."

Anne shook her head, smiling. "Okay. You go practice your reading, and I'm going to start a fire."

"Okay, Mommy." Liddie skipped down the hall to her bedroom.

Anne set the kindling atop a starter log piece, then lit the pile. In minutes, crackling and popping filled the room along with the distinct smell of a fireplace. Anne grabbed the cordless from the kitchen counter, plopped down onto the couch in front of the fire, and dialed the paper's number.

"Blue Hill Gazette," Grace answered.

"Hey, you."

"Hi, Anne. How's everything?" Grace asked.

"Good. Listen, I have a couple of things I'd like to run by you and look up in the archives. Is tomorrow after school good for me to come by?"

"Sounds great. I have an interview set up in the afternoon, but you know your way around the archives. So what do you want to look up? You know you can't tease a reporter. Curiosity would kill me," Grace said.

Anne chuckled. "It seems my aunt Edie had a part in a movie back in 1950."

"You're kidding?"

"Nope."

"I kid you not, that woman was just amazing. Just when I think I've learned all about her, you come up with some totally opposite aspect of her that I knew nothing about," Grace said.

Anne laughed. "Welcome to my world."

"Well, come on by tomorrow. I'll look forward to seeing you."

"Okay. Bye." Anne set the phone down just as Ben and Ryan stomped back inside. They backed up to the fire, although it wasn't giving out much heat just yet.

"We carried up four loads each," Ben said, breathing hard. "We stacked them right by the back door."

"You did?" Anne stood and headed to the counter, already reaching for her wallet.

"Yes. And we walked Hershey, then filled up his food bowl and gave him fresh water," Ben said. Ever since he'd adopted the dog from the humane society, he'd been as responsible as he'd promised.

"Well, then I think you boys deserve payment for your hard work." Anne handed them each a five-dollar bill. "Is that fair?"

"Thanks, Mom!"

Ryan smiled too. "Thank you, Mrs. Gibson."

"Now, why don't you two finish up your homework before dinner? That way, after the kitchen is cleaned up, you boys can work on your project," Anne said.

They rushed to the kitchen table, snagging backpacks as they went.

Anne checked on Liddie, then she went into her bedroom to change into her sweatpants. She pulled her hair back in a ponytail, then slipped on her slippers before grabbing the phone from her bedside table. She didn't want to wait too late to call Mildred, who was an early-to-bed, early-to-rise woman.

"Hello, Anne," Mildred answered right after the first ring.

"Hi, Mildred. I hope I'm not catching you at a bad time," Anne said, sitting on the chair in the corner of her room.

"Of course not, dear. I just finished my dinner. Is everything okay?"

"We're all fine. I just had a question about Aunt Edie," Anne said.

Mildred chuckled. "I suppose we'll never learn everything about that friend of mine, will we?"

Anne laughed as well. "No, I don't suppose we will."

"Well, what is it this time? Perhaps I can help."

"Does the movie title *Summer Swoon* mean anything to you?"

"Oh my. Isn't that a blast from the past?"

"You've heard of it?"

"Oh dear, that was a high point of Edie's young career. She had a bit part in the movie, only a couple of lines, but she milked it for every minute she could."

"I just found a movie poster and lobby placard with the movie title, and I found Aunt Edie's script."

"Oh my. I can't wait to see that," Mildred said. "It was a great time. We had a party for her and everything. I'll have to dig through my old photos and see if I can find any of that night."

"I hope you find them. Thanks for looking. Anyway, I'll let you go. I just wanted to run the question by you," Anne said.

"I'll look for those photos. Oh, it was quite grand."

"You have a good night, Mildred."

"You too, dear. And hug those kids for me."

"I will," Anne said before hanging up the phone. Well, she'd tried. Maybe she could find something in the *Gazette's* archives. Surely, a local girl having a part, even a bit part, in a real Hollywood movie would warrant at least a mention in the local paper.

After she checked the boys' homework, fed everyone, and cleaned the kitchen, she stirred the fire, then got Liddie settled in her room playing dolls and let the boys bring up their favorite two books of plans.

"Look, Mom. We've narrowed it down to these five," Ben said, thrusting both hardback books into her lap and pointing at the yellow sticky notes marking the pages. "Which do you like best?"

She flipped through and looked at them all. While all five were very similar, there were also very distinct differences between them. "It doesn't matter which one I like best," she said. "It matters which design you boys like best."

"That's just it, Mrs. Gibson. We like different ones," Ryan said.

"Yeah, we were kinda hoping you would break the tie," Ben added.

"There are five to choose from. What if I don't pick either of your choices? Then what?" Anne asked.

"Then we decided we'd tell you which two we like best and let you choose between them," Ben answered.

Anne shook her head. "I'm sorry, boys, but no. You both are equal project managers. Sometimes that means learning to compromise and work together." She handed the books back to Ben. "You two will have to figure it out amongst yourselves."

The boys wore such confused and disappointed expressions that she almost laughed. A knock at the door saved her from having to explain any further.

She opened the door. "Hi, Alex. Come on in out of the cold."

"Thanks." He moved immediately to stand in front of the fireplace. "It's colder than cold out there since the sun went down."

"Is it snowing, Uncle Alex?" Ryan asked.

"No. Not even a flurry. Just bone-deep cold."

"Can we go get one other book, Mom?" Ben pleaded.

"I thought you guys had it narrowed down?" she asked, taking a seat on the couch.

"Well, since we can't decide, we thought maybe we'd go through another book we liked and see if we can agree on one of those," Ben said.

"Smart thinking. Go ahead," Anne said. "Just make sure you turn off all the lights down there when you're finished."

"Okay. Thanks." The boys scrambled toward the stairs that would take them down to the library.

Alex ran his hand over his face. "Thank you again for getting Ryan and watching him today. And for the tree house idea. He's more excited about this than anything."

"It's good for them to have a project to occupy their time, and it's productive. Matter of fact, I have to run by Grace's after school tomorrow. Why don't you let me get Ryan too, and I can take him to the site after we're done? He'll help keep Ben busy while I'm digging through the paper's archives."

"I can't ask you to watch Ryan again," Alex said as he moved to sit on the couch beside her.

"Good thing you aren't asking then. I am. It will help me."

Alex grinned and she noticed the crookedness of his smile. How had she forgotten that?

She dismissed her thoughts. "So did you hire the cleaning lady?"

Alex nodded. "I did. She came by and got it all cleaned up. Did a great job, and fast too."

"Good. So you're set to work tomorrow?" Anne asked.

"We are. Patrick and I finalized the blueprints today. It's really going to be something. It's a renovation but more of a historic preservation."

Right up Alex's alley. He loved that kind of thing.

"I can't wait to see it when it's finished."

"So what are you digging around in the paper's archives for now?" Alex asked.

Anne chuckled, then began to tell him about Aunt Edie in her movie debut.

CHAPTER FIVE

"Mom, can we please go over to the park while you're here? It's so boring at the paper," Ben whined as they stepped out of the car in front of the *Gazette's* office on Wednesday. He and Ryan had worn downtrodden faces the entire drive over.

For Anne, the park was a place of happy memories of playing there as a young girl. She would swing on the big swings with the creaks and squeaks, higher and higher, until she thought she was flying. There was a peaceful small pond and a gorgeous rose garden. Aunt Edie had belonged to the park's garden club, and there was now a brass plaque set in the planter of Japanese rosebushes which the garden club placed there in Aunt Edie's honor. Anne had taken Ben and Liddie there many, many times. It was just down the street from the *Gazette*, but over the last month, there'd been reports of someone knocking over the benches and tossing the trash from the cans.

"Please, Mom?" Ben begged.

It wasn't as cold out as it had been yesterday, and they wore their coats. Both boys looked as heartbroken as Hershey did when she made him stay on his porch when the kids were outside playing. And those incidents last month had occurred at night, and it was broad daylight now. She let out a sigh. "Okay, *but*, I want you back in thirty minutes. I mean it. Not thirty-two or thirty-one minutes, thirty minutes exactly. Understood?"

Both boys' heads bobbed. "Thanks, Mom. We'll be back then, I promise," Ben said before turning with Ryan and racing down to the main entrance to the park.

"I want to go to the park too, Mommy," Liddie said as she tugged on Anne's hand. "Can I go too?"

Anne smiled down at her daughter. "No, sweetie. Not this time."

"But I'm big like Ben." Her bottom lip quivered.

Best to nip the pouting in the bud before the tears filled those big, brown eyes. "Liddie," Anne said, "we're here for your project. To find out the details behind Aunt Edie's acting in that movie."

Liddie's lip pushed back in. "Oh. I forgot."

Anne smiled. "Well, come on." She pushed inside, and the familiar bell rang out from above the door. Grace appeared from her office in a flash. "Hey, Anne. Hi, Liddie." Grace had barely reached thirty and had blonde hair, blue eyes, and skin so flawless and pale it almost looked translucent. She was beautiful, inside and out.

Liddie ran to Grace and wrapped her arms around her waist, giving her a big hug. Grace hugged her back. "I've missed you, sweet Liddie. How are you today?"

"We're searching for my project," Liddie proclaimed.

Anne laughed. "We're *re*searching for your project."

Liddie nodded. "Yeah. What Mommy said."

Grace chuckled.

The bell sounded again, followed by the door opening. A man wearing a tattered fleece pullover and jeans with rips at the pockets and knees stepped inside. He had a full beard, very unkempt, that matched the messiness of his hair.

Grace moved to greet him, her hand extended. "Hello, Mr. Thatcher. Thank you for coming in."

He shook her hand. "Thank you for seeking me out." His voice was deep and unwavering, yet held a gentle tone.

Anne took a step forward. "Hello. I'm Anne Gibson, the town's librarian."

He held out his hand to her. "Pleased to meet you, ma'am. I'm Denny Thatcher."

Anne shook his hand, trying to determine his age. It was hard to tell since there were deep lines of stress etched into the cut of his face. If she had to guess, she'd say maybe early forties. Entirely too young to be this beaten down by life. Although he didn't look as if he were disenchanted with life. "Nice to meet you as well," she said. "This is my daughter, Liddie."

He squatted to get on eye level with the little five-year-old, and smiled. "Hi, Liddie. I'm Denny."

"Hi, Denny," Liddie said. "I like your beard."

"Thank you," he said.

Anne took Liddie's hand.

"Well, you know your way to the archives, Anne," Grace said. "Denny, if you'll come with me to my office."

Anne and Liddie made their way down the hall to the large room that held the archives of the paper issues. It was also home to two microfiche machines, as well as various boxes of storage items. Even so, the room wasn't dusty, and no distinct odor of "old" filled the space.

Setting her purse on the table, she checked the binders for the year 1950, then pulled the microfiche. She showed Liddie how to load the microfiche, then began scrolling through until she came to the issues around May. Sure enough, she found an article featuring Edie.

According to the article, Edie was cast in the movie *Summer Swoon* soon after she'd graduated high school. A big production was made in Blue Hill when the movie released, including a large party to honor Edie and a special showing.

Mildred had said it was a grand party. Anne could only imagine how wonderful it probably was. She hoped Mildred could find those pictures.

Anne set the machine to make copies of the articles, then checked her watch. The boys only had about ten more minutes before they were due back. She needed to hurry because she didn't want them to interrupt Grace's interview. She grabbed the copies and slipped them into her purse, then put everything back in order before taking Liddie's hand and leading her back to the front of the office. They reached the foyer area just as Denny Thatcher stepped out of the building.

"What was that all about?" Anne asked Grace after Liddie ran to the waiting area and began to flip through magazines.

"Denny used to be a loan officer at the bank. When the mortgage industry crashed, Denny found himself out of a job. Times have been tough for everyone for several years, and Denny was unable to find another job. He lost his wife and his house. He's been living on the streets and in shelters ever since." Grace shook her head. "It's sad. He's a good guy. His wife divorced him and left Blue Hill. Poor Denny's had a rough go of it."

"You know him well?" Anne asked.

Grace shrugged. "I met him through a feature I did on the soup kitchen, hoping to get more donations. I'm hoping by doing an article on him, someone will take a chance and hire him for something. Living on the streets has to be hard. Blue Hill doesn't have a homeless shelter but Deshler does. When there's space available, he stays there."

"What does he do when there isn't space?"

"He sleeps on the street," Grace answered. "It breaks my heart, but some homeless men like Denny, they're good guys. The problem is, single women like us can't offer to let them sleep on our couches."

Anne nodded but wondered. Maybe Alex needed someone else on his crew. Anne didn't know how well a former mortgage officer would work in construction, but she could at least ask and maybe show Alex the article when it ran and make a subtle suggestion.

The boys rushed through the door, Ryan staring at his watch. "We made it, Mrs. Gibson. Twenty-eight minutes exactly."

Anne smiled. "Good job, boys."

As Grace spoke to Ryan, Ben moved next to Anne. "Mom, who was that guy who just left here?"

Anne ran a hand over Ben's head, smoothing his hair. "He was here to see Grace, honey."

"But, Mom, that's the guy who sometimes slept in the warehouse."

Before Anne could reply, her cell phone rang from her purse. She dug around and finally put her hand on it after the second ring. "Hello?"

"Anne," Alex's voice cracked. "Are Ryan and Ben with you?"

She watched as Ben joined Ryan and Grace laughing about something. "Yes. Right in front of me. Why?"

"Oh, good." The relief was clear in Alex's voice. "Michael's here because we had another incident of vandalism, and I called the police."

"Oh no," she said. Still, how did that relate to anything having to do with Ben and Ryan?

"Yeah, it's not too bad. A little worse than last time. Anyway, Michael got notice just a second ago of a report that Ben and Ryan were seen with a group of teenagers over at Rosehill Park."

Anne's stomach tensed. "Is that wrong?" she asked, turning away from the boys and Grace. "For teenagers and kids to be in the park?"

"No, but this particular group of teenagers are under investigation regarding the vandalism to the park over the last month or so," Alex said. "So when Michael got the report, I wanted to make sure the boys were with you, and they are."

"Alex," she stepped into Grace's office so the boys wouldn't overhear her side of the conversation. "The boys were playing in the park for about thirty minutes." Her heartbeat seemed to reverberate inside her head. "They got back about five minutes ago, but for about thirty minutes before that, they were in the park."

"Oh." A long pause followed before Alex said, "I think you need to bring the boys here, Anne. Michael wants to talk to them."

"Okay," Anne said. "We'll be there soon." She ended the call.

"Everything okay?" Grace asked from behind her.

Anne shook her head as she faced her friend, then quickly told her about Alex's call.

"Goodness. I don't think the boys would be running with teenagers like that," Grace said.

But her reassurance didn't quite soothe Anne's gnawing fear. "I don't know, Grace. They could. It seems Ben isn't the type to offer up information about what he's doing. I had no idea he and his friends were playing in the Kombses' warehouse when it was empty," Anne said. "It's scary to think that Ben might be in close proximity to such teens. What would teenagers want with some nine- and ten-year-olds anyway?"

"I don't know," Grace said. "Look, I'm almost done here. Why don't you let Liddie stay with me, and I'll bring her home later? Maybe she can paint my nails for me...she likes that."

Anne reached out and hugged her friend. "Thank you, Grace. I really don't want her at a construction site, and I certainly don't want her listening to Michael question the boys. You know how that would turn out."

Grace laughed. "Yeah. The phrase 'little pitchers have big ears' was coined for kids like Liddie. Don't worry about us. She loves painting my nails, and I haven't had time to do them in weeks. We'll have fun."

Anne nodded, then rounded up Ben and Ryan. She told Liddie about Grace's offer, and Liddie jumped up and down and clapped her hands. Anne kissed Liddie, thanked Grace again, then ushered the boys into their coats and outside.

Although she wanted to believe the best about her sweet son, Anne thought it would be better not to mention to the boys about the teenagers in the park. That way, when Michael asked them, she would be able to tell by Ben's face if he knew what was going on.

At least she thought she'd be able to tell. Lately, though...

"Wow, what happened here, Uncle Alex?" Ryan asked as soon as they entered the theater.

Anne pulled up short. The paint streaks that had been there last night were gone, but there were random splashes of paint on the opposite wall and covering the ticket counter glass, as well as the refreshment stand area.

"Some vandalism. You boys remember Michael Banks?" Alex asked as Michael stepped in behind him.

Anne felt rather than saw Ben stiffen up as Michael moved closer to them.

"Hi, boys. We're going to have to stop meeting like this," Michael said in a teasing tone.

Neither Ben nor Ryan seemed to appreciate the humor.

"I understand you were at Rosehill Park this afternoon," Michael said.

Ben and Ryan nodded in unison.

"What were you doing there?" Michael asked.

Ben looked at Anne. "We had permission to be there. Mom said it was okay for us to go."

She smiled. "I did. And you were only gone for thirty minutes. You followed my instructions exactly." She could only hope her verification reassured her son.

"You aren't in trouble for being there, Ben," Alex said.

"Right. I just want to know what you did there," Michael clarified.

"Oh." Ben stared at the ground. "We just ran around a little."

"We skipped some stones at the pond," Ryan added sheepishly.

Ah. That explained Ben's reaction. She'd told him to be careful when skipping stones there because boys usually ended up tossing rocks at each other for fun…until someone got hurt.

"Was it just you two together?" Michael asked.

Ben and Ryan locked gazes.

"Well, we saw other people," Ben said.

"But it was just me and Ben hanging out together," Ryan finished.

"Did you recognize any of the people you saw?" Michael asked as he jotted in his notebook. "Maybe someone you know or might have seen around?"

Ben swallowed. "We saw some older guys."

"Older?" Michael asked.

"Teenagers," Ryan said.

"Did you recognize any of them?" Michael asked.

Ben and Ryan both dropped their gazes.

"Boys, Officer Banks asked you a direct question," Alex said.

Both of them nodded but didn't look Michael in the face. Anne's chest went cold. Had they really been with some teenage boys?

"Ryan," Alex said in a sterner tone, "who did you recognize?"

Ryan looked at Alex. "Brent Masterson," he choked out.

"Who?" Both Alex and Michael asked together.

"He's been going out with Britney, that's how I know him. He asked me if I've seen her," Ryan said.

Anne was confused. "Who is Britney?"

Ryan looked at Anne. "Britney's dad manages the lumberyard. I see Britney sometimes when I go with Uncle Alex to get supplies."

"Ah," Alex said.

At least that made sense. Anne studied her son, who was still staring at the ground. So there was someone else whom Ben recognized. "Ben," Anne said softly but sternly, "was there anybody else you recognized?"

Ben nodded.

"Who?" Michael asked.

"Jed," Ben whispered.

"Jed?" Michael asked.

Ryan nodded.

"My *son* Jed?" Michael asked.

Both boys nodded. "I recognized him because he sometimes came and watched Tim when he played softball with us."

"Is that it? Anybody else?" Michael asked, but the muscle in his cheek tweaked.

"There was another guy with them, but I've never seen him," Ben offered.

"I don't know him either," Ryan said.

Alex and Michael exchanged looks. "Guys, why don't you go check out the paint samples Buddy has in the other room? Maybe you could give me your opinion on which color you think would look better with the new carpet."

The boys rushed off as if a monster were on their heels.

"I'm sorry," Alex told Michael.

Michael shook his head. "I didn't know Jed was hanging out with some older teens. Especially not ones who are old enough to date."

Anne's heart ached. "What are the boys thought to have possibly done?"

"The vandalism in the park, but we're also looking into a connection between that vandalism and the vandalism here, as well as any connection to the fire," Michael answered. "There are some older reports on file of some instances of vandalism at the Kombses' warehouse. There might be a connection there."

The warehouse! Anne laid a hand on Michael's arm. "Remember Ben said he'd seen a man sleeping in the warehouse sometimes?"

Michael nodded.

"Well, Grace is doing a feature on Denny Thatcher, and as he was leaving the newspaper office, Ben saw him and told me that he was the man sleeping in there," Anne said, but her stomach knotted as she said the words. "Not that I think he had anything to do with the fire. He seemed like a really nice man who has just fallen on some hard times, but I thought you should know. You might talk to Grace and see how to get in touch with Denny if you need to talk to him. To see if he saw anything." She knew she was rambling, but she really didn't mean to direct any accusations in Denny Thatcher's direction.

"Thanks, Anne," Michael said. He slipped his notebook into the inside pocket of his police jacket. "I'd better head back to the station and get this report filed. We'll call you if we have any more questions, Alex." He nodded at them both. "Thanks again."

Anne felt even worse watching him walk away. "I hate that Jed's even remotely involved. It has to put Michael in such a hard position."

Alex nodded. "It always breaks my heart a little when Ryan gets in trouble, even though I know it's all part of growing up."

Anne nodded, understanding completely.

"Hey," Alex said, his voice getting lighter. "I want you to meet the cleanup lady I hired. She did an awesome job with the first mess and came as soon as I called this afternoon."

"I saw that all the paint had been cleaned off that one wall and the movie poster cases. I just hate that it's happened again." Anne fell into step alongside Alex as he led her around to the hall beside the refreshment stand.

There were paint splashes all over one side of the walls in the hall and halfway down the other, where a woman scrubbed at the mess.

"Lisabeth?" Alex said.

She dropped her sponge and stood, smiling as she looked into Alex's face. She was a little shorter than Anne's five-foot-seven-inches with a trim build, but sporting obvious female curves in her hugging jeans and cross-tied scrub shirt.

Lisabeth's curly blonde hair encircled her face like that depicted in pictures of cherubs. Even from the few feet separating them, Anne could make out the spattering of freckles across the bridge of Lisabeth's nose. But it was the sparkling of her green eyes as she looked at Alex that drew Anne's focus.

"Anne Gibson, this is Lisabeth Matthews," Alex introduced them. "Lisabeth, not Elizabeth," he said with a smile.

"Hi," Anne said, putting on a bright smile. What kind of name was Lisabeth, not Elizabeth?

"Hello," Lisabeth replied, finally pulling her stare from Alex. She turned just enough that Alex couldn't see her face as she obviously sized up Anne, letting her scrutiny roam up and down Anne's length.

Anne's back straightened of its own accord. "I haven't seen you around town. Did you just move here?" she asked, struggling to keep her tone light and friendly.

"I rent a place in Deshler," Lisabeth replied without smiling. She turned back to Alex. "And I've been lucky enough to be hired by this kind, handsome man." Her voice raised an octave on the last three words as she put her hand on Alex's forearm.

"Oh, you're being too generous. You're a great worker," Alex said. "I'm lucky you put your application on file recently."

Anne's jaw almost dropped. Alex Ochs was flirting. With Lisabeth Matthews.

And Anne wasn't quite sure how she felt about that.

Chapter Six

"I think I'll have it framed and put in the History Room," Anne told Wendy, pointing at the movie poster of *Summer Swoon*. She could see it with an ornate, gold-colored frame. Maybe a red mat to match the movie title.

"And maybe I'll put the lobby placard in this front glass case. Aunt Edie would probably have gotten a kick out of that," Anne said.

Wendy laughed. "Probably."

Anne wished she'd thought to check back with Mildred about the pictures. Any of those would look great set around the lobby placard. Especially if there was one of Edie and Mildred together on that night.

"Liddie has about finished her project. It looks really good. The copy of the lobby placard is in the center of her poster board, then she included a copy of Aunt Edie's picture and the article in the *Blue Hill Gazette*," Anne said.

"Sounds really good. My poor Justin. He's having the roughest time with the project. He can't decide what he wants to use, but he's assured Chad that he doesn't want to use a poster board. He wants a *real wood* display, whatever that means," Wendy told her.

"Oh my." Anne couldn't smother the chuckle.

"But it's really *my* tree house," Ben's raised voice slipped from the hallway.

"We're both project managers," Ryan argued.

"It'll be in my backyard, so I should get to choose."

Wendy's eyes widened at Anne. "Uh-oh. Sounds like trouble brewing."

"I'm on it," Anne said as she sped down the hall to find the boys standing toe to toe, each holding a hardback book of blueprints.

"Boys, what's going on?" she asked in a no-nonsense tone.

Neither spoke for a minute, they just stood and glared at each other.

"Boys…"

"Mom, we still can't agree on a design. I say that if we can't agree, I should be the one to decide since it's my backyard. Right?"

"But you said we were both project managers," Ryan added.

"Boys," Anne began, "you *are* both project managers. Sometimes to be successful, you have to learn how to work together. You need to figure out a way to decide, even if it's putting the page number of each of your choices in a hat and picking it that way. Once decided, even if it wasn't what you wanted, you should still give it your best attention and focus and work together because that's part of being a team."

"But, Mom—" Ben started.

"No buts. If you two can't figure it out in a peaceful way, the whole project is shut down. Understand?" Anne put her hands on her hips for emphasis.

"Okay," Ben said, but he didn't sound too optimistic.

"Okay, Mrs. Gibson," Ryan said.

"I don't want to hear any more raised voices, understand?"

"Yes, ma'am," the boys said together.

She smiled. "Good. Figure it out." She turned and headed back to the counter where Wendy sat waiting.

"Were you able to limit the bloodshed?" Wendy asked.

Anne took a seat on the stool beside Wendy. "Barely." She chuckled and shook her head. "I don't know how you do it with seven of them. I'm pretty sure I'd be in a straightjacket ninety percent of the time."

Wendy laughed. "Nah, you'd handle it just fine. I've seen you go into your management mode."

"Management mode, huh?" Anne grinned.

Wendy slouched on the stool. "Speaking of Ryan, I heard about the vandalism at Alex's work site. Is there any news on that?"

Anne shook her head. "Not that I know of. It's not really any permanent damage, I don't think. More of just a real hassle and a lot of cleanup."

"That's so sad. Do you think Alex needs any help with the clean-up work? I can put my kids to work helping if he needs it. We could make a big day of it. Have a covered dish, everybody cleaning…I bet a lot of people in the community would pitch in and help," Wendy said.

"Oh no. He doesn't need help," Anne said, stopping Wendy before she dived in. That was so Wendy—to see someone who needed something done and just step in and make it happen. "Alex actually hired someone."

"Really? Who?"

Anne ran her fingernail along the chipped edge of the counter. "Lisabeth Matthews. Says she rents a place over in Deshler. Do you know her?" Anne worked to keep her voice light. She knew Lisabeth had a crush on Alex — women just knew these things, but Alex had been flirting right back.

Anne wasn't used to seeing Alex flirt with anyone besides her, and that was a long time ago. She didn't quite know what she thought about it.

Wendy rubbed her chin. "The name doesn't ring a bell. Is she from here?"

"I don't know. She really didn't say all that much to me."

"What does she look like?" Wendy asked.

"About five-five, I'd guess. Slim. Petite. Curly blonde hair framing her face. Green eyes. A few freckles on the bridge of her nose," Anne rattled off, trying extremely hard to sound bored with the description.

"Huh," Wendy stared at Anne. "About how old?"

"I'd guess around my age, early thirties." Anne remembered the predatory look in Lisabeth's eyes. And her name itself. "Maybe late twenties," she amended.

"I don't think I've met her. If she lives in Deshler, how'd Alex come to hire her?" Wendy asked.

"Apparently, she'd recently put in an application. After the first vandalism incident, he called her and she went right over."

Wendy propped her chin in her hand. "Do tell."

Anne shrugged and crossed her arms over her chest. "She does a good job and goes as soon as she's needed, according to Alex."

Wendy sat up straight on the stool and narrowed her eyes at Anne. "Okay, what gives about her? Why don't you like her?"

"I never said I didn't like her. I don't know her enough to like or dislike her," Anne said, standing and straightening bookmarks stacked on the counter.

Wendy laughed. "Anne Gibson, I can tell when something's bugging you, and something about Lisabeth Matthews bugs you. Now, fess up."

"Well..." Anne still didn't know how she felt about everything, so it was hard to explain. "I just saw the way she flirted with Alex. I don't want him to get hurt."

"Oh. It's like that, huh?" Wendy asked, leaning on the counter.

"She's obviously got a crush on him and he flirted back. We don't know her. She could just be playing with him, and I don't want to see his heart get broken."

"Again?" Wendy asked.

"Ouch." Anne shook her head. "That was a long time ago, Wendy. We were kids. Right out of high school."

"I know, and I didn't mean it ugly toward you. I just meant that you care about him so you don't want to see him get hurt," Wendy said.

"Right. I mean, he's my friend, so of course I care about him. He's been great to me and the kids ever since we came back to Blue Hill. I don't want any of my friends to get hurt." Anne ran out of breath, so she just stopped.

"And you're just concerned because you don't know her, right?" Wendy asked.

"Right."

"If Alex were dating someone from here in town, someone we knew, then you wouldn't worry so much, right?"

"Right." But Anne didn't feel as sure. Was all this because she was *jealous*?

"You know, let me ask around and see what I can find out. Our high school team plays Deshler's, so Chad knows some people over there really well. We could do a little checking," Wendy said.

"No. I'm sure Alex checked out her references before he hired her." Anne certainly didn't want Alex to think she was checking up on him and a woman who seemed interested in him. Besides, she didn't know that Alex was interested in Lisabeth. He was such a kind and gentle soul that he might not have even realized he was flirting.

Anne almost laughed at herself. Alex had told her himself that he hadn't dated much, practically not at all since he'd taken over raising Ryan several years ago. He probably didn't even understand that Lisabeth was flirting with him.

"Well, okay. If you think it's not necessary," Wendy said.

"I'm just being a worrywart."

The door whooshed open and Remi and Bella rushed in, their clear faces shining with excitement. "Oh, good, Mrs. Pyle, you're already here," Bella said.

Wendy laughed. "Of course I'm here. I've been volunteering every Thursday afternoon for months. What are you two up to on your day off?"

"We just left the young adults' group at church," Remi started.

"And we're in charge of the Winter Wonderland dance later this month," Bella finished.

"Oh, that's always so much fun," Wendy said.

"The what?" Anne asked.

"Every year, the church's young adults' group hosts a Winter Wonderland dance to raise money for their special project. The whole town shows up. It's quite the big event," Wendy explained.

"This year, Bella and I are in charge of everything," Remi said. "The theme, the decorations, the refreshments, the music… everything."

"We're glad you're here, Mrs. Pyle, because we wanted to ask both you and Mrs. Gibson if you would be willing to help guide us in the planning stage," Bella said.

"We understand you're both busy, and we wouldn't expect you to actually do the work but just to help us come up with some good ideas," Remi finished.

"Well, I think that sounds like fun," Wendy said. "When is it?"

"The last Friday of this month. From eight until eleven," Bella said.

"That's about right. I'm in." Wendy nodded. "What do you think, Anne?"

"I think it sounds like fun too. Count me in as well. Happy to help out," Anne said with a smile. The thought of a dance sounded like it could be a great time. Good for the community. Good for the church.

Liddie ran into the room. "What's fun, Mommy?"

"Uh." Anne looked at Wendy for help. "I'm guessing kids don't go to the dance?" Of course not. Kids at a dance. What was she thinking?

Wendy shook her head no. "But the youth group has a great setup for babysitting the kids in the back of the church while the grown-ups enjoy the Winter Wonderland."

Liddie hopped from one foot to the other. "Winter Wonderland...is it snowing again?"

Anne laughed. "No, sweetie, it's something for grown-ups at church, and Remi and Bella are in charge. They asked Wendy and me to help them in the planning."

Liddie wrinkled her little nose. "Oh. That doesn't sound like fun to me. Can I watch cartoons, Mommy? Please?"

Anne limited how much time the kids spent watching television or playing on electronics, but Liddie hadn't watched cartoons all week. "Okay, sweetie," Anne said. "But only until I come up to start dinner."

"Okay, Mommy," Liddie said as she bounced to the staircase.

"Well, we need to get home," Remi said.

"Once we get all the notes from the meeting tonight written out, we'll set up a time for us all to get together and brainstorm, okay?" Bella asked.

Wendy nodded. "Sounds like a plan."

"Great. Thank you. Both of you," Remi said.

"Bye, girls," Anne called out as the girls headed out.

The door to the library opened, and a trail of cold air snaked around to the counter just as Alex walked in. "Man, it's really getting colder out there. I thought because we had higher temps yesterday that we might be in a warming trend, but it sure doesn't feel like it out there right now," he said.

"I heard it's going to be even colder this weekend with another chance of snow on Saturday," Wendy said.

"I hope not. We're having to work on Saturday to make up for some of the work time we've missed because of the vandalism."

"Anne was telling me about that," Wendy said. "Do the police have any leads? Any suspects?"

Alex shook his head and leaned against the counter. "Not that they've told me. Or Patrick. He came by this afternoon to check on things. He's thinking about hiring an outside security firm, but I told him I didn't think it was necessary. Nothing's been taken and just time-consuming messes to clean up have been made."

"Anne said you hired someone for cleaning up?" Wendy asked.

Anne sucked in air. Why did Wendy have to bring up Lisabeth? The last thing she needed was for Alex to think she'd been talking about her and him. Them. Or not them. Not together.

She swallowed the groan against her own random and conflicting thoughts.

"Yeah, Lisabeth Matthews. She's been a godsend," Alex said.

"Lisabeth Matthews. *Hmm.* That name doesn't ring a bell," Wendy said.

Anne wanted to strangle Wendy.

"She lives in Deshler and just recently decided to expand her cleaning business to include construction sites. She put in an application several weeks ago."

"Oh," Wendy said, "she has a cleaning business?"

"Well, she works for herself, taking the cleaning jobs she can get," Alex answered.

"I guess she had some pretty good references?" Wendy asked, sneaking a wink at Anne, who *really* wanted to strangle her now.

"To be honest, I didn't check. When she put in the application, I never thought I'd have a need to use a site-cleaning crew, so I never checked her references."

"I see," said Wendy. "What's she like?"

"She's sweet and hardworking. Gets along great with all the guys. Is truly a delight to be around. She makes me laugh all the time, which considering why she's there, is saying something," Alex said. A smile lit up his face as he spoke and his expression went…dreamy.

There went that tightness in Anne's gut again.

Judging by the way Wendy's eyes narrowed, she caught the change in Alex's expression and voice too. "She must be very pretty."

"Why would you say that?" Alex asked.

"Because you seem a little smitten with her," Wendy said.

Alex's cheeks brightened.

Anne swallowed. Since when did Alex blush?

"I'm not smitten. I just think she's really sweet," he said. "She is pretty, but that's beside the point." The pink in Alex's cheeks deepened.

Yeah. Right.

Alex cleared his throat and met Anne's stare. "About tomorrow…"

She smiled. "Need me to pick up Ryan from school and bring him here?"

"I'm sorry to keep asking you, Anne. I just need to get a good start on this job. Mom and Dad invited him to spend Saturday with them before they leave again on Sunday, so I promise not to ask you to watch him then."

Anne waved at him. "Please. I enjoy having Ryan over and he's no problem."

"Except when he and Ben threaten to draw blood," Wendy interjected.

Anne was seriously going to throttle Wendy Pyle! If only she didn't love her so much, but Wendy truly spoke first and thought second. Maybe having all those kids made her just spit things out because she didn't have time to dance around any issue.

"They had an argument?" Alex asked.

"A difference of creative ideas is more like it," Anne answered. "Trying to decide on a plan for the tree house."

"Ah. They're still at odds over that?" he asked.

Anne nodded. "I told them that they needed to make a choice, even if it was pulling the blueprint selection out of a hat, and that once they did that, they would need to accept it and move on together, no matter what."

"How'd that go over?" Alex asked, looking relaxed and comfortable once again as he leaned on the counter.

"Pretty good, I think." Anne scrunched her nose. "I even talked about compromise and working together and all those boring adult things we have to deal with every day."

Alex laughed, and Wendy did too. "Bet they weren't as interested in that as just having you pick between them," Wendy said.

"How'd you know?" Anne asked.

Wendy grinned. "Seven kids, remember?"

"Right." Anne grinned. "Anyway, they cooled it so they either took my advice and worked it out, or both are holding out hoping the other will give in."

"Well, I guess we'll find out soon enough," Wendy said.

"Maybe a break for them on Saturday will be really good for them, then," Alex said.

Anne nodded. "Maybe. But I'm glad Ryan will be here tomorrow. They need to learn to figure it out."

And Anne needed to figure out why the sight of Alex looking all dreamy over Lisabeth Matthews bugged her so much.

Chapter Seven

"I can't believe it's happened again. This is getting ridiculous," Alex was saying to one of his workers as Anne walked into the theater. He turned as her footsteps sounded on the floor. "Anne, what are you doing here?"

"Ryan left his backpack at the library last night, and I know the boys have an English paper due Monday," Anne said, shivering against the cold she'd just stepped out of.

"Thanks, but you didn't have to bring it by. Especially in this cold weather. I would've come and got it." Alex sounded more than a little distracted.

"To tell you the truth, it's nice to get out for a little while by myself on a Saturday." Anne was so grateful that Wendy had called this morning and invited Ben and Liddie over to play with her kids. Anne had left the library in good hands with Remi, dropped the kids off at Wendy's, then brought over Ryan's backpack. She still didn't quite understand why she'd felt compelled to bring it by. She just had a gut feeling that she should.

"Well, I appreciate it," Alex said.

"What's wrong?" Anne asked.

"Vandalism."

"Again?"

He nodded. "Come see." He led the way down the hallway adjacent to the refreshment counter, the one Lisabeth had been cleaning yesterday. "We got the walls in here primed yesterday evening so we could start on the painting today. Just look at it now." He waved at the hallway.

Paint streaks lined the walls. Trash and debris littered the entire hallway. Some pieces of paper were stuck to the paint on the walls.

"This is horrific," Anne said. She took a step toward the hallway, but Alex grabbed her arm and stopped her.

"Nails." He pointed to an empty box lying almost at her feet. "Almost four boxes are empty. Strewn all over the floor."

"Oh, Alex, I'm so sorry." She reached out and gave him a quick hug. "I know how awful this must be for you."

"I'm here, Alex," Lisabeth announced from behind them.

Alex and Anne both turned. Lisabeth marched right between them and stopped, staring at the hallway. "Oh my. It seems my work here is never done."

"I'm sorry, Lisabeth," Alex said.

"It's not your fault, Alex." Lisabeth looked at him as if he were the last piece of a double chocolate cheesecake.

Anne pressed her lips together to stop from saying the obvious. Of course it wasn't Alex's fault. She was almost disgusted that Alex apologized to Lisabeth. Hello? This was the woman's job. He was paying her to clean things up. She should be happy to have to come back.

"Don't you worry, not even a little bit," Lisabeth said, squeezing Alex's arm, "I'll have this cleaned up in a jiffy so you can get to work." She rolled her little cleaning cart behind her. The side of it ran into Anne's leg.

Lisabeth tossed Anne a smile as fake as the one on Liddie's Barbie. "Oh, I'm sorry. Excuse me."

Anne took a step back, and Lisabeth pulled the cart into the hall.

"Maybe you shouldn't have anything touched until the police can come by and file a report," Anne said.

"Already talked to Michael about an hour ago, as soon as I got here and saw the damage," Alex said.

"What did Michael say?" Anne asked.

Lisabeth paused, cocking her hip out and staring at Alex.

"He instructed me to send him some photos." Alex waved his smartphone. "Already taken and sent."

"Are you sure that's enough?" Anne asked, staring at the damage. "Maybe once he has a chance to look at the pictures he'll decide he needs to come out. Or, maybe he'll want to send a forensics team or something."

Lisabeth made a great show of rolling her eyes.

Anne was wrong when she'd told Wendy she didn't know Lisabeth well enough to like or dislike her. It was official—she disliked her.

Alex snorted. "I doubt it, Anne. I know Michael's our friend and all, but, well, you know he just might have a conflict of interest in this."

Because of Jed.

Anne shook her head. "I don't think so, Alex. Michael's a cop down to his very core."

"Maybe, maybe not," Alex said, "but I can't afford to pay my crew to just stand around twiddling their thumbs. I already had to send everybody but Buddy home for the day until everything can get back to ready. Buddy and I will prime the walls after Lisabeth finishes."

Lisabeth smiled so coyly at Alex, even tilting her head just so a lock of curls fell across her cheek. "Oh, I understand, Alex. Time is money. I'll get right on this for you." She turned slightly, just enough that Alex couldn't see her face, and shot Anne a wish-you-would-disappear look.

Oh, as if. Anne wasn't sure if she was jealous or if she just didn't like the flirty nature of Lisabeth, but either way, she'd had enough. She needed to figure out if Alex was as enamored with Lisabeth as the woman obviously was with him.

Anne looped her arm through Alex's and turned him away. "Well, since you can't do anything right now, why don't you let me buy you a cup of coffee over at Coffee Joe's?" The popular place was a small shop nestled between a sporting goods store and health food store, only a few blocks from the school, right across the street from the police station. Joe's offered ice cream cones, sandwiches, and a variety of mouthwatering bakery items besides the wide variety of coffee drinks and teas.

"Sounds like a great plan, but I'm buying you the coffee for coming all the way over here to bring back something Ryan left," Alex said.

Anne glanced over her shoulder to see Lisabeth throwing daggers with her stare. Anne smiled up at Alex. "Then let's get going." She caught Lisabeth's hateful glare from the corner of her eye.

Too bad.

They took Anne's car for the short drive over to Coffee Joe's. The cold air rushed around them as they trudged into the coffee shop. The mouthwatering aroma of some type of pumpkin pastry welcomed Anne as they joined the line at the counter that ran the length of the room. They gave their orders to the barista, then moved to the end of the long counter and waited. In minutes, they received their steaming cups of coffee and found a little table in the corner to sit.

Anne inhaled deeply the rich aroma of her java. Aunt Edie had been the first person to introduce Anne to the wondrous flavor of a strong brew when Anne had turned thirteen. Aunt Edie had shared the coffee early one Sunday morning before the service when Anne would join the church. Aunt Edie had told Anne, "If you're of the age of accountability and able to profess Jesus as your Lord, then you're old enough for a cup of joe." At first, the rich, bold flavor had almost made Anne gag, but she'd drunk the whole cup because it felt like a rite of passage with Aunt Edie. Now, that was exactly how she loved her coffee.

"I'm a little concerned that Michael didn't want to come out and take a report," Anne said calmly.

"Me too. I mean, I know it's hard because Jed's name has been mentioned but so have Ryan's and Ben's, and we're both trying to get to the truth of who is behind the vandalism here and at the park, as well as the fire," Alex said.

Anne nodded and set her cup on the small round table between them. "That concerns me too, how the boys' names keep popping up."

"Me too." Alex took another sip of his coffee, closing his eyes as he did. Funny how she'd never noticed that habit of his before now.

"Did you know the boys played in Marcus Kombs's warehouse sometimes?" she asked.

Alex shook his head. "I had no idea. Did you?"

"Not a clue, which makes me wonder how many other things they're doing that we're unaware of." Anne ran her finger along the rim of the cup. "I mean, if we didn't know they were playing in the warehouse, and apparently know a lot of teenage boys, what else don't we know? It bothers me."

"Have you talked with Ben about your concerns?" Alex asked.

Anne shook her head and took another sip of coffee. "Not yet, but I decided after Liddie goes to bed, I'm going to have a heart-to-heart talk with him. I want him to understand that I need to be aware of things like this."

Alex nodded. "Good idea. I think I'll have a chat with Ryan too. They need to understand we're not trying to hinder their fun, but trying to protect them."

Anne crossed her arms over her chest. "It terrifies me to think of the danger they could have been in inside that warehouse. Or with those boys. Ben is nine and Ryan just ten. They have no business hanging out with boys who are dating. Ben still wears Spider-Man pajamas, for goodness sakes."

"I know. Ryan still sneaks into my bed whenever there's a bad thunderstorm. He's terrified of lightning," Alex said. He laid his hand over Anne's and squeezed. "We'll make them understand how important all of this is."

His touch felt different somehow. Warmer. Stronger. More...intimate.

Anne's mouth went dry as she pulled her hand back and grabbed her coffee. She took another drink, noticing that she trembled just a bit. What was wrong with her? This was *Alex*. They'd been friends forever.

But they'd also been a couple before too.

No, that was so long ago. A lifetime ago. She hadn't thought about them as a couple in a really long time. Had Lisabeth's interest in Alex made Anne see him in a different light? An older light?

"Hey, you two. What are you doing here?" Grace asked as she walked up to their table.

"We had another incident of vandalism at the work site. While it's being cleaned, we decided to have a cup of coffee," Alex said.

"Another incident?" Grace asked, pulling up a chair and sitting.

"This one is a little more aggressive," Anne added.

Alex nodded. "Not just spilling and splashing paint. This one took more time. And we lost four boxes of nails. Yeah, it's only four boxes of nails, but those things add up on a job."

"I'm so sorry, Alex," Grace said. "Hey, I have an idea. Why don't I do a feature on the theater and the renovations and mention the vandalism? Maybe that will encourage anybody who might know something to come forward."

"That's a great idea, Grace. Thanks," Alex said.

"You should contact Mr. Rollings and get some information too," Anne said.

"I will." Grace pulled out her notebook and jotted some notes. "Oh, and I can get in touch with Marcus Kombs and add in information about the fire."

"That sounds awesome," Anne said.

Grace stood. "Yeah. I'm going to grab my coffee and then get started on this so I can get it in the next edition."

"Oh, hey," Anne said, standing. "I'll be right back, Alex." She led Grace to the line. "Listen, I hope I didn't cause a problem, but yesterday, I mentioned to Michael that Denny Thatcher was the man Ben saw sleeping in Mr. Kombs's warehouse a time or two. I really didn't mean to make him a suspect, but Michael needed to know."

"It's okay, Anne. The truth is the truth. My article on Denny will be in the next edition of the paper too, so maybe he'll get a job and won't be homeless anymore so he won't have to resort to sneaking into abandoned warehouses to sleep out of the cold."

"You know," Anne began speaking as the idea sparked, "I wonder if the church has ever considered opening up some of the Sunday school rooms during the winter nights for homeless people."

Grace shrugged. "I don't know, but I bet you could mention it to Reverend Tom. He'd know if it was something to even consider."

Anne nodded. "I think I will talk to him." She glanced back at Alex. "I'd better finish my coffee. I think Alex is chomping at the bit to get back to work."

Grace tilted her head. "Did I interrupt something when I came in?"

Anne's pulse hitched. "What do you mean?" Anne swallowed.

"I saw Alex holding your hand, which isn't a big thing, but the look on your face when I walked up… I don't know, you looked different. Like maybe it was more than a friend holding another friend's hand?"

Anne shook her head. "No. We were just talking about Ben and Ryan and how worried we are that they've been places and with people we weren't aware of." Well, at least that part was the truth.

Grace smiled. "Oh. Okay. I guess my imagination just moves a little into left field on occasion."

"No worries. I'll talk to you later, okay?"

Grace nodded.

Anne returned to Alex, who finished off his coffee. "Sorry about that," Anne said. "I just wanted to let Grace know I mentioned Denny Thatcher to Michael. Her article about Denny is going to be in tomorrow's paper."

"I wonder if Michael located him," Alex said.

"I don't know. I don't believe Grace knows either." Anne took the last sip of her coffee.

"Well, I'd better get back to the site. Check on Lisabeth's status," Alex said, standing.

Anne let him help her into her coat. "Lisabeth seems like a nice enough kid," she volunteered as they stepped out into the cold.

Alex laughed. "Kid? Anne, she's only a few years younger than us." He opened the driver's door of Anne's car for her.

She waited until he was inside and the engine warming up to reply. "I guess maybe it's her level of maturity that makes me think of her as a kid." Wow, was she really being catty? That was so unlike her.

"You think she's immature?" Alex asked.

Anne put the car in gear and backed out of the parking lot. "I just get that impression. Maybe I'm wrong." Anne realized she really was being catty. And she didn't like that about herself. She would have to do some serious personal introspection soon.

"*Hmm.* I don't see her as immature. She's been nothing but a very hard worker."

And a very serious flirt, Anne thought but kept the sentiment to herself. Poor Alex was totally unaware of the woman's interest in him.

"She's always got a great attitude and she makes me smile," Alex said, smiling even as he talked about her.

Maybe Anne was wrong and he was aware of Lisabeth's interest in him. Maybe it wasn't just a crush. Anne pulled the car up to the front of the theater.

Alex unfastened his seat belt. "You aren't coming in?" he asked.

She shook her head. "I know you have work to do, and I need to get back to the library. Are you and Ryan having dinner with your parents?"

He nodded. "They leave tomorrow for another mission trip, so we want to have a family dinner before they go."

"Then I'll see you at church tomorrow. Thanks for the coffee," she said.

"Anytime, you know that. Good luck with your talk with Ben."

"And yours with Ryan," she said as he climbed out of the car. She gave him a wave, then drove off, proud of herself for resisting the urge to go in with him and watch Lisabeth's reaction. She really needed to figure out her catty attitude.

Maybe it was Lisabeth's attention to Alex that made Anne think about him in a different light. Or maybe it was that her heart was telling her it was time to open up to loving again.

Or maybe she was just crazy.

Back at the library, she'd barely gotten settled in and let Remi head on home when a tall, handsome man walked through the door. He wasn't just handsome, he was model-perfect handsome with broad shoulders on a very muscular frame with thick, wavy black-as-night hair and eyes as blue as Alex's. He couldn't be more than forty, but he had the posture and confidence of a man much older.

"Hello," he said as he approached Anne at the front desk. He had almost a Southern drawl. Enchanting.

"Hi," she said breathily. Up close, she could see his long, curled eyelashes that most women would die for. His jawbone was defined and his nose perfectly straight. The man was *beautiful*.

"I don't believe we've had the pleasure of meeting." He smiled, revealing perfect teeth. Was there anything about the man not perfect?

Anne smiled back. "I'm Anne Gibson, librarian."

"I'm Eli Wallington, owner of the newly established Wallington Construction, and I'm delighted to meet you." Yes, it was definitely a Southern drawl she'd detected. Charming.

"Welcome to the Blue Hill Library. May I help you find something?" Anne asked.

"I'm looking to locate some of the archived blueprints for some of the historic buildings in downtown Blue Hill. I was told you are the lady to see." His smile should require a permit—it could be that lethal to women.

"Who told you that?"

"Coraline Watson. Lovely lady I had the pleasure of meeting up with several weeks ago as I set about opening my business."

Ahh. Coraline. She was a neighbor of Mildred's and a self-proclaimed avid birdwatcher, but it was common knowledge among the townsfolk that ever since Coraline moved to Blue Hill over a dozen years ago, she'd kept up with most everybody's history. Still, Anne liked her. "How is Coraline? I haven't seen her the last couple of weeks."

"She's charming and knowledgeable and smart as a whip," Eli said.

Anne grinned. "That she is." She moved around from behind the counter. "Let's see, the archived blueprints for Blue Hill's historic buildings, the ones we have, are in the History Room." She led the way to the front of the first floor.

The room's walls boasted sunset colors, with sepia photographs of the town's rich railroad history hanging on the walls, the pictures Anne had paid top dollar to have made from damaged negatives. It housed dark cherry wood bookshelves and a beautiful study with chairs upholstered in fabric in rich, jeweled colors. A large oriental rug centered the room.

Anne showed Eli to the long, drawer-style shelves that held copies of blueprints. "The listing of what's in each shelf is here," she said, pointing to the index encased at the end of the shelf. "You just look up the building, and if we have the blueprints, then it'll show you which drawer it's in."

"Looks simple enough," Eli said, his drawl as warm as the sun that Blue Hill hadn't seen in days.

"Where are you from, Eli, if you don't mind my asking?"

He chuckled. "The accent give me away?"

She smiled and nodded.

"I'm originally from Louisiana." That explained the accent.

"What made you move to Pennsylvania?" Anne asked.

"Well, I'd like to say I came here to start a business, which would be partially true, but the heart of the matter is I came up here to be near a woman I met through mutual friends. She lived just outside of Deshler."

A man who would move across the United States for a woman? Interesting. Anne smiled.

"Unfortunately, things didn't work out between us, but I'd already started building a business here. I decided to stay and stick it out," Eli said with a grin. "And the people sure are nice as all get-out too. Not at all what I expected. I'd grown up hearing Northerners were standoffish."

"Well, I'm delighted to hear you've had a good experience. Welcome to Blue Hill. I lived in New York for college, then married and had my children there. I just recently moved back to town myself," she shared.

"You and your husband enjoying the move back?" he asked.

Slick way of asking but not asking if she was still married. Anne shook her head. "My husband passed away."

"Oh, I'm terribly sorry," Eli said.

"Thank you. It was several years ago." Saying it out loud, there was no longer a stab of grief or pain. Good memories of what she and Eric had shared, of course, but nothing else. It was...refreshing. Anne let out a sigh. "I'm very happy here."

"Well, it's a lovely town that's been very welcoming to me."

"Anne," Wendy's voice rang out.

She smiled. "And that's the sound of my children being returned." She pointed to the drawers. "Do you think you can handle this?"

"I'll be fine. Thank you."

"Okay. Holler if you need any help," Anne said as she rushed from the room.

"I will," Eli's voice chased after her. My, but the man was suave and charismatic.

And apparently, available.

Chapter Eight

"Liddie and Ben should both sleep well tonight," Wendy said as Anne rounded the corner to the front of the library. "Chad had all the kids bundled up outside, running and ripping until they're all exhausted."

Anne smiled. "Did they go upstairs?"

Wendy shook her head. "I reminded them that, while you had likely let Hershey out to run, you wouldn't have had time to play with him. Ben and Liddie took his ball and they're in the backyard giving Hershey a workout."

"Thanks for that," Anne said. "And for taking them today. They needed the fresh air, even if it's so cold out."

"I know. I went ahead and brought them over because Chad saw a few flurries." Wendy laid her coat and scarf over the back of one of the chairs by the front table.

"Are we supposed to get a lot? I didn't watch the news this morning," Anne said, taking a seat on one of the stools behind the counter.

"They're forecasting a couple of inches, but I've learned to expect the prediction but prepare for four times that." Wendy chuckled.

Anne chuckled as well. "Well, I think I'm good on groceries and water."

"What about firewood? Do you have plenty? If not, I can have Chad bring over a truckload," Wendy said.

"No, I'm good. Alex had given me a couple of cords."

"Good," Wendy said. "It'll be a fireplace kind of night tonight. Since the kids are worn out, Chad and I are planning to just sit in front of the fire together and enjoy the peacefulness."

Usually, such things didn't cause Anne to give her single status another thought. But today...

"Hey, Wendy. Do you know Eli Wallington?" she asked, keeping her voice low.

Wendy's eyes widened. "He's quite handsome."

Anne giggled. "So you have met him."

Wendy nodded. "Girl, if I were single, I'd be chasing that man down like nobody's business."

"*Shh*. Aside from his looks, what can you tell me about him?" Anne asked, glancing over her shoulder toward the History Room.

"Well, I've only met him a couple of times. Seems nice enough. Polite. Has a really cute accent, but you know that if you've met him." Wendy wiggled her eyebrows. "I'm assuming you have, which is why you're asking me about him."

"*Shh*. He's in the History Room," Anne whispered.

"Here?" Wendy's hands went to her hair and fluffed. "Why didn't you tell me?"

"He's looking up some old blueprints," Anne answered.

"I say if you're interested and he asks you out, you should definitely go," Wendy said. "You'd be the envy of every single woman in Blue Hill."

Except for Lisabeth Matthews. Well, maybe if she met Eli...no, that was meddling and Anne wouldn't meddle. At least, not like this.

"He hasn't asked me out, and I'm not interested." Well, maybe not. "I was just curious what you knew about him."

Wendy shrugged. "Suit yourself. Like I said, I don't really know him. Only met him a couple of times, but he seemed like a good enough guy to me."

Not much help. Anne made a mental note to ask Coraline when she had a chance.

Wendy's cell phone chimed. Wendy dug it out of her coat pocket and stared at a text message. "Well, I need to run. Chad says I need to pick up an extra gallon or two of milk—just in case." She slipped on her coat and wrapped her scarf around her neck.

Anne couldn't imagine how much milk they went through in a week with seven kids. Seven. Even with her two, it sometimes felt like Ben and Liddie were eating her out of house and home. "Thanks again, Wendy. Drive carefully."

"Call us if you need anything," Wendy said, then was gone, replaced by Ben and Liddie.

Wendy was right—they were worn out. Exhaustion coated both of them as they ran and gave Anne hugs.

"Did you have fun at Wendy's?" Anne asked.

"Emily, me, and Justin played tag," Liddie said, even as she yawned.

"Well, why don't you go on upstairs and wash up? The roast I put in the Crock-Pot this morning should be ready soon."

"Yummy. Okay, Mommy." Liddie yawned again, then headed to the stairs.

"Hershey's all fed with fresh water. I put one of the old blankets from the washroom on his bed in case he needed some extra warmth," Ben said.

"If it gets too cold, I guess we could let him in for the night."

Ben's eyes widened. "Really?"

"Really. But just for tonight. And only if the temperatures continue to drop," Anne said. "Go on up and check on your sister. I'll be up soon."

"Okay, Mom." Ben headed to the stairs.

Anne glanced at the clock. The library would close soon, but if it was about to start snowing, maybe she should go ahead and close. There wasn't anyone else here, anyway, aside from Eli.

She shut down the computers, then secured the desk as they did every evening. After finishing the rest of the closing procedures, she quietly walked to the History Room.

Eli stood bent over the large table she'd put in the corner, poring over a blueprint. Anne didn't want to disturb him, so approached slowly. "Eli?" she said softly.

He jumped. "Goodness, you gave me a start."

Anne smiled. "I'm sorry. I didn't want to disturb you, but I'm closing up."

"Oh, I'm sorry. I didn't realize it had gotten so late," Eli said. He reached for the blueprint spread out over the table.

"Don't worry about that. I'll put it away," Anne said.

"Oh, I couldn't let you do that," he said, lifting the blueprint.

"It's my job, actually." Anne smiled and took the blueprint from him.

"But I don't feel right about it. I took it out, so I must put it back," he said, reaching for the blueprint.

Now he was just getting weird. She set it on the table, then turned and led him to the door. "Do come back next week, though. I'll enjoy getting to know you."

He frowned for only a second, then flashed his perfect smile and gave her a nod. "And I, you, Miss Anne Gibson. Have a good evening," he said before stepping outside.

The wind nearly stole Anne's breath as she waited until he'd cleared the walkway. She locked the door behind him, turned out the front lights, and then went into the History Room. She made it a habit when she closed to always refile things left on tables. She just couldn't sleep knowing otherwise.

She checked the blueprint to see which one it was so she could look up on the index where to file it, then froze as she recognized what it was.

It was the blueprint for the warehouse that had burned down.

Anne filed the blueprint, but her mind raced as she climbed the stairs. Why had Eli Wallington been looking at those plans? Did he have something to do with the fire? What other reason could he have had for looking at the blueprint? She should tell someone. Michael?

She remembered how awful she felt telling Michael about Denny, and that had been based on Ben's eyewitness account. With Eli, she couldn't risk tainting his reputation without something solid, especially not when he was new and trying to build up his business.

Chewing her bottom lip, Anne climbed the stairs slowly. She couldn't imagine a reason for Eli to be looking at blueprints to a warehouse that had just burned down. Nothing made sense. Yet, despite his amazing good looks, he was a businessman and she had to be careful not to spread unfounded suspicions. Not without knowing more. If he came back, she would just ask him.

She didn't have time to think about it once she got upstairs and built a fire. She and the kids had a hot, filling dinner of pot roast and vegetables, but Liddie could barely eat for all the yawning. As soon as they were done eating, Anne told Liddie, "Sweetie, go ahead and get your pajamas. I'll come draw your bath now."

"Okay, Mommy," Liddie said, walking down the hall to her bedroom. That was a clear indication that she was exhausted because Liddie never walked anywhere, she normally skipped or jumped or ran.

Anne quickly set the temperature of the water and laid out Liddie's toothbrush.

Liddie put her pajamas on the counter and grabbed her toothbrush. "Mommy, please don't make me wash my hair tonight. I'm so bone tired."

Anne pressed her lips together not to laugh. Liddie was such a little mockingbird, repeating the exact phrases Anne used all the time. She kissed her daughter's head. "Okay, sweetie. No hair washing tonight. But finish brushing your teeth." She turned off the water then headed to the kitchen to clean up dinner's mess.

Ben had already rinsed and loaded their dishes. Anne was impressed but remembered hers and Alex's talk...and the talk she needed to have with her son. She finished the cleanup while Ben stoked the fire. She sat on the couch as he returned the poker to the holder.

"Ben, I need to talk to you. Sit down." She patted the couch beside her.

"What's wrong, Mom?"

She sent up a silent prayer for God to help her with the words, then took a deep breath. "I know it's been hard on you since your dad died. I can only imagine how difficult it is to be a boy without your dad."

"Mom, I'm okay. Really. We've had this talk."

"No, listen. I just want you to understand that I get that it might be hard for you, but you're old enough to understand that it's hard for me to be a single parent to you and Liddie too." Anne paused, her mind scrambling on how to continue.

"Mom, it's okay if you want to marry again. I understand," Ben said, sounding a lot older than nine.

"I don't." But she was only thirty-four, so falling in love again and getting married was very possible. At least she hoped so. "I mean, I haven't even been dating anyone." This was going all wrong. She shook her head again. "That's not the point. None of this is. I wanted to tell you that I'm worried about you."

"Why?" Ben asked, looking confused.

"Because, Ben, I didn't know you were playing in a warehouse. I didn't know you knew much older teenage boys and apparently spend time with them. Both incidents could be very dangerous for you."

"How can knowing teenagers be dangerous, Mom?" Ben asked. He didn't sound disrespectful, but he also didn't sound innocent.

"Because older boys have been known to do stupid things. Sometimes they do illegal things that can get them and anybody with them in big, big trouble," Anne said. Images of Ben smoking or being introduced to drugs or some crime nearly had her considering home schooling him and not ever letting him out of her sight.

But she knew she couldn't shelter him from life, no matter how much her maternal instincts screamed otherwise.

"I don't do stuff like that, Mom," Ben said, wearing a look of pure offense.

"I didn't say you did, Ben. You could be influenced, though. But, that isn't the issue. The issue is that you're going places and doing things I'm not aware of."

Ben stared into the fire. "I'm not a baby."

"I didn't mean to imply that you were."

"But you're treating me like one." Ben cut his stare to her.

"Benjamin Gibson, don't take that tone with me. You know you shouldn't have been in that warehouse, and that's why you didn't tell me. Because you didn't want to get in trouble," Anne's full parent-mode had flipped on.

"What if something had fallen over on you when you were in that warehouse? Or some faulty wiring caused a fire and the exit was blocked? Or what if you stumbled upon someone sleeping there who wasn't as kind as Mr. Thatcher and hurt you?" Anne was trembling now. "What would you have done then? You could have been hurt, trapped, or even kidnapped, and I wouldn't have even known where to look for you." Her heartbeat raced.

"I'm sorry, Mom. I didn't see it that way," Ben said, hanging his head.

"I know, and that's why I'm talking to you now," Anne said, evening out her tone. "I'm your mother and must take care of you, but I can't do that if you go places you aren't supposed to go and I'm not even aware. Do you understand?"

"Yes, Mom." He still hung his head.

"And I'm not saying it's bad to hang around other, older kids, but when I don't know who you're spending time with, it makes me wonder why you aren't telling me. Some people might even think that you were hiding something."

He looked up and made eye contact. "I'm not hiding anything, Mom. I promise." Moisture shimmered in his big, round eyes.

She wanted to hug him and tell him it was all okay, but she needed to be a strong parent. It was for his own good.

"I believe you, but, Ben, this can't happen again. I must know where you will be at all times. If you say you're going to be playing in the park, then that's where I expect you to be. Not down the street from the park in a warehouse."

"Okay, Mom."

"And if you meet up with some other kids while you're somewhere you're supposed to be, I would expect you to let me know who you are with."

"Okay, Mom," Ben said.

"I'm serious, Ben. I know you might think I'm being harsh, but I'm looking out for you." She left off the 'because I love you' bit because she'd never liked it when she was told that as a kid. She hadn't believed it until she had children of her own.

"Yes, Mom."

"Okay." She stood and reached for the poker. "Go ahead and take your shower. We have church in the morning."

"All right." He stood and headed toward the bathroom, but stopped at the hall. "Mom?"

"Yes, Ben?"

"I love you."

"I love you too," she answered, grateful that he ran on to take his shower because she knew she'd start crying any minute now.

* * *

Anne sipped her coffee while she waited for Ben and Liddie to finish breakfast early Sunday morning. She'd put some beef tips in the Crock-Pot on high, and already the house smelled delicious.

"Can we play in the snow when we get home, Mommy?" Liddie asked. She'd been enamored with the two and a half inches of snow that fell overnight. She loved the snow. Always had, ever since she could walk.

"Maybe," Anne said as she glanced through the newspaper.

Liddie prattled on about the snow and building a snowman — it didn't matter if there was enough snow on the ground to build a snowman or not, Liddie always tried to build one. Ben finished his breakfast and went to get ready.

"Hurry up, sweetie," Anne told Liddie, then turned the page on the paper. She always looked forward to reading the letters to the editor. Sometimes they were quite comical, especially if one of the older residents of Blue Hill got on a roll about something. Most of the people who took the time to write a letter to the editor had some very strong feelings about what they wrote in about. Very, very strong feelings.

But the letter to the editor featured in the latest edition of the *Gazette* wasn't a longtime resident of Blue Hill. Instead, it was from a Sally Langford, who seemed greatly opposed to the theater preservation. According to Sally, Patrick should consider modernizing the theater instead of preserving its historical roots. She suggested incorporating an IMAX-type theater instead of renovating the old theater. She mentioned new, reclining seats, bigger screens, and plug-in chargers for people's electronics.

"Mommy, I'm ready to get dressed now," Liddie said, drawing Anne from the letter.

"Okay, sweetie. Go brush your teeth, and I'll be in there in a minute to help you get dressed." Anne closed the paper and put the kids' oatmeal bowls in the dishwasher before heading to help Liddie.

But she couldn't help wondering just how against the theater's preservation Sally Langford was. She couldn't wait to see Grace and get her take on the letter.

CHAPTER NINE

It was a lovely service, Reverend Tom," Anne said, shaking his hand as she stepped out of the sanctuary.

"Thank you, Anne," he said, smiling as always.

"I wanted to invite you and Maggie to the house for lunch, if you don't already have plans."

"You know what? That would be nice. Thank you," the reverend said.

Anne nodded. "Good. Then we'll see you in about an hour?"

"See you then," Reverend Tom said, already taking the hand of the person behind Anne.

Anne met Alex in the entry. "How was dinner with your parents?" she asked.

"Good. They were flying out at six-something this morning," he answered as his hand automatically went to rest under her elbow.

"I'm glad Ryan got to spend some time with them before they left." Even though the Ochses lived in Blue Hill, because of their work in training missionaries, Ryan didn't see them much more than Ben and Liddie saw their grandparents.

"Yeah, he enjoyed spending the day with them, but he's anxious to get back to work on the tree house project," Alex said, taking the coat from her hand and holding it out to her.

"Thanks," she said as he eased the coat up and straightened the back collar. "I think Ben had withdrawals." She chuckled.

"Did you get a chance to have that talk with Ben?" Alex asked.

"I did. It went well." She swallowed. "How about you with Ryan?"

Alex nodded as they waited in the foyer for Liddie to finish talking with Cindy and Becca. "It went okay. This parenting is hard, huh?"

"It is." She slipped on her gloves. "Listen, I've got beef tips and rice for lunch, and Reverend Tom and Maggie are coming over. Why don't you and Ryan join us too?"

"Are you sure that's not too many of us? I don't want to put you out," Alex said.

"Don't be silly. I wouldn't have invited you if that was a problem." She saw the conflict in his eyes. "Come on, Alex. It'll be fun."

"Well, I never could pass up your cooking."

She grinned. "Good."

Liddie bounded into Anne's legs. "Mommy, can I play in the snow now?"

"Let's see when we get home. Now, where's your brother?"

"He and Ryan just went out," Alex answered. He held out his free hand to Liddie. "Ready to get home?"

Liddie nodded and took his hand, and together the three of them carefully headed to their parked vehicles.

Anne couldn't help noticing that Liddie seemed to be one hundred percent comfortable with Alex. Anne almost missed a step as she realized what she was thinking. Had she lost her mind?

Townspeople nodded and spoke to her and Alex as they made their way to the parking lot. Everyone seemed to accept her and Alex together. As more people waved and said greetings, she realized she and Alex were probably the most popular non-couple couple.

Anne wasn't quite sure what to think about that.

Alex offered to let Ben ride with him and Ryan to their house to change. Anne agreed, then settled Liddie in her booster seat before driving the short way home. She let her thoughts run their natural course as Liddie practiced singing the song she'd learned in Sunday school.

Anne thought she and Ben had come to an understanding last night, but she still didn't like the way her son's name kept coming up in the course of police investigations. The fire in the warehouse. The vandalism at the park. The vandalism at the theater. Was there even a connection between the three?

Ben had assured her that he wasn't involved in any of the situations, and she believed him, but she couldn't say the same about the police. Michael had seemed a little on the skeptical side, but now that his son was linked...Anne just couldn't be sure she would be unbiased if she were in his shoes. On the other hand, it was apparent that Josie had her own uncertainty, but she didn't seem to head up any of the investigations.

Anne parked the car and helped Liddie up the back staircase. "Change into your play clothes, sweetie, and hang up your dress."

"Can I put on my outside clothes to play in the snow?" Liddie asked as they burst into the living room.

Anne grinned. "Sure. But let me check you before you go out," she said. Liddie was apt to put ski bibs over a bathing suit and declare herself suitably dressed.

As Anne changed from her dress into an old, worn, comfortable pair of jeans and loose cable-knit sweater, she continued thinking about the three incidents…and the suspects.

First there were the teenagers. Jed and Brent were the two Ben and Ryan had named. It was possible they were involved in the vandalism in the park. They were in the park, which made Anne a little curious. What were two teenage boys doing hanging out in a park? Wouldn't they be at some type of cooler hangout? It was very likely that the park acts of vandalism were connected to the theater's.

And what about Eli Wallington? He was new and just starting a new construction business but was looking up the blueprints for the same building that just burned down? For what reason?

Anne reached for her slippers as she sat on the edge of her bed. Finally, what about Sally Langford? Sure, it might be far-fetched to think she might have had something to do with the vandalism at the theater just because she wrote a letter to the editor against the preservation, but it was worth considering. Although, if Sally had been responsible for the theater vandalism, that would mean there was no connection between the vandalism of the theater and the park, and she wouldn't have likely had anything to do with the fire.

All of it made Anne's head ache.

"Mommy, I'm ready," Liddie announced, standing in Anne's doorway.

After approving Liddie's attire and granting permission for her to go outside as long as she stayed in the backyard, along with giving the instructions to let Hershey out to play, Anne went into the kitchen to put the green beans and rice on to cook, and preheat the oven for the dinner rolls.

It was less than five minutes later when a knock rapped on the door, then Alex's voice trailed into the kitchen, "Anne?"

"Come on in," she replied, setting the rice's burner to simmer and covering the pot with a lid.

"Ryan and Ben decided to play outside with Liddie and Hershey," Alex said.

"Ben better not get his good shirt messed up," she replied. It was unlikely, since his coat provided ample coverage. Like the other boys at church, he wore jeans and a nice button-down shirt to services most Sundays.

"Want me to call him in?" Alex asked as he hung his coat on the hooks behind the back door.

"No. He'll be fine with his coat over it."

Alex sniffed. "It smells great in here. What can I do to help?"

She could always count on Alex to step in and help out...in the yard, with the kids, in the kitchen.

No, she needed to stop letting these thoughts of fancy creep up on her all the time.

"Um, you could set the table, if you'd like," she said.

"I'm on it, Chief." He automatically went to the sideboard and pulled out a tablecloth.

Anne turned her attention back to the kitchen, refusing to notice how handsome Alex looked in his jeans and how the blue of his sweatshirt set off the blue in his eyes.

The timer on the rice cooker had just gone off and Alex had just called the kids in when Reverend Tom and Maggie arrived.

Moments later, everyone sat around the table and joined hands for Reverend Tom to offer up grace.

"Guess what, Mommy?" Liddie spoke as soon as the plates were passed around.

"What, sweetie?" Anne asked.

"I got to be a 'ciding factor," Liddie said proudly.

"A what?" Anne asked as Reverend Tom, Maggie, and Alex all hid smiles.

"I got to choose which tree house Ben and Ryan build."

"You did?" Anne asked Liddie as she set her daughter's plate in front of her but looked at Ben.

"Yep!"

Ben nodded. "We just couldn't agree on a plan, so we agreed to let Liddie be the deciding factor in which one to build." He snuck an extra roll onto his plate, but Anne let it slide.

"She picked the one I'd wanted," Ryan offered. No question he was clearly happy about Liddie's selection.

Alex frowned, but Anne gave a gentle shake of her head to him. She studied Ben's face. He didn't look out of sorts. "So it's final now?" she asked.

"Yep. We did what you told us to do: agree to a way of deciding and then be happy with whatever plan won," Ben said.

Wasn't exactly how she worded it, but the meaning was the same. Anne was proud of her son, and of Ryan. "Good job, boys. That's what working together is all about."

Both of them beamed as they grabbed their forks.

"That's an important lesson to learn," Reverend Tom said in between bites. "Blessed are the peacemakers. Remember that. I promise you, it will come in handy down the road."

Alex chuckled. "That's the truth."

"We're going to start measuring today. After lunch," Ryan said. "Would you help us, Uncle Alex?"

"Sure. As soon as the kitchen is cleaned up, I'll be happy to help you," Alex said.

"Can I help too?" Liddie asked.

The unspoken answer was clear on both Ben's and Ryan's faces.

Maggie leaned over the table and said to Liddie, "I was hoping after lunch that you would show me all of your dolls. I so enjoy seeing them."

Liddie bobbed her head happily and went about finishing her lunch.

Soon, the boys were finished eating and begging to be excused and let outside. Once Anne made sure they carried their empty plates into the kitchen, she excused them.

"Mommy, can I be excused too?" Liddie asked.

"Carry your plate to the kitchen and you may."

Liddie did, then stood beside Maggie's chair.

"Liddie, leave Mrs. Sloan in peace," Anne said.

Maggie smiled at Liddie. "I'm almost done, then I'll come to your room to see your dolls, okay?"

Liddie nodded and bounced toward her room.

Anne watched her go, then zoomed in on the conversation between Alex and Reverend Tom.

"It's been more of a hassle than destroyed," Alex was saying. "Paint all over the place, trash everywhere, and boxes of nails stolen."

"I thought they were in the hallway," Anne interrupted.

Alex shook his head. "After Lisabeth had them all picked up, only about one box was recovered. We had four boxes, so that would mean that three are missing."

"I didn't realize," Anne said. "You know, all the vandalism has been minor. Very minor, considering."

"What do the police make of that?" Reverend Tom asked. "Are they thinking it's kids?"

"Maybe," Alex answered, his gaze locked on Anne's. "Michael is heading up the investigation, I think."

"I didn't see him in church this morning. He must be working the case," Maggie offered. She turned to look at Alex. "Who is this Lisabeth you mentioned?"

"She's the new lady I hired to clean up the mess the vandals make. Lisabeth Matthews. She's pretty amazing," Alex said, his blue eyes almost sparkling.

Anne's insides twisted. Oh. Goodness. She was jealous.

Really? Now? She'd been around Alex since she moved back to Blue Hill but only lately had she begun to really *think* about Alex. Was it because of Lisabeth's interest in Alex that Anne started seeing him as an available man? Or, was she just being possessive?

"I've never met her," Reverend Tom said. "Is she new to town?"

"She lives in Deshler. I'll have to invite her to come to church," Alex said.

Anne stood and grabbed the tea pitcher from the counter. "Would anyone like more tea?" she asked, filling her own glass.

Maggie held up her own glass for Anne. "Alex, it sounds like you might be taken with this lady?"

Alex blushed. Anne turned away and put the pitcher back on the counter. She took a moment to concentrate on breathing normally before returning to the table.

"I'm sorry, I don't mean to pry," Maggie said. "I'm just pleased to see you interested. You're a wonderful man, Alex, and I'd like to see you happy. I don't believe I've ever seen you date anyone."

Anne shifted uncomfortably in her chair. When she glanced up, she met Reverend Tom's sympathetic look. Maggie hadn't grown up in Blue Hill, but Reverend Tom knew all the town's past secrets, including the fact that Anne and Alex had been high school sweethearts and that Anne had broken Alex's heart when she went away to college.

Alex cleared his throat and stood. "I think I promised two young men that I'd help them take some measurements." He carried his and Maggie's plate to the kitchen while Anne grabbed Reverend Tom's.

Maggie stood. "And I believe I have some dolls to look at with a certain young lady."

"Guess that leaves you and me to clear the table," Reverend Tom told Anne.

"Don't be silly. I'll do this later," Anne said, waving a hand over the kitchen counter.

"Anne, I'm sorry Maggie made you uncomfortable. She doesn't know about your past with Alex."

Anne glanced about. She and the reverend were alone. Maybe she should unburden her worries where Alex was concerned. "Reverend Tom, I'm having a bit of a struggle."

He sat on one of the chairs. "About?"

"Alex." She slipped into the chair beside him.

"Because of this Lisabeth?"

She nodded.

"And you might be feeling just a little jealous?" Reverend Tom asked.

"How'd you know?" She felt relieved that she didn't have to say it. Admitting it out loud would make it…real.

The reverend smiled. "It's natural, Anne."

"It is?" Nothing about how she was feeling felt natural.

"Of course. You and Alex have a romantic past. It wasn't a tug on your heart when you came back because you are a widow, but now, more time has passed, and you and Alex have fallen back into a comfortable relationship. You're friends. Your kids are best friends. You enjoy being around each other. It's natural for those old romantic feelings to resurface."

"Is it wrong?" she asked.

Reverend Tom patted her hand. "Of course not, Anne. You both are good, Christian adults. You are both responsible and single. Whatever romantic feelings you have, they can be very good for you two."

"But that's just it. I don't know how I feel, and I'm not certain Alex feels anything toward me except friendship."

"Ah, then that, my friend, is a totally different matter. When it comes to knowing if you love someone, that's something only you can decide."

That was her problem—she just didn't know.

CHAPTER TEN

"Good afternoon," Eli Wallington greeted Anne on Monday afternoon.

Without meaning to, Anne smoothed her slacks behind the library's front counter. "Hello. Are you back to look at more blueprints?" she asked.

"Yes, I am." His smile was more than merely disarming, but Anne was increasingly curious about what he was doing looking at plans of the warehouse that had burned down.

She fell into step beside him to the History Room. "I'm curious what you're working on."

He laughed, a deep laugh that echoed off the walls. "Haven't you heard, curiosity killed the cat?"

"I have heard that, but I'm not a cat, so I guess I'm safe," she said, noticing he failed to answer her question. Of course, he was under no obligation to do so, but the fact that he was so closed mouthed seemed very suspicious.

He flashed her a dazzling smile as they paused near the drawers. "I'm researching a project I'm considering taking on. Is that enough to satisfy your curiosity, Miss Librarian? I'm afraid my potential client won't allow me to say more."

From someone else, his teasing might have come across as offensive. With Eli Wallington, it didn't. She grinned. "I guess it'll have to do." Maybe Marcus Kombs had offered Eli's company the job of rebuilding his warehouse and Eli was doing research before he agreed to take on the job. That wouldn't make him suspect, but instead would prove he took due diligence in his work ethic.

"Anne!" Grace's voice trailed down the hallway.

"In the History Room," Anne called out, knowing no one else was in the library this afternoon. Well, except Ben and Ryan, who were, of course, huddled at their table in the Nonfiction Room with their notepads and pencils, working on calculations of materials required since Alex had helped them measure.

"What are you doing in here—" Grace stopped short as she stared at Eli. "I'm sorry, I didn't realize you were with someone." She smiled up at him, her eyes widening. "I don't believe we've met. I'm Grace Hawkins, editor of the *Blue Hill Gazette*."

"It's a pleasure, Ms. Hawkins. I'm Eli Wallington of Wallington Construction."

"Nice to meet you. Wallington Construction?" Grace asked.

"We're new," he said, his voice almost mesmerizing.

Grace stood, silent. Anne struggled not to laugh. Very few times had she ever seen Grace Hawkins speechless because of a man. She needed saving.

"We'd better let you get to your business, Eli," Anne said, looping her arm through her friend's. "Come on, Grace." She led her back to the front of the library.

"That man is beautiful," Grace whispered.

Anne laughed. "He is quite handsome."

"No, Anne, that man is beautiful." Grace mockingly fanned herself. "If it were a couple of decades ago, I declare, I'd swoon."

Anne continued to chuckle and shook her head. "Swooning would probably be right up his alley. He's from Louisiana."

"Ah, I thought I heard an accent." Grace shivered. "Is he single?"

"Yes, I do believe he is," Anne said, enjoying seeing her friend flustered a little. Grace was usually very calm, cool, and confident, so the way she acted right now was quite the difference.

"Not that I'm complaining, but did you stop by for a reason?" Anne asked.

"What?" Grace shook her head. "Yes. I wanted to let you know that I heard Mr. Kombs is finally back in town. I have an appointment to interview him about the fire tomorrow."

Anne nodded but remembered her thought about Eli working for Mr. Kombs. "Do you know when he got back in town?"

Grace shrugged. "Yesterday or day before, I think. Why? Is it important?"

Anne shook her head. "I was just curious." It really didn't matter. He could have called Eli with the initial offer. After all, Eli said a *potential* client, not a client.

"Well." Grace slipped off the stool. "Guess I need to get outta here." Her gaze shot down the hall toward the History Room. "Unless you need me for anything."

Anne chuckled. "I'm fine. Go on. Get."

"Call you later," Grace said as she left.

"Bye." Anne chewed her bottom lip. Grace sure seemed taken with Eli. Anne could certainly understand that.

Interesting times in Blue Hill. Interesting.

* * *

"You have watched Ryan more than a few times lately, Anne, and I want to take us all out for pizza. I insist," Alex said as he stood in the front of the library late Monday afternoon.

"He insists, Mom. Come on," Ben begged.

"Yeah, Mrs. Gibson. We really want you to come," Ryan joined in.

Not to be excluded, Liddie added, "Me too, Mommy. I want pizza."

"Fine. Fine. If you're all going to gang up on me." Anne held up her hands in mock surrender. "We'll go."

Liddie clapped and jumped up and down while Ben and Ryan fist-bumped. Alex grinned. "Aww, you know you love pizza from Stella's."

Stella's Pizza was a hole-in-the-wall place just a couple of blocks down from the high school. The shop's rather shabby decor was offset by affordable prices and mouthwatering pizza that had kept it in business all these years. While Anne could remember Stella at the pizza joint when she'd been a teenager, the place was now run by Stella's daughter and son. The pizza was still as delicious.

Everyone piled into Alex's four-door pickup truck for the short ride over. The snow had all melted, and the temperatures were sitting in the high thirties. Even the wind had decided to calm, leaving Blue Hill as the peaceful, beautiful town the residents all loved.

As soon as they stepped into Stella's, the familiar spicy smells washed waves of memories over Anne. The five of them found a table with patched, red vinyl padded seats and a red-and-white tablecloth.

"I want cheese. Extra cheese," Liddie announced before either Anne or Alex could grab a menu from between the shakers of parmesan cheese and red pepper flakes.

"Yes, Liddie, we know," Anne said with a smile.

"How about you, boys? What sounds good to you?" Alex asked.

"Beef," Ben said.

"Pepperoni," Ryan said at the same time.

"How about a beef and pepperoni?" Alex asked.

The boys both nodded. Alex looked at Anne. "Okay with you?"

"Sounds great."

The waitress came and took their order, then returned shortly with their iced teas. The boys told Anne all about the tree house, while Liddie interjected random building suggestions that were more funny than practical. Enjoying the attention, she began to make them sillier until the pizzas came.

The table was silent as they devoured the two pizzas. As soon as the pies were gone, the kids begged to go play video games in the corner. Alex and Anne dug up a couple of dollars' worth of quarters and sent the kids to play. They nearly ran over the single lady coming in.

"Excuse me," Ben said.

The young woman smiled. "It's okay," she answered as she slipped into the booth right behind where Anne and Alex sat. Anne smiled at her, trying not to stare at her head of flaming red corkscrew curls.

Anne took a sip of iced tea, then focused on Alex. "So how was work on the theater today? No incidents of vandalism?" Anne asked casually. No vandalism meant no cleanup. No cleanup meant no Lisabeth. It was awful of her to think that way, she knew, but she couldn't help it.

"No, thank goodness. We started on the front ticket counter. Did you know that movie theaters used to be glamorous, like music halls or opera houses? The ornate spectacle of the movie-going experience extended out into the actual look and feel of the cinema. Patrick wants to bring some of that elegance back," Alex said, his face full of animation.

"I've seen pictures."

"They don't do these places justice. Patrick's theater was originally built in 1942, back when movie revenues exploded. Property owners vied to build the most lavish, elaborate, attractive theaters," Alex explained. "These plain buildings soon morphed into a unique architectural genre—the movie palace— with luxurious designs, a giant screen, and, beginning in 1953, stereophonic sound."

Anne smiled. "So what will the front ticket counter look like?"

"You've seen pictures of the box office outside the front, basically a glass box with a single person inside?"

Anne nodded.

"It'll be like that, but with lots of crown molding and ornate plaster work. Rich jeweled tones. The heavy red drapery with gold piping and cords," Alex said.

Anne grinned.

Alex shook his head and gave her a sheepish grin. "I'm rambling, aren't I?"

"It's okay. It's great to be excited about your work, and pre-serving part of Blue Hill's history is an added bonus," Anne said.

"Excuse me, but are you talking about the movie theater?" the girl with the red curls leaned over closer to them and asked.

Alex's chest almost physically puffed out, and he turned around to face her. "Why, yes, we are. My company has been hired to do all the preservations and restorations."

The young woman's face grimaced. "It's disgraceful! This town has enough historic pulls draining it. The theater should be modernized. Bring in new technology. Get the economy thriving again." As she spoke, her curls jutted through the air like little shards.

Anne couldn't even find her voice, she was so shocked. That someone had the nerve to eavesdrop, and then be just plain downright rude...

Alex's face was getting deeper red with every word she spoke. "I'm sorry you feel that way, but it's really the owner's choice, and he has elected to preserve the beauty and elegance of the theater from back in its original days."

"That's why there aren't any jobs here anymore. That's why the economy is stagnant, because everyone is caught up in preserving the past instead of moving into the future where there are more employment opportunities."

"No offense meant, but we'll just have to disagree. I think the history of Blue Hill is vital to the town, and its residents," Alex said. "Preserving something that was once majestic and beautiful and an important part of the town's past isn't disgraceful. We're a town full of a rich heritage, of which we're very proud."

"But that movie theater, if modernized, would bring in bigger named, first-run movies, which would bring in more money to the area. Those old historic theaters have what, one or two screens?

The modern theaters house at least eight and up to twenty. That would mean a huge influx of needed employees." The young woman's voice had risen.

Anne shifted. "I'm sorry, Miss — I'm sorry, what's your name?"

"Sally. Sally Langford."

The woman whose letter to the editor in opposition of the preservation that was printed.

"Ms. Langford, I understand you're very passionate about the subject," Anne began, deliberately lowering her voice to encourage whispering, "but you need to understand that Blue Hill residents love our history. We embrace it. And we encourage the retelling of our past to the next generation so the history lives on." Like the photos and movie posters of Aunt Edie's.

Goodness, if they disregarded all the fascinating history of just Edie Summers alone, that would be a tragic loss to the remembrance of Blue Hill.

"Isn't there enough history preserved in this backwoods town? I moved here with the expectation that the economy was on the rise with the Diamond District plans," Sally said.

Ah. The Diamond District, which was a development on the west side of town that had built up not long before the last recession. The plan was a small, upscale shopping plaza to attract boutique tenants from Blue Hill, Deshler, and surrounding towns. Despite the tasteful landscaping and cozy retail spaces, the development had struggled to retain their desired high-end tenants. Once the economy tanked, the development had no choice but to house a more eclectic mix of shops and offices that were in a constant struggle against Blue Hill's thriving downtown.

"The Diamond District developer had good intentions, but you can't blame the historical sites in Blue Hill on its failure," Alex said.

"And really, it doesn't matter what any of us think," Lisabeth came up to the table and stood beside Alex.

Anne bristled as Lisabeth continued, "Because the owner of the theater wants it preserved, and since he's the sole owner, it's his right to do with the property as he chooses." She smiled as she laid a hand on Alex's shoulder. "On top of that, I heard the Blue Hill town council is discussing listing the theater in the town's historical building registry, which would guarantee the preservation of the building by assisting the owner with funding for said preservations."

Sally Langford grabbed her ticket from the table and stood. "You people don't even realize how much this little preservation deal could be costing this back-thinking town," she said before storming to the register to pay her bill. Anne made a mental note to ask someone to check Sally's background. She seemed just a little too passionate about the theater's renovations.

Alex pulled out the chair at the end of the table, between him and Anne, and gestured to Lisabeth. "Have a seat, Lisabeth. I didn't even see you come in."

She smiled and sat, her eyes only on Alex. "I just ran in to pick up an order I called in. I couldn't help overhearing her tirade, and it just made me angry." She touched his hand. "I know you don't need me to defend you, and I'm sorry if I was out of line, but the way she came across as so condescending to you...well, it just upset me."

Anne was pretty sure the three slices of pizza she'd just eaten were threatening to change directions.

"I think it's sweet," Alex said.

Yep, Anne figured, she was going to be sick. Really sick.

"Would you like to join us?" Alex asked.

"Oh, the kids are almost out of quarters, Alex, and it's a school night," Anne interrupted. "Besides, Lisabeth said she had called in an order. We don't want to keep her." She forced her smile to cover her clenched teeth.

Lisabeth narrowed her eyes as she finally looked at Anne. She opened her mouth to say something, just as Ryan, Ben, and Liddie returned. Liddie crawled up in Anne's lap while Ben drained what was left of his tea.

"Uncle Alex, can we go now?" Ryan asked, stepping between his uncle and Lisabeth. Anne wanted to hug the child.

"Ryan, don't be rude. This is Lisabeth Matthews. She does some work for my company," Alex said. "Lisabeth, this is my nephew, Ryan, and Anne's kids, Ben and Liddie."

Lisabeth flashed a toothy smile at Ryan and Ryan alone. "Hello, there. My, you're as handsome as your uncle. Good looks must run in the family."

Ryan frowned. "Everybody says I look like my dad."

"Do you? He must be very handsome," Lisabeth said.

"He was. He died in a car wreck with my mom. Uncle Alex raises me," Ryan said very matter-of-factly.

Lisabeth's eyes widened and she had the decency to turn red. "I'm sorry."

"Do you get to use a hammer?" Liddie asked. "I like to use a hammer, but Mommy and Alex don't let me use it a lot. They say it can be dangerous."

Alex chuckled. "It can be dangerous. Especially in your wild-girl hands," he teased, reaching across the table to tweak her nose. Liddie giggled in response.

Lisabeth glared at Anne for a split second before she stood. "I'd better get my pizza and let you guys get out of here. It was nice meeting you kids." For just that moment when she addressed the kids and her smile wavered, she clearly looked uncomfortable and unsure.

Anne realized, to the outsider, the five of them probably looked like a normal family out having pizza. The realization didn't bug her. Maybe it should, or at least make her wonder, but she just accepted it as fact.

Alex scrambled to his feet. "It was nice seeing you. I mean, outside of work."

And he just had to go and show interest. Or was he just being nice? Anne honestly couldn't tell.

Lisabeth smiled. "It was nice seeing you too. I'll talk to you later." She tossed Anne a victorious gloat before heading to the cash register.

Well, it was more than official... Anne truly didn't like Lisabeth Matthews.

* * *

Tuesday morning brought even warmer temperatures to Blue Hill, almost teasing the town into believing spring had sprung.

Even though the bluebells wouldn't bloom until April, the stalks around the library looked full and ready for buds. Some of the crocus flowers were already opening to the warming rays of the late February sun.

"Anne, I found them," Mildred said as a way of greeting as she waltzed into the library.

Anne looked up from the scattered brainstorming ideas she'd been having with Wendy, Remi, and Bella. "Found what?"

"The pictures, of course." Mildred's tone was clear that Anne should have automatically known what she was referring to. "The ones of the party for Edie's movie debut at the theater."

"Oh!" That was exciting. Anne took the offered envelope and gently pulled out four photographs. Wendy, Remi, and Bella crowded around her to see.

The first picture was of the theater's marquee. Just like she'd seen in movies and old pictures, the movie title, *Summer Swoon,* was lit up with hundreds of little lightbulbs. Underneath and smaller, was "starring Blue Hill's own Edie Summers." Anne smiled, imagining her aunt's pure pleasure at seeing her name in lights, literally.

Anne carefully flipped to the next picture. This one depicted a very young and beautiful Edie, dressed to the nines in a strapless formal dress with soft pleats below the neckline. A wide, satin pleated sash with long satin streamers ran down the hips of the full, sweepy skirt. In the black-and-white photo, it was hard to tell the color of the light dress. Edie stood in a vogue-style pose under the marquee, her smile as big and bright as ever.

"She's beautiful," Anne whispered as she ran her finger along the edge of the photograph.

Mildred smiled. "Ah, she was. That dress was to die for too. It was a Fred Perlberg—yellowish lime net over taffeta. She looked stunning. It truly was her night."

"She must've been in her element," Wendy said.

"That she was," Mildred confirmed.

Anne flipped to the next photograph. It was of Edie standing beside the movie poster in the glass case outside the theater, her hands showing off the poster. She wore the same beautiful dress, and the same exuberantly happy smile. This was the photograph Anne wanted to use to display next to the lobby placard.

The last picture was a little out of focus, but Anne could still make it out. It was a photo of the credits at the end of the movie, listing Edie in the role of Betty.

"Do you mind if I have copies made?" Anne asked.

"Of course not, dear," Mildred said. "That's why I brought them over."

Anne went back to the photo of Edie by the movie poster in that stunning dress. "She looks so elegant and famous."

Mildred nodded. "That night, she was both."

"That's it!" Remi exclaimed.

"What?" Anne and Wendy asked in unison.

"The theme for the Winter Wonderland dance," Remi said.

Anne raised a single eyebrow. "What's that?"

"Classic Hollywood," Remi announced, clearly pleased with herself.

"Oh, that's good," Bella said.

"I like it," Wendy added. "You can use decorations from big Hollywood movies."

"I'm sure I have a lot of movie memorabilia in some of my old boxes," Mildred said. "I always did love a good movie."

"Do you think we could use a copy of your aunt's movie poster, Mrs. Gibson?" Bella asked. "And maybe blow up copies of the photographs?"

"Oh, that would be really cool," Remi said.

"I think that would be lovely," Anne said. "And I'm sure Aunt Edie would have been over the moon with the idea."

"We could go with a black-and-white color theme too, to bring out the black-and-white pictures," Bella suggested.

"Oh yeah. Black and white, classic Hollywood, Winter Wonderland," Wendy said. "This is great, girls. Should be the best Blue Hill's ever seen."

Remi and Bella grinned from ear to ear.

Anne was pretty sure Aunt Edie would have been grinning just as big. She would've been a movie hit again.

CHAPTER ELEVEN

I just wondered if you could do a little background check on Sally Langford," Anne told Grace over the phone Tuesday afternoon. She'd just finished telling Grace about Sally's outburst at Stella's Pizza. "There was definitely something going on with her, I just don't know what."

"I'll see what I can dig up," Grace said. "By the way, has Eli Wallington been back in?"

Anne chuckled. "No, he hasn't. Why? Are you interested?"

"Well, he *is* a beautiful man." Grace sighed.

"So I've noticed. To answer your question, no, I haven't seen him today."

"Okay then. I'll call you if I find out anything," Grace said, disappointment evident in her tone.

"Thanks." Anne watched as Alex walked toward the reception desk at the library. "I've got to run," she said into the phone.

"Okay. I'll call you as soon as I find out anything. Bye."

Anne hung up the phone and smiled at Alex. "How was work on the theater today?" She couldn't wait to show him the pictures Mildred had brought over. Maybe if he saw the original marquee, he could restore it to a similar design.

"Not great. We had another incident." Alex sounded as tired as he looked as he took a seat on the stool beside her.

"Oh no. What happened?" Anne asked.

"A little bit more than just a mess this time, although they did make a mess," Alex said. "This time, in addition to covering the entire refreshment counter with paint and throwing around drywall scraps, I'm missing some handheld equipment. Nothing too expensive, just some hammers, screwdrivers, and one of my old drills." Weariness rode his every word. "And the paint wasn't any we had onsite, so the vandals brought it but took the can because we didn't find it."

Anne patted his hand. "Did you call Michael?"

Alex nodded. "He came out and filed a report. He even brought a forensics crew to look for evidence because the investigation has nothing new."

"Nothing?"

"According to Michael, they haven't been able to find and question Denny Thatcher since Grace's interview ran, and the investigation into the teenage boys is still ongoing." Alex ran a hand over his face.

Anne felt horrible. "Can't the police have someone patrol that area more?" she asked. "Especially since it seems this isn't going to stop anytime very soon."

"Michael says they're doing the best they can in that department. Patrick and I discussed the option of hiring a private security officer, but he hasn't been able to find out yet," Alex said.

"I hate that he'd have to cover such an additional expense." Goodness knew if she had to think about hiring private security for the library, she'd have her work cut out for her. The money from Aunt Edie's estate was plenty enough to cover the costs incurred with reasonable remodeling, as well funding the trust to pay Anne's salary. The town council members had agreed to enter into a fifty-year-term lease that allowed for public usage of the specified portions of the building for a nominal rental fee, but security certainly wasn't included in any lease or trust.

"It's getting to where he might not have a choice," Alex said.

"I'm so sorry." Anne wished that he didn't have to go through this over and over again. It had to be beyond frustrating.

Alex shook his head and smiled, but it was a polite smile that didn't reach his blue eyes. "But, enough about my ongoing battles. How was your day? Was Ryan any problem? I really hate your having to watch him all the time."

"*Shh*. Ryan's not any problem and it's not a chore. He helps Ben with Hershey, he's patient with Liddie, he minds, and he feeds Ben's enthusiasm over the tree house, so stop apologizing for him being here. If I didn't want him here, I wouldn't keep volunteering to pick him up, okay?"

Alex held up his hands in mock surrender. "Okay, okay." He grinned, a genuine one this time. "So how was your day?"

She laughed, even as she knew they sounded like a couple. It seemed odd to have these thoughts and not share them with Alex. But, of course, she couldn't.

"Just another exciting day in a small-town library," Anne said, then remembered Grace's interest in Eli. Blue Hill *was* a small town and most people knew each other, or at least knew *of* each other. Especially if they were in the same line of work. "Hey, do you know an Eli Wallington?"

Alex sat up a little straighter. "I do. Why?" Was that defensiveness?

"He's come into the library a couple of times. Explained his new business, so just thought I'd ask if you knew him," Anne said.

"Oh." Alex leaned against the counter, resting his elbow there. "I've seen some of his job portfolio and his work is legitimate. Good quality. I think he's a little overpriced in his bidding, but that's probably just because he isn't used to small-town pricing yet."

If Alex said his work was legit, he most likely had nothing to do with the warehouse fire. That made Anne happy, and she smiled.

Alex frowned. "I've heard most women think he's handsome and go all gaga over him, but I don't know. I mean, if you like that sort of look." He shrugged. "I can't say how he is as a person. I think there's more to somebody than just their looks."

Wait a minute. Alex sounded…almost…jealous.

"Oh, I totally agree," Anne said, carefully studying Alex's expression in his eyes. "It's what's inside a person's character that counts."

"Is that why you asked about him?" Alex asked.

"What?" Oh. Oh. *Ohhh.* "Not for me. I'm not interested in him." Well, not really. "I mean, he's handsome and charming and has that endearing Southern accent, but I'm not interested in him like that," Anne stammered. Great. It sounded like she protested too much.

Alex stood and grinned. "Anne Gibson, are you flustered?"

This was wrong. All wrong.

"No. Let me back up. Eli came into the library to look at some old blueprints. He introduced himself, and I would be lying if I said he wasn't handsome and charming. But you know me, I was more curious about what he was looking at than his looks. A friend of mine came in another time he was here and thought him attractive and charming as well, and I think she might be more interested in him than what he's viewing at the library. That's why I asked you," Anne explained in a rush of words.

"I see." Alex rubbed his chin. "What old blueprints was he looking at that made you curious?"

Ah, Alex knew her too well, and he hadn't missed her interest.

"Blueprints of the Kombses' warehouse."

"Really?" His eyebrows went up with his question.

"Why? Is that bad?"

"I guess not. He put in a bid for the theater," Alex said.

"He did?"

Alex nodded. "He was a little high for Patrick and his insurance company. And I don't think he was as interested in restoring back to the original design." He shrugged. "But then again, a lot aren't. Like Sally Langford, apparently."

Anne smiled along with him. "She was quite the pill, wasn't she?"

Before Alex could answer, the kids came running into the front of the library. "Uncle Alex, come see. We finished marking with the string just like you told us," Ryan said.

Not to be outdone in excitement, Ben added, "And we finished our materials list and have it ready for you to look over too."

Liddie, on the other hand, seemed rather bored with the tree house plans. "Mommy, can I go play with my dolls?"

"Sure, sweetie. It won't be long before I'm up," Anne said, giving her daughter a quick hug before Liddie skipped away.

"Boys, Alex is tired. He's had a long day. Why don't you show him tomorrow?" Anne suggested.

But Ryan wasn't accepting that. He turned on his puppy dog eyes and begged, "Please, Uncle Alex? It will only take a minute. Just look at it."

Alex threw his hands up and smiled at Anne. "How can I refuse?" He stood. "Lead the way, boys."

"Come on, Mom. You too," Ben said, taking her hand.

"Okay, okay. Let me tell Bella. I'll catch up with you," Anne said. She used the cage-style elevator to the second floor where Bella was shelving books in the Children's Room after toddler Story Time from this morning. "I'm running out back, and then to the house. Please close down the library for me."

"Will do," Bella said.

Anne had just reached the backyard and could see where the tree house base had been cordoned off with wooden stakes and white string when she picked up the accusation in Alex's tone. She picked up her pace.

"Ryan, where did you get this box of nails?" Alex asked. He held a black cardboard box with white and red lettering and markings.

"What's wrong, Uncle Alex? Can't we use those nails?" Ryan asked.

Alex shook his head. "That isn't the point, Ryan. I want to know where you got them," Alex said.

"Alex," Anne deliberately lightened her tone. "Is there a problem?"

He held up the box. "Look familiar?"

Now that he mentioned it, the box *did* look familiar. She remembered. "From the theater," she said. Her heart flipped.

He nodded at her, then turned back to the boys. He knelt in front of them, getting eye to eye with his nephew. "Three boxes of these nails went missing from my work site at the theater during one of the vandalism incidents. So I'm going to ask you again, Ryan Slater, where did you get these nails?"

Ryan's bottom lip quivered for just a second. "We didn't steal them, Uncle Alex. I promise."

"We didn't," Ben added.

"No one said you did," Anne told the boys, "but we need to know where you got them."

"A man gave them to us," Ben admitted.

"A man?" Alex asked, standing.

Ryan nodded. "Yes, sir."

"Who was it?" Anne asked.

Ben shrugged. "I don't know his name."

"Ryan?" Alex asked his nephew.

"I'd never seen him before," Ryan said.

"When was this?" Alex asked. "When did a man give you a box of nails?"

Anne couldn't blame him for his disbelieving tone, but she was more than a little willing to hear the boys out.

"Yesterday," Ben said.

Alex threw Anne a look that clearly said he wasn't buying their story.

"Where were you when the man gave you the nails?" Anne asked.

"Right here," Ryan answered.

Now Anne's pulse raced. A man had approached the boys here, yesterday, just outside the library. Just outside her home. How many times had they played outside while she cooked or was in the library? Liddie! What about all the times Liddie had been outside swinging with only Ben out with her?

"A man you don't know came here yesterday and just gave you a box of nails?" Alex asked, shaking his head. "Boys, you have to know how crazy that sounds."

"We were out here, double-checking the measurements and figuring out the building materials, just like you told us to do," Ryan started, "when a man came up."

"He was really nice and asked us what we were building," Ben said. "We told him, and then he looked over our plans and told us we'd done a good job so far."

Anne's heart threatened to explode in her chest.

"He said he wanted to help us, but I told him my uncle was helping us," Ryan said.

"But he walked to his car and came back with a box of nails and gave it to us," Ben said. "He told us that's all he had with him that he could spare, but if he found some other stuff we might be able to use, he'd bring it by."

Ryan nodded. "That's what happened."

"It's the truth, Mom. I promise," Ben said.

Anne looked at Alex and saw her own concerns mirrored in his eyes. Was it possible some kind stranger had just come across the boys building at the right time? Seemed highly unlikely...and it didn't matter. A stranger had approached her child and Alex's when she wasn't watching. It could've been a totally different scenario they were dealing with right now instead of just a box of possibly stolen nails.

So much for her grand talk to Ben about her needing to know things to keep him safe.

Alex's cell phone rang. He dug it out of his pocket. "It's Michael," he told Anne before he answered the call and took a few steps away.

"Mom, I promise, we didn't do anything wrong," Ben whispered.

"The man really just gave us the nails," Ryan added.

Heaven help her if she was just being gullible, but Anne believed them.

"Was there anything you remember about the man? Maybe his hair color?" she asked.

Both boys shrugged. What did she expect? Boys didn't take a lot of notice of adults they didn't know.

"It's okay," she told them, even though she was already thinking about the possibility of putting up a fence around the backyard. She'd do anything to keep the children safe.

Alex came back, pocketing his phone. "Ryan, go get your backpack. We have to go."

"Are you mad, Uncle Alex? We didn't mean to do anything wrong," Ryan said.

"We won't use the nails," Ben offered.

"It's okay, boys. Run on up to get your stuff. We're right behind you," Anne said. Once the boys were out of earshot, she told Alex, "I believe them."

"Maybe. I don't know. Michael said they just got back all the test results from the crime scene stuff."

Maybe there'd be a lead. "And?" she asked as she started back toward the library. She kept the boys in sight until they stepped inside the house.

Alex shook his head as he fell into step alongside her. "Nothing. He said there wasn't one bit of forensic evidence left on anything, anywhere."

"That sounds impossible. Did Michael say that was normal?"

"No. He said it's very unusual. He said the only thing they found on anything from the theater is traces of an organic compound, which is only natural since Lisabeth only uses environmentally friendly cleaning supplies in her business."

"How is that possible, Alex? Your crew does work after Lisabeth cleans, so there shouldn't be any traces of her cleaners without at least some traces of your crew behind. Not to mention the vandals."

Alex stopped as they reached the door. "I can't explain it, Anne. Neither can the police. They're totally baffled." He gestured toward the door. "And now this...some strange man coming and giving the boys a box of nails? A box just like the ones missing from the theater?" Alex shook his head. "You know me, Anne. I don't buy into coincidences much. What are the odds that the boys would be given the exact same nails as went missing?"

"Are they a popular kind of nail? That brand and size and whatever, I mean?"

"Probably the most popular, but again, what are the odds?"

"I don't know, Alex, but I believe them. They might not have offered up information before, but I don't think they've ever flat out lied to us. I don't think they would start now."

"So you think a man just randomly showed up with a single box of nails to give them?" Alex asked.

"I know it sounds crazy, and maybe that's another reason I *do* believe them."

He stared at her for a long moment. "Then we need to be more careful with them."

"My thoughts exactly," Anne answered. Ben would be most unhappy that she would now be into super-supervision mode, but it couldn't be helped.

The kids' safety had to come first.

CHAPTER TWELVE

Wednesday turned out even warmer than Tuesday had been, with the temperature creeping up to almost forty with nothing more than a gentle breeze. Spring seemed to be lurking just around the corner, ready to make an appearance at any time. Anne wished it would hurry up. She was ready for the bluebells covering the hill by the library to come into full bloom. She loved looking out the windows and seeing the cheerful blossoms. She loved her home.

Except she didn't feel as safe as she usually did, and she wouldn't until she could figure out what strange man had approached the boys. After she'd picked the kids up from school earlier, she'd settled the boys in to doing their homework and Liddie playing Barbies, but Anne knew it wouldn't be much longer before the boys itched to go outside. Especially since it was so nice out. No way could she let them just go out. Not until she figured out something about the strange man who'd given them a box of nails. Besides, she had to meet Alex at the police station in just a bit. Luckily, Wendy would be here soon to watch Liddie and the library.

She'd wanted to call the police yesterday, but Alex had talked her into waiting. It was possible the boys weren't being entirely truthful, although Anne believed they were. Alex said he would call Michael and report the incident. Neither Anne nor Alex wanted the boys in danger, nor did they want them frightened. Alex had called earlier and said he'd missed Michael but had spoken with Josie, who took the report. She asked that they bring the boys to the station to give their statements around four this afternoon.

Anne had barely returned from brushing her teeth when her cell phone rang. She checked the caller ID and smiled. "Hi, Grace," she answered.

"Hi. How's it going?"

Anne grinned into the phone. "He hasn't been by again," she teased.

"I didn't ask," Grace said.

Anne chuckled. "But you wanted to know."

"Maybe," Grace said with a little laugh. "But, I wanted to let you know that I pulled some information on Sally Langford. You were right, there is something off about her."

Anne knew it! "What?" she asked.

"Sally Langford went to college at Penn State, just east of us in State College. Seems that there, she had a little run-in with campus police," Grace said.

"Really? What kind of run-in?"

"A 'defacing of school property' type of run-in."

Anne widened her eyes. "Oh."

"I know. I know," Grace said, her voice building with excitement. "According to records, she was affiliated with a group who protested the use of mice in the labs. A bunch of them were seen spray painting the building housing the Applied Research Lab with defaming phrases."

"Was she arrested?" Anne asked.

"No. Apparently she wasn't caught. None of the group technically was, and they weren't formally charged, but they were all brought into the dean's office and reprimanded." Anne swung her legs as she played with a pen sitting on the counter.

"So she has a past with vandalism as a form of protest," Anne mused out loud. Much like the minor vandalism at the theater.

"What are you thinking?" Grace asked. "I can almost hear the squealing wheels in your mind spinning around."

"Consider this—what if the fire had nothing to do with the vandalism at the theater?" As Anne spoke it out loud, she realized it made sense, honestly. "We only think the fire was set because of what Josie Bolling said on the scene, really. What if the cause of the fire is nothing more than faulty wiring?"

"I think Michael said they're pretty certain the fire didn't just break out due to faulty wiring. They know an accelerant was present," Grace said.

"Okay, maybe a homeless person who was sleeping there might've accidently set the fire without even realizing it." Anne spoke even faster to ward off Grace's argument. "That isn't to say Denny Thatcher is responsible. If Denny knew he could crash in the warehouse sometimes, it stands to reason that another homeless person might know the same, right?"

"Yes, I suppose," Grace said, but the uncertainty was clear in her tone.

"For the sake of argument, we know it's a possibility. So if the fire was a totally isolated incident, let's take it out of consideration."

"Okay," Grace said.

"Then that leaves us with the park vandalism and the theater's renovations defacement, right?"

"Right."

Anne took a deep breath. "We've jumped to the conclusion that the acts of vandalism are connected because of the nature of the crime, but maybe we've been wrong."

"Continue," Grace said.

Anne picked up a pen and began doodling on a scrap pad of paper. "The mess in the park happened a month ago. Has there been anything else since then?"

"Not that I know of, but I can check."

"I haven't heard anything, so let's say there's not been anything new. If that's the case, then there's a good chance those responsible for messing up the park are not the same ones who are vandalizing the theater," Anne spoke with more authority as she went on, almost sure she was on the right track. "Think about it, the park was an isolated incident. Maybe some kids out playing one night. A one-time thing. But the theater? They've had three incidents so far in less than two weeks. Not the same MO at all."

"I see your point, Anne. So if you're right in thinking each event is separate, maybe that's why the police haven't been able to solve anything because they're looking to connect them all."

"Yes," Anne said. "And if they are all separate incidents, then Sally Langford is a primary suspect in the vandalism at the theater." Something occurred to her. "When did you run the first article about the theater being restored?"

"The day after. Remember, I talked with Mr. Rollings at the fire and then followed up. I made the mention then that he was interested in restoring the theater in the article," Grace said.

"So right from the beginning, it was public knowledge that the theater was going to be restored and not modernized," Anne said.

"Correct."

"And we know Sally is very passionately opposed to restoration instead of modernization, and we know she has at least one incident in her past where she vandalized property in support of something she feels passionately about."

"I get it. Let me try to do some more digging. Maybe you should call Michael and run these thoughts by him," Grace suggested.

Maybe she should. Michael might be more than willing to follow up on her theory, because if she was right, then that would mean Jed wasn't involved in the acts at the theater. "I think I will," Anne decided.

"I'll call you if I learn anything more," Grace said and hung up.

Anne dialed the police station. She was put on hold briefly after asking for Michael.

"Officer Banks."

"Hi, Michael. It's Anne."

"Hi, Anne. What can I do for you?"

She quickly told him what she'd told Grace. When she finished, she was nearly out of breath.

"I hadn't heard about your encounter with Sally Langford," Michael said. "I'll be sure to follow up on her."

"Thanks, Michael. I really appreciate it."

"No problem. I understand you and Alex are bringing Ben and Ryan in for their statements in a little while."

"Yes, we are."

"It's scary to think a stranger came right up to them in your backyard."

"Very scary."

"I'm glad you filed a report. So many people nowadays don't."

Anne hesitated, recalling Alex's initial reaction. "You don't think it sounds too far-fetched, like something the boys might have made up?"

"It's because it's so outlandish that I believe their story. Most kids, if they're lying, would tell you they found the nails or they were just there."

She hadn't considered that, but it was true.

"Anyway, we'll do everything we can, Anne. I promise you that."

"Thanks, Michael."

"I'll see you soon."

Anne handled some library return items that needed attention, then smiled as Wendy entered.

"Thanks for coming to watch Liddie and the library," Anne said after Wendy had stowed her purse in the bottom drawer of the counter.

"Not a problem. I still can't believe a man just waltzed into your backyard like that."

"It scares me," Anne admitted.

"I would expect so. I'd feel the same way," Wendy said. "But are the boys sure they didn't recognize the man? Even if it was just a patron from the library who might have heard them talking about the tree house and remembered he had a box of nails in his car? Maybe they were afraid they'd get in trouble so the details got a little fuzzy."

"I don't know, but I'm sure the police are trained in ways to question to get information the person may not even realize is important," Anne said.

Wendy nodded. "And Michael's a good guy. He's a dad, so he knows how to talk to kids."

"Michael won't be the one questioning, I don't think. Josie took the report," Anne told Wendy.

"Josie Bolling?"

"Yes. She was a couple of years behind me in school. She's nice," Anne said.

"She seems to be. I don't know her well. I just see her around and sometimes at church." Wendy pulled a tube of lip balm from her pocket and swiped it over her lips. "I have to admit, with everything going on lately, it makes me wonder what's happened to Blue Hill."

"Me too," Anne said. She hadn't realized how much she'd missed her hometown until she'd come back. Now it was home, not just physically, but in her heart.

And she would go to great lengths to protect her home.

* * *

"Are you sure we aren't in trouble?" Ben asked, his nervousness obvious as they made their way into the Blue Hill police station.

"No. Of course not. We just need you to tell the police about the man who gave you the box of nails is all," Anne answered.

Her reassurances didn't seem to make much difference as both Ben and Ryan were pale as bleached sheets.

Alex reached the counter first. "Hi. Josie Bolling told us to come at four," he told the uniformed lady standing behind the counter. He rested his hand on Ryan's shoulder. "These young men are here to give their statements."

She smiled down at Ben and Ryan. "I'll call Officer Bolling right now and let her know she has some handsome visitors waiting." She lifted the phone on her desk. "Josie? You have two very handsome young men at the front desk for you." She looked up at Alex. "Their names?"

"Ryan Slater and Ben Gibson."

The lady gave their names, then hung up the phone. "She'll be right with you."

"Thank you," Anne said, keeping her arm around Ben's shoulders.

Within minutes, Josie appeared, her blonde hair bobbing. "Come on back," she said as she motioned them down the hall. She stopped at a closed door and opened it, gesturing them inside. There were four chairs on one side of a long table, and two on the other.

"This is our interview room. It's easier to talk in here because there aren't phones going crazy or people running around," Josie said as she sat in one of the two chairs.

Anne helped get Ben in the chair, then took a seat beside him. Ryan sat beside Ben with Alex on the other side of him.

"Now, boys, I want you to tell me exactly what happened about the day you got the nails," Josie said, opening her notebook and tapping her pen against the paper.

Ryan took a deep breath, then started speaking. "We were outside Ben's house, the library, like his mom said we could." He glanced at Anne.

Smiling, Anne nodded.

"We were by the old tree in the backyard that has the tree swing. We decided to build our tree house there, but the design we picked is really more of a fort with just a ladder to get on the roof," Ben added.

Ryan nodded. "Right. We were double-checking the measurements and figuring out the building materials, just like Uncle Alex told us to do."

"Mr. Ochs had helped us mark off the boundaries already, but we had to double-check so we could make sure we know how much of all the materials we need," Ben explained.

Josie nodded. "And then what?"

"A man came up behind us," Ryan said. "He asked us what we were building."

Ben nodded. "We told him about our tree house fort. We showed him the plans we'd picked out."

Ryan grinned at Josie. "He told us we'd done a good job so far. Then he offered to help us, but I told him my uncle already was."

"He walked off and I thought he was leaving," Ben said, "but he came back with a box of nails and gave it to us. He told us that's all he had with him that he could give us, but if he found some other stuff we might be able to use, he'd bring it."

"And then he left," Ryan finished.

Josie slowly finished writing and then chewed on the end of her pen. "And neither one of you recognized him? Not even maybe just having seen him once in a store or something?"

Ryan and Ben both shook their heads.

"Was he tall?" Josie asked.

Ben shrugged.

"Kinda," Ryan said.

Josie stood up. "Alex, come stand on this side of me. Anne, would you stand on my other side?"

Once the three of them stood in a line, Josie asked the boys, "Now was he closer to how tall I am, or Anne is, or Alex is?"

"Uncle Alex," Ryan said at the same time Ben said, "Mr. Ochs."

"Well done," Josie told them. "How tall are you, Alex?" She sat down and motioned for Anne and Alex to sit as well.

"I'm six one," Alex said.

Josie jotted in her notebook. "Quick, both of you tell me what color hair he had. On one, two, three..."

"Black," both boys said in unison.

"Perfect. You guys been practicing?" Josie asked.

"No, ma'am," Ben said.

"I'm just teasing you," Josie said.

Anne really appreciated the young officer making the questioning seem like a game. Both boys had visibly relaxed and actually seemed to be having fun.

Josie tapped the pen against her chin. "Now, what was he wearing? Um, Ben, quick, what color were his pants?"

"Blue jeans," Ben said, sitting on the edge of his seat and swinging his legs.

"Ryan, what color shirt?"

"Red," Ryan said without missing a beat.

"You guys are really good," Josie said. "Now, both of you, close your eyes."

They did. Anne had to admit, she was almost tempted to close her eyes too, Josie was so compelling.

"No peeking, okay? Now, think back to that day. To that man. I'm going to ask you to just nod or shake your head to the questions I ask you. Don't answer out loud. Okay?"

Ryan and Ben nodded.

"Good. Did he have glasses?"

Both of them shook their heads no.

"Did he have a moustache?"

Head shakes.

"Did he have a beard?"

Head shakes.

"Did he have a tattoo?"

Head shakes.

"Okay, good job. You can open your eyes now," Josie said. "You boys did excellent. Now tell me, was there anything different about this man?"

Ryan shook his head.

"He talked funny," Ben said.

Anne stiffened. He hadn't mentioned that before.

Josie leaned forward and grinned, wrinkling her nose at Ben. "Funny how? Like this?" She'd raised her voice really, really high like a falsetto.

Ben and Ryan giggled.

"No. Not like that," Ben said.

"Like this?" Josie used an overstated deep voice.

"No," Ben said as he and Ryan laughed.

"No?" Josie said, tilting her head. "Then how? Show me."

"He kinda talked a-like-a this," Ben said in an exaggerated Southern accent.

Anne gasped. She only knew one man who had a Southern accent and that was Eli Wallington.

CHAPTER THIRTEEN

A nne, may I speak with you?"

There was no mistaking that accent. Anne turned slowly from shelving the books in the Nonfiction Room. "What may I help you with, Mr. Wallington?"

He frowned and put his hand over his heart. "I'm demoted to 'Mr. Wallington' instead of Eli now? You must be very upset with me."

She put her hands on her hips. "You put terror in my heart. You approached my son and Ryan while they were alone, you gave them something very peculiar, and you never even bothered to tell me? Of course I'm upset with you. Who does that?"

"I'm so sorry, Anne. I never dreamed such a gesture would create such havoc for you."

"You didn't consider that a strange man approaching my child on my own property wouldn't cause me to be upset?" She shook her head. "You must be clueless, sir."

"Anne, Anne…allow me to explain, like I did to the police." His hypnotic eyes pled with her to listen. To understand. To forgive.

"I'm listening," she said but crossed her arms over her chest.

"I thought the boys recognized me from here. When I approached them, neither seemed alarmed."

"Why would you approach them in the first place?" Anne interrupted.

"I was going to my car when I noticed two boys standing by a tree, looking at the ground. Neither seemed to be moving. I was concerned."

Anne narrowed her eyes. "If you were concerned, you should have come inside and told me."

Eli nodded. "You are correct. I should have. But I didn't. Instead, I approached the boys. They didn't seem alarmed, so I assumed they recognized me from the library. I asked them what they were doing, and they explained their intent to build a fort. They showed me their plan and their mapped-off area, and I told them they'd done a good job. I offered to help and was told they already had assistance. I merely wanted to also pitch in, so I gave the boys what I had in my car, a box of nails."

Anne shook her head. "Why would you do that? Give them anything?"

Eli's perfect skin tone reddened. "Quite honestly, I recognized one of the boys as your son, and I wanted to do something nice for him to make you happy."

Oh. How was she supposed to respond to that?

"I want to be your friend, Anne, and I thought, perhaps, by doing something nice for your son, you would think well of me."

Anne opened her mouth to say something, realized she had nothing, and closed her mouth again. What was she supposed to think? Be flattered? She was. Kind of. Or should she think he was a little too smooth, like making an attempt to get in her good graces by taking a shortcut?

"I'm very, very sorry to have worried you or caused you even a moment of concern, Anne. I didn't think, and that comes from me not being a parent. I humbly beg your forgiveness," Eli said, his charm oozing from his every pore.

It took a very big man to come immediately and apologize. The Bible did instruct her to forgive as God continually forgives.

She let out a sigh. "You're forgiven."

His smile broke out, and it was almost as if a ray of sunshine beamed down on her. How could she have stayed angry with him?

"But don't you ever do something like that again. Ever."

He gave a low bow. "You have my word, madam."

She shook her head and grinned. The man was incorrigible, but he just might make a good date for Grace. "Now, I have to ask you something."

"Anything. Name it."

"Tell me why you were looking at the plans for Marcus Kombs's warehouse that burned down."

"Ah, my dear Anne, if I could, I assure you that I would. Unfortunately, due to my work agreements to keep jobs or potential jobs confidential if requested, I can't tell you."

Well, she couldn't argue with someone's strong work ethic, but it didn't help that she still didn't know. She guessed she would just have to trust him.

"You know, after reading the library newsletter, I got to thinking. I'd be more than happy to teach a Handyman 101 class here at the library."

"Well, thank you. I'll have to look over the schedule and see where we can slot you in," Anne said.

"I'll await further instructions then," Eli said. "Well, I better let you get back to work. I just wanted to come over and apologize in person."

"I appreciate that."

"Also, one evening, if you're free, I'd enjoy having dinner with you."

Her mouth went dry. "Um…"

He chuckled. "You don't have to say anything, Anne. I was just letting you know of my interest. I'll see you later." He turned and left.

Anne leaned against the doorframe. He was handsome and kind and considerate and, in a roundabout way, had sort of asked her out, yet she hadn't jumped at the chance. Because of Grace? Or, because he wasn't Alex?

* * *

"But I can work on the fort plans at home," Ben said as Anne parked the car in front of Rosehill Park.

"Well, you can do that later. Today, I wanted to take you and your sister to the park to play," Anne said, helping Liddie out of her seat. She was glad Ben was so dedicated to the project, but she wanted him to have fun just playing as well.

They locked the car, then headed to the slides. Liddie ran, reaching the biggest slide before Ben. Anne smiled and took a seat on the bench. The fresh air of the almost spring-like afternoon smelled so good. The sunshine felt good on Anne's face as she switched her glasses for her prescription sunglasses.

Liddie squealed as she slid, then ran around to climb the tall steps again. Just recently Anne had begun letting Liddie climb up so high without having Ben right behind her. Liddie was proud of her accomplishment, and Anne was too, but at the same time, a little sad that her children were growing up. It felt like only yesterday she and Eric had brought Liddie home from the hospital.

Car doors slamming turned Anne's head. Four teenage boys ambled toward the area by the pond, laughing and shoving each other as they walked. They seemed like a tight-knit group of boys, and very comfortable with each other.

Anne glanced at Ben and Liddie, who had moved from the slides to the swings. Both were pumping their legs, going higher and higher.

A peal of deep laughter rang out from the group of teen boys. Anne turned to stare, and recognized Jed Banks.

Those boys had to be the group the police were investigating for vandalizing the park. Anne watched as they sat on the back of one of the benches by the pond. They didn't appear to be doing anything, wrong or otherwise. They seemed to just be hanging out with each other and talking.

Another car door slammed behind Anne. She made sure Ben and Liddie were still swinging, then glanced over her shoulder. An older woman with a teenage boy approached the group of four boys. Anne stiffened. What if there was trouble? She dug her cell phone from her purse and held it in her palm, ready to call the police if the need arose.

The teen with the older lady sat on the bench with the group of boys, and the older lady turned and headed along the sidewalk, toward Anne. The boys, now five, walked in the opposite direction on the sidewalk, toward the nature trails around the other side of the pond. Anne's curiosity nearly choked her as the older woman drew nearer.

Ben and Liddie continued to swing, their laughter carrying on the gentle breeze. Anne smiled as Liddie pumped her little legs faster, trying to go as high as her brother.

"They're adorable," the older woman said, a little breathless.

Anne scooted to the other end of the bench. "Thank you. Would you like to sit down?"

"That'd be lovely. Thank you." She sat. "I'm Shirley Edwards. Just moved into Tarryville, up the road, about six months ago, but they don't have much in the way of parks."

"This park is lovely," Anne said as she took stock of the lady sitting beside her. Shirley Edwards had to be in her late sixties or early seventies. Her hair was a beautiful white, not the dingy gray many older women had. The sun shone on her face, and Anne could detect the shimmer of cataract implant lenses in her eyes.

"And it's a beautiful day," Shirley added.

"It certainly is." Anne glanced down the sidewalk to find no sight of the boys. "Do you come here often?"

Shirley nodded, her short, curled hair sweeping gently over her ears. "I've been coming here at least twice a week, if I can make it, for the last three months or so. My grandson enjoys visiting with his friends."

Ah. The opportunity presented itself to ask. Anne smiled. "Your grandson?"

Shirley nodded again. "Billy. He's fourteen."

Anne waited for further explanation. None came, so she pressed on. "Does Billy go to school in Blue Hill?"

"Oh no. He goes to a specialty school." Shirley lifted her face to the sun and closed her eyes.

Well, Anne decided, she'd just have to flat out ask. "I couldn't help but notice the boys your grandson went off with. I know one of them, and know he attends school here in Blue Hill. "

Shirley smiled and looked at Anne. "And so you're wondering how Billy and these boys are friends, right?"

Anne felt the blush but nodded.

"It's okay. I'd ask the same questions," Shirley said. "Billy is deaf. Almost a year ago, Billy's father, my son, got a career opportunity that is a once-in-a-lifetime chance but involved him moving out of state to a place where there isn't a special school for the deaf. My son was willing to pass up the opportunity, but after much thinking and prayer, I decided to step in. I moved into their home to be with Billy so my son could take advantage of this opportunity."

Tears welled in Anne's eyes, and she desperately wanted to give Shirley Edwards a hug. A big one.

"Billy has been struggling in his ability to read lips. Especially hearing teenagers. The therapist said teens don't use the same movements in speaking, so she encouraged Billy to be around more hearing teenagers to improve his skill." Shirley smoothed her long coat over her knit slacks. "The problem is that Billy doesn't have many hearing friends."

Anne watched Ben and Liddie move to play on the monkey bars.

"So I reached out to a friend of mine who lives here. You might know him—Barney Stockbeam?"

Anne nodded. "Oh yes. He's the one who usually so graciously plays Santa in our Dickens of a Christmas event."

"Yes. Well, Barney suggested I come over to Blue Hill to meet some teenage boys around Billy's age. I thought that was a grand idea, so I met Barney at the park, and sure enough, we found a few boys who were around Billy's age and a little older."

Anne's admiration of the woman's spunk grew. "So you introduced Billy to them?"

"Well, yes," Shirley said with trepidation in her voice. "But before I brought Billy around, I explained to the boys about him being deaf and needing to practice his lip reading. I offered to pay them to hang out with Billy for a couple hours a week, but they refused me." She paused. "They told me they would be his friend and help him because that's what Jesus would have them do," she said, her voice cracking.

Anne's heart thumped wildly. Not only was this woman amazing, thoughtful, and determinedly full of grit, but those boys...Michael should be proud of his son and those friends of his. She would make sure Michael found out what kind of character they had. No boys who would turn down easy money and cite Jesus as the reason were behind any vandalism. She wouldn't believe that.

"So twice a week, weather permitting," Shirley said, "I bring Billy here to the park for a couple of hours. He gets to hang out with his friends and practice lip reading, and I either sit and read or make new friends." She smiled at Anne.

"Funny you should mention reading because I happen to be the librarian in Blue Hill," Anne said.

The two ladies talked about books for about thirty minutes, until Liddie and Ben came to the bench.

"Mommy, I have to go," Liddie said.

Anne stood. "Then we'd better leave." She took Shirley's hands. "It was such a pleasure to meet you. I hope to see you again."

"Of course," Shirley said. "If the weather allows, we're usually here on Tuesday and Thursday afternoons from three thirty until five."

"Mommy!"

"Bye," Anne told Shirley, then rushed with Liddie and Ben to the car.

Once home, Anne checked on Bella in the library and found everything in order, so she went upstairs to get Ben started on his homework and set Liddie to practicing her writing. She sat down at the kitchen table to write out checks when the phone rang.

"Hello?" She slipped the cordless between her shoulder and her chin.

"Hey, Anne," Alex said.

She grabbed the phone and smiled. "Hi, Alex. Is anything wrong?" she asked, worried he needed her to get Ryan.

"Nothing's wrong. I just heard from Michael."

"And?"

"Their forensic unit learned the paint the vandals brought of their own is a specific brand that isn't carried here in Blue Hill," Alex told her.

"Really?"

"Oh, it's available in other towns and readily available online but nowhere here in Blue Hill. Michael said the police would try to figure out how to determine if anyone in Blue Hill ordered any of this particular paint in the last ninety days."

"They can do that?" Anne asked.

"I don't know, but I'm just excited because it's the first real lead the police seem to have," Alex said.

"I'll be praying they figure it out. And soon."

"Oh, and Eli Wallington came by to apologize about the whole deal with the nails and the boys," Alex said.

"He came by here as well to apologize." And kind of ask her out, but Anne didn't mention that.

"I respect that," Alex said.

"Me too. Hey, speaking of what I respect, let me tell you about some young men I respect." Anne explained about Shirley and her grandson and the four teenage boys. "I just don't think the boys could vandalize the park, then turn around and be extraordinarily nice to someone and cite Jesus as the reason."

"Me either. Have you told Michael?"

"Not yet. I probably should call him now. I wouldn't want anyone to wait to tell me something so admirable about one of my kids," Anne said.

"I'll talk to you later," Alex said. "Bye."

Anne dialed the police station's phone number and was put on hold only for a minute before Michael answered. She quickly told him about Shirley's grandson and Jed and his friends. Michael was silent for a long moment afterward.

"I—I'm stunned," he finally got out.

Anne smiled, even though tears pooled inside her own eyes, blurring her vision. "Michael, Jed and his friends acted so admirably, there's no way they could be behind any vandalism. You have to know that."

"Wait a minute. Did you tell me Shirley said she'd been going there every Tuesday and Thursday for the past couple of months, from three thirty until five?"

"That's what she told me," Anne said. "Why?"

"Hang on just a second." The sound of papers shuffling came over the phone connection, then Michael came back on the line. "The vandalism at the park occurred on the twenty third of last month, a Thursday between three and four thirty."

Anne smiled against the phone.

"Where did she say she normally met them?" Michael asked.

"She didn't say exactly, but Jed and the boys were waiting near the bench on the west side of the park, just before the pond. I'm sure you can ask Jed."

"I will. This just might help me establish not only their alibi, but also might give me a lead if she saw anything."

"I hope she can remember something. She said she only missed when weather wouldn't permit her to go there."

"I'll be sure and check the weather report for that day. Thanks, Anne. For calling, and for making a point to tell me about Jed and his friends. It really means a lot," Michael said.

"I know. It would to me if it were about one of my kids. I'll talk to you later," Anne said just before hanging up. Her heart felt loads lighter. She could only imagine how Michael felt.

She would be on top of the world, despite not having all the answers.

CHAPTER FOURTEEN

"Anne, I found this in the corner of the Nonfiction Room. I assume Mr. Ochs left it, because I believe that's his company logo on the battery." Remi handed an old drill to Anne.

Taking it, Anne flipped it over. The entire bottom, including the battery, was covered in nicks and scratches and even a couple of gouges, but faintly detectable was what might be the edge of Alex's company logo. "Thanks. Alex must've left it when he picked up Ryan on Wednesday," Anne said, although she didn't remember Alex having a drill with him, nor could she think of why he would've carried it into the Nonfiction Room. "I'll take it to him after I leave the school."

She slid it under the checkout counter by her purse and checked the time. Only a little under an hour until she had to leave to go to the school to help Liddie celebrate the entire kindergarten's Heritage Day. Liddie had worn one of Aunt Edie's brooches on her dress for the special day. Anne had remembered to charge the battery to the camera and put the camera in her purse so she wouldn't forget it.

"Good Friday morning, dears." Coraline Watson entered the library, slipping three of the new releases into the bin for returned books.

"Good morning, Ms. Watson," Remi said, smiling. "I have your two books that you requested. Would you like me to go ahead and check them out for you?"

"Please, dear." Coraline's green eyes twinkled from behind her thick glasses. "Hello, Anne."

"Hi, Coraline," Anne said. "How are you?"

"Fabulous. Last evening, I caught a glimpse of a Saw-whet Owl roosting in a spruce along the park. He was beautiful."

Coraline did love her bird-watching. Next to people-watching, it was her favorite hobby.

"I've only seen pictures of owls. Now that I think about it, I don't believe I've ever seen one in person," Anne said.

"That's a shame, dear. Beautiful birds, simply beautiful." Coraline hugged her sweater closer around her. "You should come bird-watching with me sometime. I try to go just at dusk over to the park."

The image of Coraline at the park, alone, at dark sent little sparks of trepidation along Anne's spine. "I hope you aren't going alone, Coraline."

The older woman laughed. "Oh, don't you worry about me, Anne. I'm quite capable of taking care of myself. For instance, just last month as I was in the park hoping to catch sight of a Pileated Woodpecker, two young men came toward me. One of them pushed over a trash can. I confronted him and told him to pick it up."

Anne gasped. "You didn't?" Surely Coraline knew how dangerous that could be? Yes, this was Blue Hill where there was much less crime than in other towns but still…

"Oh yes, I did," Coraline chuckled again and shook her head. "One of the little hoodlums asked me who was telling him, and I told him I was a member of the garden club and wouldn't tolerate such nonsense. He and his buddy had a right good laugh about that."

Anne could see Coraline doing something like that.

"What happened, Ms. Watson?" Remi asked.

"Well, he asked me who was going to make him pick it up, and I told him my buddy Mr. Smith & Wesson in my pocket," Coraline said with a smile.

Anne's eyes widened. "You carry a gun?"

"Of course not. Don't be ridiculous," Coraline said. "I had my binoculars in my coat pocket, but it could easily be mistaken for a gun, I suppose."

Remi chuckled while Anne wanted to tell Coraline how incredibly dangerous that could have been for her.

"So what happened then?" Remi asked.

"Well, they changed their tune right quick. They apologized, picked up the trash can, then hustled off." Coraline reached for her books from Remi. "Punks don't scare me. I've been taking care of myself long before those hooligans were even born. Those boys are nothing more than cowards." She shook her head and clutched the books to her chest. "Knocking over trash and overturning benches…those are cowardly acts."

"Who is performing such cowardly acts?" Eli rounded the corner and smiled. "Miss Coraline, if anyone is messing with you, cowardly or otherwise, you just let me know and I'll take care of them for you."

Coraline's cheeks pinked up. Apparently even the older woman wasn't immune to Eli Wallington's good looks and Southern charm. "Eli Wallington, you make a woman's head turn," she teased.

"But I only have eyes for you, Coraline," he said as he wrapped an arm around her.

She laughed and planted a kiss on his cheek. "You are an incorrigible flirt, but I love it." Coraline grinned at Anne. "Isn't he something?"

Anne smiled and nodded. "Oh, he's something all right. *Scoundrel* comes to mind."

Eli put a hand over his heart. "I'm hurt."

Anne and Coraline laughed together, then Eli joined in. "Okay, okay," he said, "I give up."

"Coraline, you should call the police. I think it's very possible you might have run off the boys who vandalized the park," Anne said.

The older woman nodded. "I suppose I might have. I'll call this afternoon."

"Good," Anne said. She turned to Eli. "Not to be rude, but I'm going to have to leave soon for something going on at my daughter's school. Did you stop by for something specific?"

Eli nodded. "I did. I have something for the boys and thought this time I'd bring it directly to you."

She had to give the man points for playing smart. "What did you bring them?"

"It's a crate of nails, screws, a couple of old hammers, and some other miscellaneous items I thought they could use. Also, we had several pieces of plywood left over from a job, along with some two-by-fours. I left everything in a pile by the tree of their build site."

"That's very nice of you, Eli. Thank you." Anne felt a little odd about accepting, but it wasn't really *her* accepting, it was for the boys, and they needed all the donations they could get because they were ready to start seeing some progress. "Ben and Ryan will be ecstatic."

Before Eli could respond, Bella burst into the library. "Oh my goodness! You would not believe how amazingly all the decorations are coming along for the Winter Wonderland dance. Mrs. Farley had gobs of old movie and Hollywood stuff she's going to let us use."

"Oh, Mildred would have plenty of that kind of stuff," Coraline said with a nod. "Like Edie, I don't think she throws anything away."

"That reminds me," Anne said. "I've decided to let you borrow the movie poster of Aunt Edie, but I need to get it matted and framed first." It had taken her some time to decide to let the girls borrow it. A copy wouldn't be the same. But, she'd argued with herself, had she and Liddie not gone looking in that particular trunk in the attic, she wouldn't have found it and had it anyway. "I'll try to get that done first thing next week."

Bella smiled. "Thank you, Mrs. Gibson. Since your aunt was such a prominent member of Blue Hill, we'll make the poster the centerpiece of the dance's decorations."

"That's lovely, dear," Coraline said. "Your aunt would have enjoyed being the focus after all this time."

"You know," Eli interrupted, "not that I know much about decorating for dances, but I do know how to build frames." He smiled at Anne. "Why don't you let me make a custom frame for the poster?"

"Oh, you don't have to do that," Anne said at the same time Remi and Bella both said, "Thanks."

Anne shook her head. "Really, Eli, thank you, but I'll get it done this week."

"Don't be ridiculous, Anne, let the man make a frame for Edie's poster," Coraline said. "You know she would have loved having something custom made for her big movie debut."

True. Anne hesitated. "If you're sure it's not a problem."

"I'm sure." Eli grinned. "Why don't I go ahead and take the poster's dimensions so I can start on it this weekend?"

"That is so sweet of you, Eli," Coraline gushed. "I have to run, everyone, or I'll miss my tea date. I'll see you all soon."

"Bye," Anne said, leading Eli to where she'd put the movie poster in the drawer for safe keeping.

After Eli took the measurements of the movie poster, he left, and Anne had time to freshen up just a bit before leaving for the school. She drove to the school and finally found a parking space — every parent must have been able to attend.

"Hey, Anne," Wendy called out to her as she made her way toward the three-story brick building.

"Hi. Looks like the kids will have a great turnout," Anne said as she fell into step beside Wendy. "Liddie was so excited this morning, she didn't even fuss when I French braided her hair." Normally, the little girl would cringe and jerk away, saying Anne was pulling it too tight.

Wendy chuckled. "I'm just grateful my kids let me put clean clothes on them."

Together, they squeezed into the old school building along with all the other parents. They made their way down the halls to the gym, where all the kids' projects were set up on display.

"Liddie said something about winning ribbons. Any idea what she's talking about?" Anne asked Wendy.

"They'll give out a bunch of awards on the projects," Wendy said as she led Anne to available chairs in the rows set up in front of all the displays. "First they'll talk about the project and how proud they are of all the kids and all that. Then, they'll give out award ribbons. Each of the kindergarten teachers give out several ribbons to their students' projects for best display or most research, or something," Wendy explained with a shrug. "It's a big deal for the kids, and we parents kinda like our kids to get a ribbon too."

Anne nodded. She hoped Liddie would get a ribbon for something, only because Liddie would be so incredibly excited.

While they waited, Anne told Wendy about Shirley Edwards and her grandson. Wendy was practically in tears, and then Anne told her about Coraline.

"I hope she called the police and told them about the kids in the park. It could be the lead they need," Wendy said.

Anne nodded. "I hope so too."

Further conversation halted as Mr. Bailey, the principal, turned on a microphone. "Hello. Hello. Is this on?" A squeal sounded. "Good. Welcome, parents and guests. We're so pleased to have you join us for the kindergarten Heritage Day celebration. The students will be joining us in a just a moment, but we wanted to take a second first and tell you how pleased all the kindergarten teachers are with the students' projects. A lot of that comes from the parental support, so we thank you." He clapped, and the audience joined in a bit.

"A lot?" Wendy leaned over and whispered to Anne. "How about *most* of it? These projects wouldn't get done without us parents buying the boards and helping the kids find the stuff to use, then helping to make sure they don't hot glue their hair to the display. Maybe they should give the parents award ribbons." She chuckled.

Anne nodded as Mr. Bailey introduced the three kindergarten teachers as each led their class into the gym and directed them to the smaller chairs set up for them. Anne waved as Liddie waved back.

"The ribbons are already on the individual projects, but the students haven't been informed yet," Mr. Bailey said. "So please, join me in appreciation as each awardee's name is called." He then introduced each teacher, who bestowed the coveted award ribbons for their class. Miss Reed, Liddie's teacher, went last. Miss Reed was also Justin's, one of Wendy's sons, teacher.

Miss Reed wore her long black hair straight without bangs. While it didn't look thick, just the sheer length of it appeared to overpower the very petite woman. "Hello, everyone. Thank you again for coming. Our classes had some outstanding projects, and I hope you'll take the time after the assembly to view the projects on display."

Anne found her palms a little moist and wiped them on her jeans. She could only imagine how nervous Liddie must be.

"Like the other teachers, I have four ribbon awardees. Most Creative Display goes to…Katherine Logan."

Applause sounded.

"Next, the Best Use of Material goes to…Cindy Jacobs."

Applause sounded again.

"The Most Original Display goes to…Beth Norris."

Anne clapped with the others, but her chest hurt. She really wanted Liddie to win a ribbon, but she also knew with only one ribbon left, both Liddie and Justin Pyle couldn't get one.

"And last, but certainly not least," Miss Reed said, smiling big, "The Best Overall Display goes to...Liddie Gibson."

Anne almost jumped out of her chair, clapping as hard as she could. Best Overall was huge! Liddie had worked so hard, and Anne was so proud of her.

"Congratulations," Wendy said, clapping just as hard as Anne. "She'll be thrilled."

"Thanks. She's over the moon, I'm sure," Anne answered but wondered how else she could respond. "I'm bummed Justin's project didn't get a ribbon."

Wendy laughed. "I'm not. I'm just glad he turned it in on time."

"Thank you all for coming. Please, allow your child to take you to look over other projects from their class. We hope you enjoy your time with us this afternoon," Mr. Bailey, the principal, said.

Anne couldn't get to Liddie fast enough.

"I won a ribbon, Mommy!" Liddie bounced from one foot to the other. "Best Overall."

Anne swept her daughter up into a hug. "Congratulations, sweetheart. You did amazing." She held her for just a second longer, breathing in the moment. This was a memory she'd cherish forever.

"Congratulations, Liddie," Wendy said.

Liddie grinned. "Thanks, Mrs. Pyle."

Anne allowed herself to be led through the maze of project displays before the bell finally rang that the assembly was over.

She gave Liddie a final hug. "I'm so proud of you, Liddie," Anne whispered as she let her daughter go.

Liddie skipped back to line up with the rest of her class. Anne turned and found Wendy waiting for her by the door. "Justin didn't want to look at any displays that weren't all boy," she said with a laugh.

Anne and Wendy headed to the parking lot together.

"Did you see the project with the crown because the girl's mother was a pageant winner?" Anne asked.

Wendy nodded. "A bit brazen of the mom, but I can't say it surprises me."

"*Ahh.* I loved the display with the baseball glove that belonged to a Philadelphia Philly. It was really neat," Anne said.

"Yeah. That's probably why he won Best Overall in Mrs. Hoskin's class," Wendy said as they reached the parking lot. "Well, I'd better get going. Won't be long before the kids are out of school, and I need to do the grocery shopping first."

"I'll see you later," Anne said, turning to her own car.

"Bye."

Anne got behind the wheel of her car and fastened her seat belt. She turned over the engine and let it warm a little while checking her cell phone. No missed calls. That had to be good. She set the phone in the console, then started to put the car in gear. Movement from the corner of her eye made her rest her foot on the brake.

A woman rushed from the back part of the school where the kitchen entrance was. She rushed across the concrete.

Anne pushed her glasses back up to the bridge of her nose, and even then, squinted to be sure she was right.

The woman turned as she reached a car, her face clearly visible to Anne.

Anne's eyes hadn't deceived her — the woman in such a hurry was none other than Lisabeth Matthews.

What was she doing there? Did Lisabeth have any children? Maybe so, otherwise why would she be at the elementary school? But if she had kids, wouldn't they go to school in Deshler where she lived?

Anne put the car in gear and eased out of the parking space. She intended to find out a little more about Lisabeth Matthews.

And she told herself all the way back to the library that it had nothing to do with any jealousy issue. Just curiosity.

Not jealousy at all.

CHAPTER FIFTEEN

"Hello, Anne," Alex said, smiling as he walked toward her. "I didn't know you were coming by the site today."

"I was out at Liddie's Heritage Day anyway." She nodded toward the ticket counter. "That's beautiful."

Alex's eyes lit up. "It does look really good, doesn't it? Patrick's thrilled with how it's turning out."

"You should be very proud, Alex. It's beautiful."

He blushed, just a little, and bent his head. "Thanks, Anne."

She didn't mean to embarrass him, so she changed the subject quickly. "No more acts of vandalism?"

Alex shook his head. "The men on the crew and I have been taking turns standing guard every night since the last episode, and we have not had a single incident." He grinned. "Patrick is so pleased that he's paying us extra for the service since he wasn't ever able to hire a security firm, even though it means we're starting a little later than usual. I'm letting the crew sleep in to make up for the time we're taking turns being here all night."

"That's wonderful, Alex," she said, then hesitated. "So I guess Lisabeth hasn't been doing any work for you lately."

"No. Why?" Alex asked.

"I just thought I saw her leaving the school today," Anne said. "I wondered if maybe she had a child there."

Alex shrugged. "I'm not sure, but I don't think she has any children. She told me she'd never been married. You're probably mistaken about whoever you saw being her."

"I guess," Anne said but wasn't convinced. She didn't even want to think about how it made her feel that Alex automatically assumed she'd been mistaken. She forced a smile. "I know you're busy and I don't want to keep you, but since I was out, I wanted to see the progress you're making." She pulled the drill out of her purse. "And I wanted to return this to you."

Alex took the drill, and frowned.

"It is yours, right?" Maybe she was mistaken and it was someone else's.

"It's mine all right. Where did you get this?"

"Remi found it in the library. I guess you left it when you came by to pick up Ryan the other day," Anne said.

"I didn't leave it at the library," Alex said.

Now Anne frowned. "Then I'm confused. If you didn't leave it there, how'd it end up in my Nonfiction Room this morning?"

"I don't know, but we should find out." His expression had sobered into deep lines of concern between his brows.

"Alex, what's going on?" Anne asked, her nerves bunching.

"This drill was the one stolen from this site, Anne. The one the vandals took." His eyes were wide.

"Then how did it get into my library?" she asked even as her heartbeat skipped rhythm.

"That's what we need to find out. Maybe we should run it by the police station and let Josie or Michael look it over," Alex said.

"I touched it. So did Remi," Anne said.

"I don't think that's the main issue. It was listed as stolen property, so we should definitely let them know it's been recovered."

"Right." Anne hadn't really thought about that. Then again, she was still trying to wrap her mind around the idea that the drill had been stolen and then just showed up in the library.

Alex placed his hand under her elbow. "Why don't we run there now, then grab a sandwich for lunch? Will that work, or do you need to get back to the library?"

"No, that's fine. I want the police to have this information."

"Let me tell Buddy that I'm leaving. I'll be right back," Alex said, heading toward the back of the theater.

Anne moved closer to the ticket counter. Alex and his company had done quite a remarkable job. It looked almost like part of the original theater.

"Okay, I'm ready to go," Alex said as he returned. He led Anne to his truck, guiding her with his hand under her elbow and carrying the drill in his other hand. After he unlocked the door and helped her inside, Alex moved around to the driver's side.

They drove a few miles in silence until Alex said, "So... how's your morning been?"

Anne smiled. There was always the quiet comfortableness between them, easy because they'd been friends for so long. "Liddie's Heritage Day project won Best Overall Display in her class. She got a ribbon, and she's so happy."

Alex grinned while keeping his eyes on the road. "I bet she's quite proud of herself."

"She is, and I'm quite proud of her too," Anne said.

"As you should be." Alex grinned wider and stole a glance at Anne. "And I bet your aunt Edie would've been pretty pleased as well."

Anne laughed. "She definitely would've been. Oh, Alex, she so loved Liddie and Ben." So many times, she wished her aunt were still alive to be around the kids more. Now that they lived in Blue Hill, Anne would love for Aunt Edie to be here to laugh and share with. Anne missed her dearly.

"I know she did." Alex smiled. "Do you remember when you brought the kids here a few years ago?"

Anne nodded. "We had such a great time with her. The kids loved her."

"After you left, all she ever talked about was playing hide-and-seek with Ben and how precocious Liddie was. To be honest, I got a little sick of hearing about your visit," Alex teased with a chuckle. "Over and over and *over* again."

Anne laughed too. "*Mmm*. Thanks for sharing that, Alex. These kinds of memories are pretty awesome to hold on tight to." They were like hugs from special loved ones.

Alex didn't say anything, just found a parking spot for the truck at the police station and rushed around to open her door. He gallantly led her inside. "We'd like to see Michael Banks, if he's available," Alex told the officer standing behind the counter.

Michael arrived a few moments later. "Hey, you two."

Alex didn't smile. "We have some news."

Michael's smile vanished. "Come on back," Michael said, leading the way to the interview room. "More vandalism?"

Alex let Anne step into the room first. "No. The drill I reported stolen in one of the vandal attacks has been recovered," he said, pulling the drill out from under his coat and setting it on the table.

Michael cocked his head. "I don't understand."

Anne took a seat. "Let me back up and explain. Could you both please sit down? You're making my neck hurt."

Both men sat.

"This morning, Remi brought me this drill and said she'd found it in the Nonfiction Room of the library," Anne said. "This is where Ben and Ryan have been set up working on their project. When Remi gave me the drill, I just assumed it was Alex's and he left it there when he'd come to pick up Ryan on Wednesday. This morning, I had to go to the school for Liddie's Heritage Day celebration anyway, so I took the drill with me. After I left the school, I took it to Alex at the work site."

"And it *is* mine, but it's the one that went missing after one of the acts of vandalism," Alex interjected. "It's listed in the police report."

Michael looked at the drill, then Alex. "Are you sure it's the same one?"

Alex nodded. "I didn't check the serial number, but yes, I know it's the same one."

"You have no idea how it got into the library?" Michael asked Anne.

She shook her head. "Like I said, I didn't ever see it there. Remi found it this morning in the Nonfiction Room when she was opening the library. She, too, thought it was Alex's, so she brought it to me."

"It is mine—it's just the one that was taken from the site," Alex finished.

Michael pulled out his notebook. "We'll run the drill through forensics, and we'll need both of your fingerprints, as well as Remi's," he said. "Now, Anne, how often are the library rooms tidied?"

She tried not to bristle, understanding he was doing his job. "Every afternoon, we shelve any books that have been returned that day that we didn't have time to shelve. Then, every morning, we check each of the rooms and make sure the trash cans are emptied and the shelves and tables are dusted. It's part of our opening procedures."

"So Remi opened this morning and that's when she found the drill?" Michael asked.

"Yes."

"Who closed the library last night?" Michael asked.

"Bella, Remi's sister, but she didn't find the drill," Anne said, "which is very unusual. Both Remi and Bella are very thorough and have strong work ethics. If the drill had been there, she would've seen it." So when was the drill left?

"Who has been in that room?" Michael asked, moving on.

"Oh." Anne blinked as she shrugged. "I can't tell you how many people might have gone in there to get a book. Ryan and Ben have been set up in there during the afternoons, but while they're at school…it's hard to say."

"Anything you can give me would help, Anne," Michael said.

"Well, I can pull the records of any books checked out of that room this week," Anne said. "That's an easy report to pull." Three clicks and it'd be in Excel form. "I can e-mail it to you as soon as I get back to the library."

Michael nodded. "Do that," he said, looking up from his notebook. "Have you noticed any strangers hanging around the library?"

"Not that I can think of," Anne said, pushing away the image of Eli Wallington. He wasn't a stranger. Coraline thought highly of him. Even Alex seemed to respect him. She couldn't cast suspicion on him for no reason. He'd been nothing but nice to the boys.

Michael looked at Alex. "Anything going on at the site?"

"Nothing, but I've had crew members staying there every night, just to watch over the place."

Frowning, Michael said, "Just remember what I told you. No heroes and no vigilantes. If any of you see or hear something, you call 911 immediately."

"Don't worry," Alex said, "I've made sure everyone is aware of what to do. We just want the person caught."

"What did Ben and Ryan say? Had they seen the drill or know anything about it?" Michael asked.

"Ben was already at school when Remi brought the drill to me," Anne said. "I'll ask the boys this afternoon."

"Maybe I should pick up Ryan so I can ask him," Alex said.

"Don't be silly," Anne waved him off. "I'll ask the boys. If they know anything, I'll let you know immediately."

"Sounds like a good idea. Let me know if they know anything," Michael said as he shut his notebook and nodded. "Or if you think of anything else," he said, pushing to his feet.

Anne and Alex stood as well.

"I'll e-mail you the list of names as soon as I get back," Anne said.

"Thank you. I'll have forensics go over the drill," Michael said. He escorted them down the hall and introduced them to an officer who would take their fingerprints. "I'll leave you two to finish up here, but I'll be in touch." With a nod, he was gone.

Once Alex and Anne were finished with the fingerprinting, they stepped out of the police station and headed to Alex's truck. "How about Keystone for lunch?" he asked her.

"Oh, that sounds fabulous," Anne said, still wiping at her blackened fingertips with a wet wipe.

The Keystone Café, tucked in one of the historic downtown buildings, seemed to be perpetually busy no matter what time or day. The charming decor stood out with its checked white and salmon floors resting beside whitewashed brick walls. The food was both sophisticated and delicious.

Alex grinned as he backed the truck out of the parking space. "You're already thinking about the grilled cheese sandwiches, aren't you?" he teased her.

"You know me too well," she said. The café might offer Italian fare as a prime menu, but the grilled sandwiches rivaled any Anne had ever eaten in New York. A blend of four different cheeses was piled thick between two pieces of homemade sourdough bread, then heated to the perfect temperature for maximum gooeyness — Panini style. Served with a salad and an order of thick French fries…*mmm*, Anne's mouth watered at just the mental image.

Alex chuckled. "Ryan isn't big on Keystone, I guess because they don't serve regular pizza or burgers, so I never get to eat the lasagna unless I go for lunch."

"Ben and Liddie like the grilled cheese sandwiches too."

"Well, no doubt. I'm sure you force-fed them those since birth," Alex said, grinning from ear to ear.

"I did not," Anne said but laughed.

After they were settled inside the comfortable restaurant and placed their orders, Alex shared with her all the plans for the theater. She wasn't bored because she loved history, and she was thrilled to hear that the theater would bear more of a resemblance to the building's origins than to the modern theaters of the last couple of years.

"I heard you've been discussing the decorations for the Winter Wonderland dance," Alex said after their entrees were delivered to their table.

Anne swallowed her bite of mouthwatering grilled cheese, then chased it with her water. "Where'd you hear that?"

Alex waggled his eyebrows. "I know all."

Anne burst out laughing, and Alex joined her. "Okay. So I ran into Wendy when I was dropping Ryan off at school, and we were chatting and she mentioned it."

"Ah. That makes sense," Anne said, then shoved a fry into her mouth.

"You're good with all that. Wendy said the theme is going to be Classic Hollywood. Said she's making Chad rent a tux."

Anne nearly choked. "I don't think I've ever seen Chad in a tux. Ought to be a hoot."

Alex chuckled. "I don't think Chad knows her intent yet."

"He's been married to Wendy long enough to know to just go with what she wants. It's much easier," Anne said.

"You got that right."

"I think the theme will be fun for everyone, and I'm letting them use the movie poster I found of Aunt Edie's," Anne said.

"That's nice. If you want, I could build a special display frame for it," Alex offered.

Suddenly, the grilled cheese Anne had just polished off sat like lead in her stomach. "Um, thanks, but that's okay."

"Really. I'd be honored to," Alex said, smiling.

Oh, mercy. Anne took a drink of water. "Actually, Eli is making a frame for it." She wished she could look away, but her eyes were glued to Alex's face.

His smile disappeared for just a split second. "Oh. That's nice of him."

"I was going to go have it matted and framed, but Eli overheard and offered, and you've been so busy, and at first I said no, but Remi and Bella and Coraline all—"

Alex held up his hand. "You don't have to explain to me. It's nice of him to do it. I can't wait to see it when it's finished."

Anne finished off her water.

"Speaking of finished…" Alex motioned to the waiter for the check.

"Speaking of Eli… he stopped by this morning and left some wood and a crate of odds and ends of building stuff for the boys," Anne said. "He wanted to let me know so that there wasn't any confusion."

"That's smart of him." Alex slipped bills into the leatherette folder, then helped Anne to her feet and out of the restaurant. "I have to say, I respected him contacting you and me to apologize after Michael talked to him." He opened the truck door for her.

"Me too," Anne said.

There were a few moments of silence as Alex steered the truck back to the theater. "Do you like him?" Alex asked as he pulled the truck up to a stop sign and turned to stare at Anne.

"Like him?" She could feel the heat radiating across her face. "He seems nice enough."

"That's not what I meant, and I think you know that," Alex said, then turned his attention back to driving.

Anne's mouth was dry. "I actually think he and Grace would make a lovely couple."

Alex chuckled. "Does Grace know that?" He shook his head as he pulled into the theater's parking lot. "Matchmaking is never a good idea, Anne."

"Spoken from personal experience?" she asked. For the life of her, she couldn't imagine Alex playing matchmaker.

"As a victim of many matchmaking attempts over the years," Alex said, "it was extremely painful for me at first, until I just started declining the invitations of every well-meaning friend of mine."

Anne laughed. "Point taken. I won't try to play matchmaker."

Alex had barely killed the truck's engine when Lisabeth rushed toward the truck. She pulled up short when Anne opened the passenger door.

"Oh. I didn't realize you weren't alone," Lisabeth told Alex but curled her lip at Anne.

"Just getting back from lunch. Are you here to pick up your check?" Alex asked Lisabeth. "Buddy could have given it to you."

"I wanted to say hi," Lisabeth said, her flirty smile almost coy.

Anne forced a pleasant expression to her face as she raised her purse strap high onto her shoulder. "Hi, Lisabeth. I thought I saw you earlier today."

A single, perfectly arched brow of Lisabeth's raised. "Did you now?"

"Yes. At the elementary school. I didn't know you had any children."

Lisabeth narrowed her eyes for a moment, then smiled. It was a fake smile, Anne noticed, but Alex didn't seem to catch it. "I've expanded some of my cleaning positions here in Blue Hill. One of the crew at the elementary school is out on maternity leave, so I'm filling in," Lisabeth said. She turned to face Alex, putting her back to Anne. "But I'm finished at the school by ten every morning, so if you need me, I can be here before ten thirty."

Of course she could. Anne bit her tongue to hold in the words, then shook it off. "Alex, you have business to attend to, so I'm going to head on back to the library. I'll call you after I speak with the boys."

"Okay, Anne. Thanks. I'll be there to get Ryan around four thirty or five," Alex said.

"See you then. Thanks for lunch," Anne said. "Bye, Lisabeth," she remembered to add.

"Oh yeah. Bye, Anne," Lisabeth answered just before she turned to fall in step with Alex.

Anne let out a long breath, then headed to her car. She just stared at the theater as she let the car idle. Lisabeth rubbed her wrong in so many ways.

Was it all because of Alex? Surely she wasn't the jealous type. Over a friend, none the less. At least, Anne sincerely hoped she wasn't that type of woman.

CHAPTER SIXTEEN

Anne climbed down the back stairs after she'd settled Liddie at the kitchen table with her after-school snack of juice and graham crackers. The afternoon had turned warmer than anticipated, so only a jacket was needed.

The sound of a pounding hammer made Anne rush outdoors. The boys knew they shouldn't be actually building anything without an adult present! She'd told them. Alex had told them.

She rushed around the tree and—

Drew up short as Denny Thatcher froze, hammer held midstrike.

He dropped his arm. "Hi."

"Mr. Thatcher. What are you doing here?" she asked, even as she eyed Ben and Ryan. At least Ben had the decency to blush and look away. This would definitely be a topic of discussion for later, and Ben knew it.

"Just helping the boys out a little," Denny said. "I saw they were working on the plans a few days ago and asked if they would like a little grown-up muscle." He looked sheepish. "I didn't mean any harm."

Anne remembered what Grace had said about Denny and his unfortunate events. "I'm sure you didn't. The boys just failed to mention to me they would have any help, so you can imagine my concern when I heard hammering."

"Oh yes, ma'am. I completely understand," Denny said.

"We weren't sure he'd be here, Mom," Ben offered.

Anne narrowed her eyes at her son. "We'll discuss that later. Right now, I need to ask you boys about a drill I found in the Nonfiction Room this morning. Do either of you know anything about it?"

Denny nodded. "That's my fault too, ma'am. I found the drill and brought it to the boys, thinking they could probably use it."

"You *found* it?" Anne asked, even as she struggled with posing the question. Who just happens to find a drill that's listed as stolen? The person who was wanted for questioning?

"Yes, ma'am. I found it next to a Dumpster," Denny said.

Anne nodded at the boys. "Ben and Ryan, you two go check on Liddie for me and grab yourselves a bottled water."

"Mom, we aren't thirsty," Ben started to protest.

Anne silenced him with a look. "I'd like to speak to Mr. Thatcher alone. Please, go and do as I asked."

"Yes, ma'am," Ryan said, turning and racing toward the stairs. Ben was right behind him.

"I didn't mean any harm," Denny said as he set the hammer on top of a wooden crate. "I just wanted to help the boys."

"Are you aware the police are looking for you, Mr. Thatcher?" Anne asked as she reached into her jacket pocket and wrapped her fingers around her cell phone.

"The police? No, ma'am."

While it might seem inconceivable that he was unaware of such a search and that he just found a drill, Anne was inclined to believe the man. She couldn't say why, it was a feeling in her spirit.

She pulled her cell from her pocket. "They have a few questions regarding the fire at the warehouse. Why don't I call them for you?"

He nodded. "Thank you, ma'am."

She quickly dialed the station and spoke to Michael, who told her he would be there soon.

"Michael Banks is one of the policemen working the case, and he said he'd be here soon," Anne told Denny.

Ben and Ryan came back outside, Hershey on their heels. Ben handed Denny a bottled water and a pack of cheese and peanut butter crackers. The dog raced around the tree until Ryan threw Hershey's old blue ball.

"Thank you," Denny said.

Again, Anne ached at the needs of Denny Thatcher. How many more were out in Blue Hill just like him? She had to remember to talk to Reverend Tom or someone to direct her in ways to help the homeless.

Hershey ran back up to Ben, leaning against his leg. Ben patted the dog's head, then took the ball and threw it again.

"Is everything okay, Mom?" Ben asked cautiously.

"It's fine." She needed to think of something to tell the boys before Michael arrived. She didn't want them to get the impression that Denny was a suspect or anything. "It seems you aren't the only ones needing Mr. Thatcher's help today."

"Really?" Ryan asked. "He's going to help you too?"

Anne smiled. "I'm sure he would if I asked, but that isn't what I meant. Michael's on his way over here to talk to Mr. Thatcher because the police need his help too."

"Cool," Ryan said, grinning. Hershey came to Ryan this time, and dropped the ball at his feet. Ryan hurled it across the backyard. The lab shot off like a rocket.

Ben stared at Denny, then looked to Anne. "With the warehouse fire?" he asked. Even though Ben was only nine, her son was definitely astute.

Anne nodded as the sound of a truck's engine rumbled over.

Everyone turned, then Ryan broke into a sprint. "Uncle Alex, Uncle Alex..." Ben followed along with Hershey, who barked as he ran.

"Thank you, Mrs. Gibson," Denny said.

"For what?"

"For telling the boys I was helping the police." Denny took a long sip of water. "You and I both know they're taking me in for questioning."

"That's helping the police, right?" Anne asked but understood completely.

"If you say so, ma'am." He bit into another cracker, and Anne thought she heard his stomach growl.

Alex joined them at the tree after sending the boys and Hershey scampering inside, his gaze flickering over Anne's face to detect any type of anxiety. "I hear you're Denny Thatcher," Alex said by way of greeting.

Denny held out his hand. "Yes, sir."

Alex didn't hesitate to shake the man's hand. "Alex Ochs. I understand you found my drill." It was a statement, but the way Alex said it, it came out more like a question.

"Yes, sir. By the Dumpster in the alley behind the theater and warehouses," Denny answered. "I thought someone threw it away."

"You didn't think to bring it to the work site in the theater and see if it belonged to any of the crew?" Alex asked.

Denny shook his head. "I'm sorry, but I didn't." He shrugged. "It looked old and used, and I know firsthand how some items are just discarded when something newer comes along."

Anne didn't know what to say in the awkward silence that followed. Good thing she didn't have to figure out something because Michael pulled up and parked alongside Alex's truck.

"There's Michael. Come on," Alex said.

Anne and Denny fell into step with Alex as they met Michael by his car.

Denny stepped forward. "I'm Denny Thatcher. Mrs. Gibson was kind enough to let me know you've been looking for me?"

Michael opened the passenger's door of the cruiser. "Please, come with me."

"Thank you," Denny said to Anne. "For everything." He ducked his head and sat in the front seat.

Michael shut the door and nodded at Anne and Alex. "I'll let you know what we find out."

"For the record, I think he really did find the drill," Anne said. "As preposterous as that may sound."

Michael nodded. "Oh, by the way, Anne, I did speak with Shirley Edwards and Coraline about the boys in the park."

"And?" Anne asked.

"We've cleared Jed and his friends of the vandalism at the park. Coraline came in just before I got your call and is working with the sketch artist."

"That's great," Alex said. "Maybe that will be a lead on our vandalism."

Michael tapped the roof of the car. "Right now, Alex, we're investigating everything as three separate crimes: the vandalism at the park, the fire in the warehouse, and the vandalism at the theater. If we uncover a connection, then we'll proceed with that angle, but for now...they're three separate cases."

"Thanks for letting us know," Anne said as Michael got into the car.

Alex and Anne waited until Michael drove off before climbing the stairs to Anne's living area over the library.

"I should have asked Michael if he was able to follow up on Sally Langford," Anne said.

"I heard she hasn't renewed her lease at the house she's renting," Alex said. "I believe Coraline said something like that, but I could be wrong."

They stepped into the living room to find Ben and Ryan watching cartoons.

"Where's Liddie?" Anne asked.

"She's playing dolls in her room," Ben said.

Alex sat on the couch beside Ryan and grabbed the remote. He turned off the television, then turned to face both boys. "Guys, I know you're excited about the project and I respect that enthusiasm, really, I do, but you had to know that you couldn't just accept help without letting us know."

The tips of Ryan's ears turned red and Ben stared at the floor.

"It's just that we want to make sure you both are safe," Anne said. "Getting help is wonderful, but we need to know in advance. Understand?" She kept her tone soft. The boys really hadn't done anything wrong but after they'd just discussed about strangers...

"Then I guess we should tell you that Mr. Wallington has helped us too," Ben offered.

Anne smiled. "I know. He told me he was leaving the materials."

"Oh. So you knew he helped us change the design?" Ryan asked.

"No. Why did you change it?" Alex asked.

"Because we wanted to move the door to the back side instead of having it face the library," Ben said.

"Why wouldn't you come to me with that?" Alex asked.

"Because you're really busy at the theater all the time," Ryan said. "We didn't want to bother you."

Anne recognized the hurt look embedding itself on Alex's face. Her own chest tightened for him. "Boys, you can always come to me or Alex. We might not be able to get to something right then, but we're happy to help," she said.

Liddie skipped into the room. "Mommy, I'm hungry. When's dinner?"

Alex stood. "We'd better be heading home. Get your things," he told Ryan.

"You're welcome to stay for dinner," Anne offered. "It's spaghetti."

"Thanks, but I think Ryan and I need a little time tonight."

Anne smiled in understanding. "I'll see you later then."

She sent up a silent prayer that their night would be one full of love and connection.

* * *

"Mrs. Gibson, can you come in here, please?" Remi called out from the front of the library.

Carefully sliding the last book back to its proper place on the shelf, Anne stood and left the Fiction Room. She all but bounced down the spiral staircase. "Yes?" she asked as she turned toward the front desk.

"Surprise!" Wendy, Remi, Bella, and Eli all sang out together, then stepped aside to reveal the framed movie poster resting on a display easel.

Anne smiled and moved to the display. The frame itself was an intricate work of art. Swirls, curly-Qs, and clean curves were etched into the deep mahogany frame, their lines embossed with a rich gold tone. The poster had been triple matted in red, then gold, then red. Rich colors that perfectly matched the red of the title font.

"It's beautiful, Eli," Anne whispered, as if speaking too loudly might break the beauty of the moment.

"I'm very pleased you like it," Eli said, nearly startling her at his close proximity as he was just over her right shoulder.

"We wanted to see your face when you saw it," Remi said.

"Isn't it perfect?" Bella asked.

Anne turned and smiled at the girls, whose excitement was more than contagious. "It's very perfect. Thank you again, Eli, and for bringing it in on a Saturday."

"I aim to please, madam," he said, mock bowing.

"I think I'll put it back behind the counter for safety for now," Anne said. "That way, it'll be a surprise at the dance."

Remi actually clapped her hands and bounced. "That's perfect. Thank you, Mrs. Gibson, and you too, Mr. Wallington."

"Are you finished in the Fiction Room?" Bella asked Anne.

"I did the shelving, but the tables need to be dusted and the trash cans emptied," Anne replied.

"I'm on it," Bella said.

"I'll go finish in the Children's Room," Remi said as she followed her twin.

"What are you doing here on a Saturday morning?" Anne asked Wendy.

"Letting Chad have the kids this morning while I go to get my hair cut. I have to take the kids shopping at the mall in Deshler this afternoon for shoes—all seven of them." Wendy shook her head. "How do seven kids all wear their shoes out at the same time?"

Anne chuckled. She still had a hard time grasping the concept of seven kids, ranging in ages from four to fourteen.

"But I wasn't going to miss this unveiling. That will be the center focal point of the whole Winter Wonderland dance," Wendy said.

"Speaking of the dance," Eli said, turning to Anne and taking her hand. He led her a few steps away from Wendy. "Anne, would you like to go to the dance with me?"

Anne's throat held her voice hostage. No denying that Eli was quite the handsome man and charming as well…he was nice to the boys and very generous. But, well, Anne just didn't feel comfortable saying yes. "Wow. I'm flattered, really. To hear it told, you're probably one of the most eligible bachelors in town," she said, finally finding her voice.

He dropped her hand. "But you're going to tell me no."

"I know I've been a widow for several years, but I'm just not sure I'm quite ready to go on a *real* date with anyone just yet. Especially so publicly. Does that make sense?"

He smiled. "It makes perfect sense. But you are going to the dance, correct?"

"Yes. I'm going," she said. Anne wanted to let out a long sigh of relief that he took the turn down well.

"Then you must at least save a dance for me. Okay?"

She smiled and nodded. "Of course."

"Then I will bid you good-bye and see you later," Eli told her. He turned and headed for the main door. "Good-bye, Wendy."

"Bye, Eli," Wendy called out but stared at Anne. "So? Are you going to the dance with him? He is so nice looking and charming. And did you see that frame? Girl, he's got skills too," she gushed.

"Um, I told him no," Anne said.

"You what?" Wendy looked at Anne as if she'd just sprouted a second head.

"I'm not sure I'm ready to go on a real date to such a public event."

"Are you serious?" Wendy's expression read that she hoped Anne was joking. "Anne, no offense, but you've been a widow for over three years now."

"I know. It's not that," Anne said, and it was true. She was ready to move on, and the thought of romance with someone other than Eric was by no means unattractive.

"So it's Eli himself then?" Wendy probed.

"Yes. No." Anne shook her head. "I don't know. He is handsome and charming and everything wonderful, but I don't know. I just don't…I don't know how to explain it."

Wendy scrutinized Anne for a long moment, then nodded. "I get it. You just don't feel it with Eli. The chemistry."

"No, that's not it." How could she explain a little better? "I just don't know him all that well. Is he a Christian? What's his past? What are his dreams? His goals? I know none of that."

Wendy laughed. "Anne, honey, finding out all of that is the whole point of dating." She shook her head. "I've got to run or the kids will have Chad hog-tied, but you need to think about the whole dating thing. If you're not ready, you aren't, and that's okay. But if you think you might be, you need to figure out what you're looking for."

"I know," Anne muttered.

Wendy gave her a quick hug. "Pray about it. You'll figure it out."

"Thanks."

"Wish me luck. Seven kids at the mall. I might be insane," Wendy said, then grabbed her purse and left.

Alone at the checkout desk, Anne straightened all the pads and pens and every other little item on the desk. Her mind couldn't seem to get in sync with her emotions.

Was she ready to date? Her gut had immediately recoiled at Eli's invitation, yet she found him very appealing as a date. What was going on with her?

Wendy was right. She should pray and let that be the start.

Chapter Seventeen

Monday morning burst forth in Blue Hill with the promise of spring just around the corner. Temperatures climbed to high thirties early in the day as the sun shone brightly. Anne stood next to the library's flower beds, taking inventory of what she'd need to replace in the spring. She loved having a multitude of blooming flowers overflowing the flower beds. It was like a joyous explosion welcoming patrons to the library.

"Anne, your cell's ringing," Wendy hollered out the door.

"Grab it, please," Anne said as she brushed her hands against her jeans and rushed inside. Wendy handed her the phone, whispering, "It's the school."

"Hello," Anne said.

"Mrs. Gibson, this is Flores Sanchez, the nurse at Blue Hill Elementary. I have Liddie in the sick room. She's complaining of a tummy ache."

"Oh, goodness. I'll come get her," Anne said, then disconnected the call.

"What's wrong with Liddie?" Wendy asked.

"Upset stomach," Anne answered, reaching into the drawer to pull out her purse. "Probably the two pieces of pie she had last night. I warned her it was really rich chocolate." Anne had argued with herself for allowing her daughter a second piece, but Liddie had eaten all her carrots...

"It's probably nothing that lying on the couch and watching cartoons won't fix. And some Pepto-Bismol," Wendy said. "How about I run up to your place and get the couch ready?"

"That'd be great, Wendy. Thanks," Anne said as she rushed out the door.

On the drive over to the school, Anne couldn't help but notice all the buds daring to pop out on the trees and foliage. Simply beautiful. She pulled into the school's circle and parked.

"Good morning, Mrs. Gibson," the school's office worker greeted her.

"Hello, Celeste. I hear you have one of mine in the sick room," Anne said as she reached for the computer to check Liddie out.

"Yeah. She's got a tummy ache." Celeste handed Anne Liddie's backpack. "I have a feeling she'll be fine in a couple of hours. At least, that's what Flores says."

Anne nodded. "She probably ate too much pie last night."

Celeste grinned. "Well, I just might take a stomachache for pie." She pressed a button on the intercom machine behind the desk. "She'll be right out."

In less than a minute, Nurse Sanchez led Liddie into the hall.

Anne squatted and hugged her daughter. "You don't feel well, sweetie?"

Liddie shook her head. "My tummy hurts, Mommy."

"Okay, baby girl. We'll get you home and resting on the couch, okay?" Anne stood, held Liddie's hand, and pushed the backpack strap up to her shoulder. "Thank you," Anne said to the nurse and office worker.

"Get to feeling better soon, Liddie," Nurse Sanchez said.

Anne settled Liddie in her seat, then inched the car out of the circle toward the road. Just as she was about to turn onto Main Street, she noticed a car speeding into the parking lot. Anne frowned. No one should be driving that fast in the school parking lot. Should she go back in and report it to the office? Surely Mr. Bailey, the principal, would at least want to have a talk with the person.

She glanced in her rearview mirror to find Liddie's head back against the seat and her eyes closed. Anne really didn't have time, but that person...she squinted as she saw a woman get out of the car and practically run across the lot toward the back door of the school.

Anne gasped as she recognized the woman. Lisabeth.

What was she doing? Anne glanced at her watch and took note of the time: nine fifty-two. Wait a minute. Didn't Lisabeth say she was finished at the school by ten? Then what was she doing arriving at the school just before ten? That made no sense.

"Mommy?" Liddie said from the backseat. "I want to lay down."

"It's 'lie down' sweetheart, and okay." Anne drove toward Bluebell Lane, her mind still wondering about Lisabeth and whatever game she was playing.

After getting Liddie settled on the couch, with plenty of juice and a good dose of the pink stomach medicine, as Liddie liked to call Pepto-Bismol, Anne headed back down to the library to find Wendy hanging up the phone.

"How's Liddie?" Wendy asked.

"Sleepy, I think. She's watching cartoons. Thanks for setting up the couch," Anne answered.

"I just talked with Remi. She and Bella will be here in a bit. Bella will watch the library for you, and Remi is more than happy to stay with Liddie while you pick up Ben as usual," Wendy said.

"Thank you. I hadn't even thought that far," Anne said. Despite Wendy's sometimes full-steam-ahead personality, Anne didn't know what she'd do without such a good friend.

"Listen, I know it's none of my business, but Christian told me that Ben and Ryan have been arguing about their tree house, fort, whatever."

That was new. "What did Christian say?" Anne asked. Alex had spent yesterday afternoon after church and lunch helping the boys. The frame for the building was fully complete.

"Just that Ben and Ryan couldn't agree on something having to do with the design of something," Wendy said, shrugging. "I don't know."

"Did Christian say when they were arguing?" Anne asked.

"Friday at lunch at school," Wendy said. "Just thought you might want to know."

"Yeah. Thanks." She couldn't imagine what they were arguing over. Maybe they'd worked it out over the weekend or when they were working on it with Alex on Sunday. She'd still talk to Ben about it. Just something else on her plate that seemed to be heaping high lately.

Her cell rang. Anne checked the caller ID before answering. "Hi, Grace. What's up?"

"Did you hear that Sally Langford moved?"

"No, I hadn't heard that," Anne said, slipping onto the stool behind the front counter.

"Yep. Moved this weekend to Deshler. According to Josie Bolling, Sally got out of the lease she'd taken on the house here and took a job over in Deshler," Grace said.

"I wonder if the police ever spoke with her," Anne pondered out loud.

"Josie did. She said Sally had an alibi for one of the times the theater was vandalized. She was down at the town hall, trying to fight having the theater put on the historical building registry," Grace answered.

"Well, I guess that's that," Anne said. "Thanks for letting me know."

"Anytime. Hey, I heard you got the framed movie poster back from Eli."

"I did. It's beautiful," Anne said.

"I might swing by later or tomorrow and take a peek at it," Grace said.

"Good. I'll see you then." Anne pocketed her cell and checked the time. "I think I'll run up and have a sandwich and check on Liddie right quick."

"I'll be here." Wendy smiled.

After sharing some chicken broth with Liddie, who said the pink medicine had made her tummy all better, Anne returned to the library.

"Michael Banks called just a little bit ago," Wendy said.

"Did he leave a message?" Anne asked.

Wendy nodded. "He wanted to let you know that Denny Thatcher has been eliminated as a suspect in any of the open cases, and that he, Michael, would talk to you soon about some other things."

Anne smiled. "Oh, good. I like Denny Thatcher. He's really a nice man. I just hate that he's homeless." She shook her head, annoyed at herself. "I keep meaning to talk with Reverend Tom about doing something for the Blue Hill homeless."

"Hey, that's a good suggestion," Bella said, coming up behind Anne.

"What? Doing something for the town's homeless?" Anne smiled at the twins. "I keep forgetting to talk to Reverend Tom about it."

"I meant for the dance," Bella said.

"The dance is a means to raise funds for a need in the community," Remi explained.

Bella nodded. "I can't think of a better need for funds than the homeless."

"I think that's a great idea," Wendy said as she reached for her purse. "But I better get out of here and pick the twins up from Mother's Day Out or I'll be in big trouble."

"Thanks, Wendy," Anne said, then turned back to the girls. "I love the idea of using the dance as a fund-raiser for the homeless." Anne smiled. Finally…something would be done about the homeless. Maybe a shelter could be set up.

"I'll tell Reverend Tom tonight at our meeting," Remi said. "He'll figure out what we need and how much we'll need to raise. Thanks, Mrs. Gibson. It's a perfect idea."

"No, thank you girls for coming in to help this afternoon," Anne said.

"Is Liddie upstairs? Can I go ahead and go up?" Remi asked.

"Of course. She had soup not too long ago and some Pepto. Remind her to drink her juice, if you think about it," Anne said. "And girls, thank you both. I really appreciate it."

"I love Liddie," Remi said, then climbed up the stairs.

Anne's cell rang. Wasn't she just the popular lady of the day? She checked the caller ID and took in a little breath. "Hi, Alex."

"Hey, Anne. Listen, I hate to ask you this, but could you please get Ryan for me from school?"

"Of course. What's wrong?" Anne asked, leaning against the counter.

"We had another incident this morning."

"Oh no. What happened? I thought your crew was taking turns standing guard, so to speak."

"We were. Buddy left at eight this morning. I showed up right about ten and found the mess. The whole day went downhill from there. Anyway, I'll explain it all to you when I come pick up Ryan around five. Is that okay?" His words held so much more meaning in his tone.

"Of course." Good thing Remi and Bella were covering Liddie and the library, but Ryan would keep Ben occupied, and she would have a chance to talk to both boys about what Christian had said.

"Thanks, Anne, and I'm really sorry for the late notice."

"I'll see you after five," Anne said, disconnecting the call.

After checking on Liddie again, it was time for Anne to go get Ben and Ryan from school. She thanked Remi and Bella yet again, then made the short drive over. As she pulled in the car lane, she told the on-duty teacher she would also be picking up Ryan Slater again, then waited her turn. Soon, the bell rang and kids erupted from the school doors like lava out of a spewing volcano. Anne inched through the line until the boys were let into the backseat.

"Is Uncle Alex working late again?" Ryan asked as he latched his seat belt.

"Yeah, honey, he is. There was another incident at the site," Anne answered as she moved the car forward.

"Mom, where's Liddie?" Ben asked.

She smiled that her son was worried about his little sister. "She has an upset stomach so I had to check her out of school this morning," Anne answered as she pulled out of the line and into the flow of traffic on Main Street.

"What happened to the theater this time?" Ryan asked.

"I don't exactly know. Your uncle didn't have a lot of time to talk when he called. He'll tell us when he comes and picks you up."

"Mom, can we work on the fort when we get home?" Ben asked.

"Do you have any homework?"

"Nope. None," Ben said.

"Do you want a snack?" Anne asked as she pulled into the library's drive.

"We can just have some of those peanut butter cheese crackers and some juice, if that's okay," Ben said.

Anne put the car in park and turned off the engine. She twisted to stare at the boys in the backseat. "That's fine, but first, I want to know if you two have recently been arguing about the fort." She stared over the top of her glasses at them.

The tips of Ryan's ears turned red.

"Just a little," Ben said.

"But we worked it out," Ryan added.

"Worked it out fairly and both of you are okay with the way it ended?" Anne asked.

Both boys nodded.

"We decided that since Ryan's design for the building won, we'd go with my choice for the interior layout," Ben said.

"That way, it really is both of ours," Ryan said.

"Good. I'm proud that you two worked it out." Anne smiled.

"Now can we go get our crackers and juice and get to work?" Ben asked.

"Yes. Get out of here." Anne laughed as the boys raced up the stairs. She followed at a much more sedate pace. "Let Hershey out to play while you work," she called up to the boys just as they ran into the house.

She checked on Liddie, who had the color back in her cheeks, and thanked Remi again for sitting with her. Remi went back down to man the library with Bella until closing time, so Anne worked puzzle after puzzle with Liddie on her daughter's bed.

A knock sounded on the door.

"I'll be right back. You stay here and finish that puzzle," Anne told Liddie.

She opened the door. Alex stood, shoulders drooping. "Come in."

He plopped onto the couch. "I saw the boys on my way in. The fort is looking good. Almost done. I'm really proud of them."

"I am too." Anne sat sideways on the couch beside him, facing him. "So what happened today?"

Alex let out a long and heavy sigh. "Our schedule of late has been someone stays from five until ten, then someone else relieves him and stays from ten until three, then the next person stays from three until eight. I usually come in between nine and ten, Buddy right behind me. Today, I got there a little before ten and unlocked the place and found the mess." He ran a hand over his shortly cropped hair.

"How bad was it?" Anne asked.

"Paint all over the ticket booth and hammer holes destroying the hall," Alex said.

Anne gasped. "The ticket booth? Oh, Alex, I'm so sorry." She couldn't even imagine all the work and detail he'd put into that, just destroyed. It nearly broke her heart.

"Well, it's not as bad as you might think," Alex said. "I called Michael immediately and he was able to come right over and file a report. I called Lisabeth in. She was a little late coming to clean because she had to work late at the school, but that didn't matter because she was able to get most—"

"Wait a minute," Anne interrupted. "You said Lisabeth had to work late at the school?"

"Yes. I talked to her right after I called Michael, about ten fifteen or ten thirty, and she told me the morning janitor at the school had called in sick so she had to stay an extra hour to fill in.

She wasn't able to come until after eleven, but when she got there, she dug right in. Got almost every bit of the paint off the ticket booth."

Anne shook her head. "That's a lie, Alex."

"What? No, really. We'll just have to do some minor touch up."

"Not that. I mean about Lisabeth saying she was working late at the school. I saw her this morning, a little *before* ten, rushing into the school. She was in a big hurry," Anne said.

"Are you sure, Anne?" Alex asked.

"I'm positive. Liddie had a stomachache and I had to check her out. I was leaving the school and saw a car speed into the parking lot. It was going so fast that I debated going back in and reporting it to Mr. Bailey. I saw Lisabeth get out of the car and run across the parking lot and into the school."

Alex frowned. "Is it possible you're wrong about the time?"

"No. Because I recognized her and remembered that she told you she was off work at ten on weekdays, so I looked at my watch. It was nine fifty-two exactly."

"Maybe she had to run an errand or something. I don't know."

"Maybe you should ask, Alex." Anne pushed down her worry that it might just be her jealousy talking. The woman had been caught in a lie, plain and simple.

"I'm not sure it really matters, Anne."

"She lied to you, Alex. As her employer, you shouldn't be lied to," Anne said. Was he really going to just accept the lie and not even bother to ask her? Maybe Alex was as taken with Lisabeth as she was with him.

Now Anne's stomach began to ache.

"What if she had just been running an errand for someone at the school? I'd feel terrible accusing her of lying." Alex shook his head. "She did an amazing job, Anne. Got almost every bit of paint off the ticket booth. It's like she's a miracle worker."

A lying miracle worker. Anne didn't know if she could keep her mouth shut. She could abide many things but lying wasn't one of them. "I still think you should ask her, Alex."

He let out a heavy sigh. "Look, at this point, I'm not so concerned about that. She saved me a lot of time and work, and I don't usually go around accusing good workers of lying." Alex stared hard at Anne. "Why is this such an issue for you?"

"If someone will lie about little things, what's to stop them from being deceitful on big issues? I just don't like people lying to me," Anne said, crossing her arms over her chest.

"But that's the point—she may not be lying. She may have been running an errand and that's why she was in such a hurry. It's not my place to ask about one of her other jobs, Anne."

He wasn't going to ask Lisabeth, no matter what Anne said. Anne would just have to ask Lisabeth herself because she knew, deep down inside, that she wouldn't be able to let the matter drop.

"What did Michael say?" Anne asked, letting the subject drop. For now.

"He says since we know the vandal had to be there between eight and ten, we have a tight window, which is good for the investigation. He thinks he can get the video from the store's ATM across the street."

"That could be great, right?" Anne asked.

"Maybe. We don't know for sure yet which way they came in. If they are brazen enough to walk right in the front door, then the video should show them. If not, Michael says they might be able to pull plate numbers off cars in the area," Alex said. "At least it's something."

Which was better than nothing, Anne supposed.

"Mom!" Ben barged into the living room. "Mr. Thatcher is here and wants to know if it's okay if he helps us. We've almost got the roof and walls done, and if he helps, we can have it finished tonight, so please can he?"

Anne smiled. "It's *may he,* and yes." She remembered how hungry he'd been the other day. "Ben, take a couple more packs of the crackers and some bottled water down to share."

"Okay!" Ben ran into the kitchen and gathered the snacks, then flew out the door.

Alex pushed to his feet. "I should go help."

"It's understandable if you're too tired, Alex. No one would blame you for just resting for a bit."

"No." Alex shook his head. "I should be helping." He stopped at the door. "Are you coming down?"

"Not just yet. I need to make sure Liddie's all good," Anne said.

"Okay. Well, thanks again for picking up Ryan. I'll talk to you tomorrow, okay?"

"Sure."

Alex closed the door behind him. Anne stood and stared at the closed door. Was Alex really respecting Lisabeth's work privacy, or was he attracted to her and not wanting to know anything bad about her?

Anne sighed. It didn't matter. She would find out the truth. All by herself.

CHAPTER EIGHTEEN

I'm just glad Liddie was feeling better and able to go back to school today," Anne told Mildred. "It must have just been that second piece of chocolate pie."

"Yeah, I do that too," Mildred said.

"Do what?" Anne asked.

"Eat a second piece of pie and then later regret it," Mildred said, laughing. "Usually when I step on the scales."

Anne chuckled. As if Mildred needed to worry about being on the scales. "I'm so glad you came by," Anne told Mildred. "I miss visiting with you."

"It's finally nice enough weather that I feel like venturing out," Mildred said.

It was true. Tuesday had turned out just as sunny and warm as yesterday had been. When Ben had let Hershey out to run this morning, he only needed to wear a light jacket.

Mildred pointed at the framed movie poster sitting on the easel. "That is truly beautiful, and I know Edie would be quite pleased."

"It is lovely. Eli did a wonderful job." Anne rested her elbow on the checkout counter and put her chin in her hand.

Mildred swiveled on the stool. "What's up with you, dear?"

Anne straightened. "Nothing."

Mildred smiled and patted Anne's knee. "You aren't fooling me. What's going on?"

"I don't know really," Anne said. "Eli asked me to the dance."

"And that's a problem?" Mildred asked, no judgment in her voice.

"Well, he's handsome and charming and really generous," Anne said.

"But?"

"But…I don't know." Anne wrinkled her nose. "I told him no. Was that silly of me?"

"Only you can answer that, Anne, but if you had doubts, you were right to say no. I never thought much of those women who would rather go with just anybody than wait for the one they wanted to say yes to," Mildred patted her knee again. "Are you second-guessing yourself?"

"I don't know. I mean, I don't know him well and there are all these questions, so in that aspect, I'm not second-guessing. On the other hand, as Wendy pointed out, the reason people date is to find out the answers to all those questions," Anne said. When she said it out loud, it sounded even more confusing than it did in her head.

"True, but the question really is, do you want to invest your time and interest into finding out the answers to those questions on Eli Wallington? That, my dear, is what you need to figure out."

Anne nodded. Mildred was right, as usual, but that didn't help Anne answer what was in her own head and heart.

"I would imagine Alex's new employee would have preferred you said yes to Eli," Mildred offered.

That got Anne's attention. "What?"

Mildred smiled. "Lisabeth Matthews. She's Alex's new clean-up gal, isn't she?"

Anne nodded.

"I hear that she has her eye on Alex," Mildred said, holding up a hand. "And before you ask, you know Coraline knows just about everything going on in Blue Hill moments after it happens."

True. Anne nodded. "I think Lisabeth does have a thing for Alex." She swallowed and lifted a pen. "It's possible Alex might return the sentiment," Anne said, clicking the pen.

"Do tell." Mildred leaned in closer.

Anne explained about catching Lisabeth in the lie and how Alex refused to question her about it. "The only reason I can fathom why he wouldn't just ask her is because he likes her."

"Maybe." Mildred studied Anne's face. "Or he could be just as he says, staying out of it because he doesn't believe she lied. He may truly believe she ran an errand or something."

"Then why doesn't he just ask her?"

"Because to do so would sound accusatory. Think about it, Anne. If you were Lisabeth and you were sent on an errand at work, and someone later asked you what you had been doing because someone else saw you during that time, wouldn't you feel like you were being accused of something?"

"Well…I guess," Anne admitted.

"Of course you would. Anybody would."

Anne shook her head. "But Mildred, I really don't think she was running an errand."

"What do you think?"

"I'm not sure." And that was the truth. It didn't make sense.

"I see," Mildred said.

A minute passed in silence. Then another. And another.

"Anne, may I ask you a personal question, since you brought up the subject?"

"Of course, Mildred. You may ask me anything. You know that."

"Does it bother you more that you think Lisabeth might be lying or because Alex might be interested in Lisabeth and there's a chance they will become a couple?"

Ouch. Hard question. One Anne didn't have an honest answer for except for the same one she kept giving herself— "I don't know."

"That's honest," Mildred said. She slipped off the stool and stretched. "I think maybe you should do a little soul searching and figure out where your feelings are, Anne. On dating. On romance overall. On Alex and how you feel about him."

"I know."

"You two have a history, Anne. A past that contains romance and broken hearts. If you find that there are still some feelings buried inside, you need to determine just how permanent you would want to be with Alex in the future, because once you go down that path again, you want to take caution that no one's heart gets damaged again."

A lump the size of Philadelphia caught in the back of Anne's throat.

Mildred gave her a hug. "I'm not saying anything's wrong with the way things turned out. I'm just saying that moving forward, I think you need to be sure of what you want."

Anne smiled. "I know. Thanks, Mildred."

"Anytime, dear. Now, I must run. I'm due to have lunch with Coraline, and you know how she hates to be kept waiting."

Anne saw Mildred out, but the older woman's wise words of advice burned against Anne's heart.

If only she could know what she really felt.

A little after noon, when Remi was settled in at the library, Anne ran to the grocery store. While Blue Hill boasted a larger, chain grocery store on the highway near the edge of town, Aunt Edie had always shopped at Newlands', and since Anne's return to town, she had adopted the quaint family-run store for most of her grocery needs.

"Hello there, Anne," Josie Bolling said.

"Hi, Josie. How's it going?" Anne asked as she stepped alongside the pretty blonde, careful to not let the plastic basket over her forearm bump into Josie.

"Good. You?"

"All good," Anne said. She wondered if it'd be considered rude to ask Josie about any of the ongoing cases. Probably, and Josie probably wouldn't tell her anything.

"Did Michael tell you that Coraline Watson's sketch helped identify two valid suspects in the park vandalisms?"

"No." Maybe this was a great break.

Josie nodded. "Michael's actually interviewing the boys with their parents today," she said. "I think we've got the right guys."

"That's awesome," Anne said.

"Well, it's partially due to you," Josie said as she put a head of lettuce in her plastic basket.

"Me?" Anne asked, surprised.

"Yes. Coraline told us she didn't even consider coming forward until you advised her to. Great call, so thanks."

"So do those suspects have anything to do with the warehouse fire or the vandalism incidents at the theater?" Anne asked. She slipped four bell peppers in a plastic bag and added them to her basket.

"We aren't supposed to discuss the cases," Josie said but shook her head emphatically, looking every bit like the schoolmate Anne remembered.

Anne nodded in understanding. "Well, I'll keep my ears and eyes open."

Josie laughed. "You do that. How's Ben doing? He and Ryan finish their tree house?" She put a package of tomatoes in her basket.

"It isn't really a tree house. It's more of a fort, I guess." Anne shrugged as she moved toward the potatoes. "Anyway, I think they're almost done. Alex and Denny Thatcher helped put the roof and walls up yesterday afternoon."

"Denny Thatcher," Josie said. "He's a really nice man. His story nearly broke my heart."

"I know. I had no idea there were any homeless people in Blue Hill," Anne said. "But the good news is, there are several people working to start a project to raise funds for the homeless here." She rounded the produce aisle and nearly plowed right into —

"Lisabeth," Anne stammered. "I'm sorry. I didn't realize —"

"Don't worry, it was an accident. No harm, no foul, right?" The hatred oozed from Lisabeth.

Maybe it was her intolerable attitude, or maybe Anne's curiosity just couldn't be contained. Didn't matter, Anne forged on with her probing. "Hey, it's a good thing I ran into you, literally, because I wanted to ask you about something, Lisabeth."

"What's that?" Lisabeth asked, the sarcasm virtually dripping off her tongue.

"Yesterday, you told Alex you couldn't go immediately to clean up his work site because you had to stay late at work," Anne said, fully aware of Josie's full attention on her and Lisabeth.

"Yeah, so? What business is it of yours?"

"He said you told him you had to stay late at work because you were covering for the morning janitor out on maternity leave," Anne pushed on.

"What's your point?" Lisabeth asked.

"Well, my point is, I saw you arriving to your job at the school and it was just before ten."

Lisabeth's mouth drew into a tight, straight line.

"Care to explain that?" Anne asked.

"Why should I tell you anything?"

"Because Alex is my friend and I'm sure he won't appreciate finding out he's been lied to," Anne said. That was basically true. If he found out Lisabeth had lied, he'd be most upset. Even if he did find her appealing.

"Look, I was late getting to the school because the traffic was horrible. There was a wreck on the inner loop through Deshler, right out by the mall, and traffic was backed up." Lisabeth actually looked a little remorseful and pathetic. "I was late getting to the school, so I needed to stay later to finish the job."

"So why wouldn't you just tell Alex that?" Anne asked. Alex would've understood.

"Because I didn't want to admit to him that I'd been late to work. That doesn't look so great to a part-time employer. What if that made him not hire me again?"

"Alex would have understood." That just showed how little she knew Alex.

"Maybe, but it wouldn't have looked good." Lisabeth tried on a smile. "Please, don't tell him, will you?"

Now Anne was between a rock and a hard place because she'd already told Alex. She couldn't lie, even though she still didn't believe Lisabeth one hundred percent. Something still felt off about her story.

"I won't bring it up to him," Anne said.

Lisabeth's smile was even more strained. "Thanks." She glanced at her watch. "I better run. Thanks, Anne."

Anne watched her go.

"That was interesting," Josie said.

Anne turned, having nearly forgotten the officer was standing there. "I guess you could say that." She nodded toward Lisabeth's retreating back. "What do you make of her, Josie?"

Josie stared as Lisabeth got into her car and drove off in her little red Volkswagen. "I can't say for certain, but her body language was screaming that she was hiding something."

Anne stared at Josie. "Really?"

Josie nodded. "Yep. I don't know what, but that girl has a secret she sure doesn't want you to know."

Interesting.

"Well, girl, I've got to run. I have friends waiting on me for burgers," Josie said.

"Good talking to you," Anne said.

Anne finished her shopping and then headed back home. She put away the groceries, threw dinner into the Crock-Pot to cook, then headed down to the library.

"Well, hello, Anne," Eli said. "I thought I might miss seeing you on this visit. I'm glad I was wrong."

"Hello, Eli," Anne said, naturally smiling at his charm. "What are you doing here?"

He put his hand over his heart. "I'm crushed." He was smiling, though.

Anne couldn't help but giggle.

"Oh, hi, Mr. Ochs," Remi said, looking toward the entrance.

Anne turned, the giggle dissipating like fog being hit by the sun.

"Well, looks like this is a party," Alex said.

"Indeed it is," Eli said, extending his hand to Alex. "How are you doing? How's the theater restoration coming along?"

"Today's going well," Alex said, shaking Eli's hand.

Anne couldn't recall a more awkward time.

Remi grinned at Eli. "Okay, I have your Handyman 101 class all scheduled. Second Saturday of March."

"You're going to teach a handyman class here?" Alex asked.

Eli nodded. "Anne finally relented and agreed to let me teach." He smiled at Anne. "Now if I could just get her to reconsider going to the dance with me."

Alex cut his eyes to Anne. She'd never wanted the ground to open up and swallow her more than she did at that exact moment. That, or she wanted to strangle Eli Wallington with her bare hands.

"Hey, if you're free, you ought to come by and jump in. We could both answer questions," Eli said to Alex.

"What?" Alex asked, finally breaking eye contact with Anne and looking at Eli.

"The handyman class. If you're available the second Saturday next month, you should come by and field questions with me," Eli explained.

"Oh. Yeah. If I'm free."

"Good." Eli stood for a moment, his gaze darting from Anne to Alex, to Remi, then back to Anne. "Well, I guess I'd better be going. Oh, how are the boys coming along with their club house?"

"It's all but finished," Alex answered.

Eli glanced at Alex and a slow smile spread across his face. "Is it now?"

"Yes. We finished the roof and walls yesterday," Alex said.

"Well, good." Eli took Anne's hand and brushed his lips against it. "Until our dance at the Winter Wonderland this weekend." He let go of her hand and waved at Remi, then left.

Anne's face and neck were hot as fire. She could only imagine the blush covering her cheeks. Alex just stared at her, a funny expression on his face.

What was she supposed to say?

Luckily, Alex's cell phone rang, breaking their stare fest. He checked the caller ID, and answered. "Hi, Michael."

Anne busied herself behind the counter while Remi lifted the returned books and walked off. Anne had just thought she felt awkward before. That was nothing compared to how awkward she felt right then.

"I see," Alex said, looking back at Anne over his shoulder.

Now what?

"Yes. Of course. Thanks for letting me know, Michael." Alex disconnected the call and slipped his phone back in his pocket. He stood in front of Anne. "Michael wanted to let us know that they've made an arrest in the warehouse fire."

"Really? Who?" Awkwardness was forgotten in the wake of such news.

"The Kombses."

"What?" Anne couldn't believe it. "Why?"

"Apparently, the warehouse had become a financial drain on Natalie and Marcus for some time now. They carried out a plot to burn down the warehouse for the insurance money," Alex said.

"That's insane." What if Denny Thatcher had been sleeping in there? Or some other homeless person?

Alex nodded. "I know. According to Michael, they planned for the fire to be set when Marcus was out of town so he'd have an alibi. They figured no one would ever suspect Natalie of actually setting the fire."

"Goodness. I never would have," Anne said.

"Michael says when the trace evidence led the police back to the Kombses, Natalie cracked under the pressure of the proof and confessed, but when Marcus found out, he refused to let her take all the blame since they'd concocted the plan together, so he confessed to his part in it all." Alex shook his head. "So they've both been charged with arson and insurance fraud. They're in jail pending a bond hearing later this week."

The lengths some people would go to. "That's just...I don't even know what to say," Anne said.

"I know. It's crazy." Alex stood awkwardly in front of the counter. "Well, guess I'd better get back to the work site."

"Did you need something?" Anne blurted out.

"What?"

"To have come here during the workday. Did you need me for something?" Anne asked, then clamped her mouth shut.

"Oh no. Nothing important."

Anne started to argue the point but saw his face and decided against it. Alex looked...different, but in a confusing way.

"I'll just see you later," Alex said, then left before Anne could answer.

Anne stood, staring at where he'd just been standing. What had he really come by for?

"Has Mr. Ochs left?" Remi asked as she returned to the front checkout area.

"Yes."

"Good. He looked a little jealous of Mr. Wallington," Remi said.

"What?"

"You didn't see his face when Mr. Wallington mentioned he'd asked you to the dance. I thought Mr. Ochs was going to get sick. And then, when Mr. Wallington kissed your hand — oh, he looked beyond ill," Remi said.

Could that be true?

All of Anne's insides twisted.

CHAPTER NINETEEN

I can't believe it's Thursday already," Bella said. "The dance is tomorrow."

Anne smiled at the girl's excitement, recalling all the dances she'd gotten in a tizzy over. "It's going to be wonderful."

"Did I tell you about my dress?" Bella asked.

"Yes," Remi answered, walking around the counter. "You've told her about your dress. And your shoes. And even that ridiculous tiara you're planning on wearing."

"It's not ridiculous. It's stylish," Bella argued.

Anne chuckled at the girls. "I'm just grateful you girls are raising money to help the homeless."

"Reverend Tom agreed that we needed to do something for the homeless. He's already assigned a committee to making a list of what is needed to turn that old hall into housing rooms for the homeless," Bella said.

Blue Hill church had been built in the late nineteenth century, and its old hall had been used for town meetings once upon a time before the town hall was erected in downtown. When it was no longer needed for that purpose, the hall was used as a gathering place for potlucks and prayer circles until the fellowship hall was later constructed. Since then, the old hall was used for storage. Reverend Tom had agreed that the hall should be cleaned and cleared out, and be set up as several bedrooms for the homeless.

"I think it's wonderful," Anne said.

Grace rushed into the library, carrying a dry cleaning bag over her shoulder. "I need your opinion," she said to Anne. "You too, girls."

Anne, Remi, and Bella stood at the ready. "Need our opinion on what?" Anne asked.

Grace smiled, her eyes flickering. "Eli Wallington asked me to the dance," she practically squealed. "Can you believe that?"

Anne nodded and smiled, even as her mouth went drier than the desert in August. "Today?"

Grace nodded. "He came by the *Gazette* and just asked me out."

Remi looked at Anne.

"That's wonderful, Grace," Anne said, finally finding her voice. "I'm sure you agreed."

"Of course. You'd have to be blind, married, or stupid to turn down Eli Wallington," Grace said, laughing.

Well, that put Anne in the stupid category.

"So what do you need our opinion about?" Bella asked, totally unaware that Eli had asked Anne to the dance first.

"Which dress I should wear." Grace laid both plastic-bag-covered hangers on the counter. She pulled the wrap up on the first to reveal a deep navy satin dress. "This one is very comfortable, but some might consider it a little low cut for a church event, even if it is a dance."

"It's very pretty," Bella said. "Let me see the other one."

Grace pulled back the plastic bag on the second dress. "This one's a little plain, but it's the popular little black dress."

"*Hmm.* Both are pretty," Bella said. She twisted to look at her twin. "Which do you like better?"

Remi looked at Anne, then back at the dresses. "Uh. I like them both. Which do you like best, Ms. Hawkins?"

"I don't know. I like them both." Grace pleaded with her eyes at Anne. "Help me out here."

"I like the little black dress. It's classy. Sophisticated, yet understated," Anne said. She had, after all, wanted to fix Grace and Eli up in the first place. This was what she wanted.

Right?

Right.

"I think I have a string of pearls you could borrow that would go with that dress perfectly," Anne said.

"Really?" Grace asked, her eyes widening.

"Yes. Let me go get them for you," Anne said.

"Thanks."

Anne rushed up the stairs. While Eli might be a catch, he was more Grace's type than Anne's. Sure, he could charm the best of them, but Anne just didn't feel the same connection she felt with...

Anne froze, hand on the banister.

Mildred's warning came back to her, replaying in her head like an iTunes playback...

"*You need to determine just how permanent you would want to be with Alex in the future, because once you go down that path again, you want to take caution that no one's heart gets damaged again.*"

Before Anne decided anything, she would really have to examine how she felt about Alex and think about what she wanted.

Anne grabbed the pearls from her jewelry box, then rushed back downstairs. "Here," she said as she handed them to Grace.

"Are you sure you don't mind my borrowing them?" Grace asked, her fingers gently caressing the freshwater strand.

"Well, I don't want you to pawn them or anything," Anne teased. "You'll look stunning with them in that dress, I can assure you."

Grace surprised her by pulling her into a tight hug. "Thank you," she whispered.

Anne pulled back, smiling. "You're most welcome." It occurred to her that Grace had never mentioned a guy or going on a date or anything like that. She was a pretty woman, vivacious, independent, and in a solid career—she should have men beating down her door.

"Well," Grace said, grabbing up the dresses, "I'd better get going. I was able to squeeze in a haircut and a manicure, but I've got to run. Thank you, girls."

"Bye."

Bella turned back to Anne and Remi. "She's going to look beautiful."

"Yes, she is," Anne said.

"It's none of my business, Mrs. Gibson, but...," Remi started.

"Let it go," Anne finished. "I'm very happy for Grace."

Remi nodded and smiled. "You're a class act, Mrs. Gibson. A real class act."

Anne wasn't so sure about that.

The library's phone rang, and Bella answered it. "Blue Hill Library." A pause. "Sure. Just a moment." She held the phone out toward Anne. "It's for you."

Anne pressed the phone against her ear. "Hello, this is Anne Gibson."

"Anne, it's Josie. Can you come down to the police station right now? There's something I want to show you that I think you can verify for me." Josie sounded almost out of breath with excitement.

"Sure," Anne said, uncertainty in her voice.

"Thanks. I'll go wait at the front desk for you."

Anne hung up. "Girls, I need to run an errand. I'll be back soon." She grabbed her purse and headed to the station.

What could Josie want her to verify?

She asked herself that question over and over during the drive to the police station. She didn't come up with an answer, but she was tingling with excitement as she parked her car.

As promised, Josie was waiting at the front desk for her. "Thanks for coming so quickly," Josie said. "Come on back." She led the way down the hall and into a conference room with a long table and a computer at the end, one with a really big monitor.

"What's going on?" Anne asked as she set her purse onto the table and looked at Josie.

"This is the feed from the ATM across the street from the theater from eight until nine forty-five Monday morning. Just watch," Josie said, pushing a button and starting the recording.

Anne pushed her glasses up the bridge of her nose. "What am I looking for?"

"I can't tell you. For you to properly identify, I can't point it out to you. Just watch and tell me if you see anything you recognize." Josie patted Anne's shoulder. "I'm sorry to make you go through all of it, but it's policy for us not to point out evidence to potential witnesses. Okay?"

Anne nodded. She was a potential witness now? What had she seen?

"Just tell me what you see that you recognize. Okay?" Josie asked.

"Sure. That's fine. Whatever you need me to do," Anne said, sitting in a chair close to the monitor. Whatever she was supposed to see, she didn't want to miss it.

"Here we go," Josie said as she knocked on the glass part of the wall giving a signal for someone to start the video.

It took her a moment to acclimate her vision to the bird's eye view of the front and side of the theater in black and white. For a minute, nothing showed up, then she saw a man leaving the theater's side entrance. He walked toward the parking lot.

"That's, um, Buddy, he works for Alex. Buddy Collins," Anne said. She noticed the time stamp on the recording. "It's eight oh three, so he must have been the one watching the theater and is leaving now."

"Good," Josie said. "Keep watching."

Anne watched for the next twenty minutes, making note of several cars she recognized going by, but none stopping near the theater. She saw a couple of the town's fitness die-hards out power walking, but they didn't even bother looking in the direction of the theater as they sped walked on the side of Main Street with the cords from their ear buds dangling to the MP3 players attached to their waists.

This was rather boring, Anne realized as she smothered a yawn. A car passed on the video. Looked like Yvette Jacobs's old Chevy. A Volkswagen inched toward the theater, pulling into the back parking lot.

Anne sat up straighter and noticed the time stamp: eight twenty-nine. The car's front right fender was in the very top corner of the video, but the plates and the full vehicle itself weren't in plain view.

But Anne recognized that car. She'd just seen it. With Josie.

She turned to Josie. "That's Lisabeth Matthews's Volkswagen Beetle. Right?"

Josie smiled. "Is it?"

Anne turned back to the monitor, then stood and got even closer. "I'm pretty sure. Maybe I'll get a better look when it leaves?"

"Just watch," Josie said.

This was what Josie had called her in for. To identify Lisabeth's car. But, did that mean…

Anne stared at the monitor as the minutes clicked off the clock. Eight forty.

Eight fifty-eight.

Nine ten.

Anne let out a sigh and relaxed the tension in her shoulders.

Nine seventeen.

Nine twenty-nine.

Nine thirty-five.

Nine forty—

Movement! The Volkswagen backed out of view.

Anne tensed, sitting forward toward the monitor. Come on, come on. Drive back in front of the camera.

And just like that, the Volkswagen sped in front of the camera, heading back into town.

"Can you back it up and pause it?" Anne asked Josie. "I want to be one hundred percent, absolutely certain."

"Sure." Josie did as Anne asked.

Not only was the Volkswagen clearly identifiable, but paused, Anne could make out the outline of Lisabeth's profile.

"That's Lisabeth Matthews and her Volkswagen," Anne said.

Josie looked at the glass, then back at Anne. "Are you positive?"

"Yes."

Josie smiled and threw a fist up in the air. "Yes! Thank you, Anne."

Anne stood. "So does that mean Lisabeth's been the one vandalizing the theater? What motive would she have? She's the one who cle—Oh! She's the one Alex hires to clean up the mess." How could she have not suspected Lisabeth?

Michael stepped into the room. "Hello, Anne."

"Hi, Michael." Had he been watching her through the two-way glass? Maybe it was policy when she was a witness.

"What can you tell us about Lisabeth Matthews?" Michael asked, flipping open his notebook and sitting down.

Josie leaned against the wall in the corner.

Anne sat back down at the conference table as well. "I don't know her well personally. She filled out an application with Alex's company for clean-up work."

"Do you know when she filled out the application?" Michael asked.

"Um, Alex said it was just before he got the theater job," Anne answered. "I'm sure he still has it on file and could tell you the exact date."

"We'll check with him," Michael said. "What else can you tell me about her?"

"Well, like I said, I really don't know her personally." Anne would not let her personal feelings intrude on the facts she told the police. This wasn't about jealousy or Alex…it was about breaking a law. "Alex says she's an amazing worker. After the incident on Monday, he said she had the ticket booth cleaned so well that he wouldn't have to do much."

"I see," Michael said.

Oh. Now a lot of it made sense. If Lisabeth was behind this, she would naturally do things that looked a mess, but that she could clean up easily enough. Makes her a very enticing employee, one who could do a job efficiently and effectively.

"Josie told me about the conversation she overheard you and Lisabeth have about her whereabouts on Monday," Michael said.

Josie turned a little red and shrugged.

"Could you tell me about it?" Michael asked.

Anne explained how she'd seen Lisabeth, and Lisabeth's excuse when confronted.

"What did she tell Alex?" Michael asked. "I mean, when he asked her."

"He didn't ask her."

Michael glanced up from his notes. "He didn't?"

Anne shook her head. "He believed that she was filling in for a janitor." She cleared her throat. "He thought perhaps I was mistaken in what I saw."

"But you weren't?" Michael asked.

"No, she claims there was an accident in Deshler that backed up traffic so that's why she was late," Anne recalled Lisabeth's excuse.

"There was no accident Monday morning in Deshler that backed up traffic," Michael said.

"I didn't think so." Anne's stomach tightened. She'd known something was off with Lisabeth but had thought that her own jealousy was clouding her judgment.

"And there was no janitor who called in sick on Monday," Josie added.

If only she'd pushed the issue more with Alex.

"What does she say about this?" Anne asked, pointing at the frozen on-screen video. "What's her excuse?"

"We haven't been able to contact her," Michael said. "We've called and we had Deshler police go by her apartment. No sign of her."

"I went to the school this morning and she's not there either," Josie said.

"Now that you've confirmed her vehicle at the scene, I'll put a BOLO out on her Volkswagen," Michael said as he stood.

"A what?" Anne asked.

Josie laughed. "BOLO stands for Be On the Look Out for. Replaced the APB code," she explained.

"Ah. If there's anything else I can do to help, let me know," Anne said, standing.

"We will. Thanks for coming down," Michael said, then left.

Josie rubbed her hands together. "As soon as I saw that bug, I knew whose it was."

"This is crazy," Anne said, shaking her head. "Have you told Alex yet?"

"Michael wanted your confirmation first. I'm sure he's calling him in right now," Josie said.

Anne couldn't imagine how betrayed Alex would feel when he found out.

"I'm not sure if she did it to keep getting jobs, so it was all about money, or if she did it because of Alex," Josie said.

"What do you mean, because of Alex?"

"Well, if she has an obsession with him, she could have kept doing the acts to cause him to call her in, so she could be close to him," Josie said with a shrug. "And if he praised her work like you implied, that would be a rush for her."

Anne shot Josie a questioning look.

"Think about it. If you have a crush on a guy and he sings your praises, you'd feel pretty much on top of the world."

"True." Anne just couldn't see being destructive as a positive thing in any light. "You know, at first, it was easy clean-up stuff, but this last episode on Monday? There were hammer holes all in the drywall. That's pretty damaging."

"Which is why I'm leaning toward it not just being about the money."

"How do you figure?" Anne asked.

"Well, I saw how you basically called her on the carpet at the grocery store. I thought she was just incredibly jealous of you, but I think now it might have been more. I think she not only is jealous of you, but was fearful of losing her connection with Alex," Josie said.

Maybe, but Anne wasn't ready to go that far yet.

"It'd been some time since Lisabeth had done a job for Alex. Maybe she thought they had a personal connection, but once the employment need was gone, he didn't call her or contact her as maybe she'd assumed he would. She was desperate. She had to do something to get his attention. What better way than to vandalize the theater again?"

"I see your point," Anne said. "And she had to have known how close Alex was to the ticket booth, so she did the least damage there, only doing what she knew she could clean up."

Josie nodded. "Remember, a special type of paint was used. One that's very susceptible to her particular cleaning products. Naturally, that would make her look like a hero to Alex, her being able to clean up something so well that he'd worked so hard on restoring."

"He was very pleased and impressed," Anne said.

"Maybe she realized you were suspicious, so knew she needed to do some serious damage," Josie said.

"Thus the hammer holes," Anne finished.

Josie nodded. "That's my theory anyway." She opened the door to the conference room. "I'll let you know what we find out, when I can."

"Thanks, Josie."

"No, thank you, Anne. You might have provided us the key to this whole case."

Anne nodded and headed back to her car. She should be happy. Happy that she helped the police with the case. Happy that she might have stopped any future acts of vandalism on the theater. Happy that Lisabeth wouldn't be around to be so snooty to her and to distract Alex.

But Anne wasn't feeling celebratory. All she could think about was how betrayed Alex was going to feel. Maybe even a little bit foolish for not having listened to Anne.

And that didn't make her happy at all.

CHAPTER TWENTY

B oys, you've done an amazing job. I'm so proud of you," Anne said as she stared at the finished fort.

Not only was the fort well-constructed, it was a nice design of an almost octagon shape. Measuring about twelve feet by twelve feet, the wooden building had a cut-out window and an old screen door. There were two-by-fours nailed into the tree alongside the fort that served as the ladder to reach the roof of the building. A three-foot tall border framed the edge of the roof, one of Anne's requirements so the boys didn't fall off easily.

Both Ben and Ryan smiled, their little chests puffing out.

"Even more than what you built, I'm proud of the way you two learned to work through your differences and the times you didn't see eye to eye. That takes maturity, boys, so I'm very proud of you," Anne said.

The boys' grins probably couldn't get any wider.

"Me too. I'm proud of you both," Alex added as he moved to stand next to Anne. "It took a lot of hard work, saving your hard-earned money, and learning to compromise. You both did an awesome job."

Anne was wrong—the boys' grins *could* get wider.

"Can I go swing now?" Liddie asked.

Anne chuckled. "Sure, honey. Just be careful not to swing too high."

"We're going to play in our fort now, okay?" Ben asked.

Anne nodded, and the boys disappeared into their new domain. She could make out the words *Spider-Man* and *Batman* between the laughter as she and Alex headed to the picnic table and sat down.

"Still nothing from Lisabeth?" Anne asked.

"Nope. Michael says he doesn't think she has enough money to really run far, so he says it's more of a waiting game," Alex said, staring out across the field that would soon be covered in bluebell flowers. "He also thinks it's possible she'll try to get in touch with me."

Anne laid a hand over his. "It'll all come out in the wash, Alex."

He grinned at her. "Your aunt Edie said that all the time, didn't she?"

Anne nodded and smiled back. "She was right too. We can try and figure out things, but in the end, after the final spin cycle, what's left will be what it is."

"I'm sorry, Anne," Alex said, his voice so sincere.

"Whatever for?"

"For not believing you. For not listening when you said she was lying."

"Don't be silly. That's nothing to apologize for," Anne said, but she did feel better that he apologized for not believing her. "She pulled the wool over a lot of people's eyes."

Like the school's head janitor. On Monday, she'd told him that her mother had fallen and was rushed to the clinic. She said she just had to take her mom's insurance card to the clinic so they'd treat her mom. The head custodian at the school, Mr. Smithson, let her run the errand on the clock.

So she'd committed a crime and gotten paid by the Blue Hill school system. Something was just so wrong with that, Anne thought.

"But I should have trusted you," Alex told Anne.

She leaned against him, nudging him. "Hey, when are you going to just accept the fact that I'm always right?"

He chuckled. "I'm learning to do that. I promise."

"Then the world will be a much better place." She laughed.

A long, comfortable moment passed as they watched Hershey chase Liddie as she swung on the old tire swing.

"Do you remember all the times we played out here on a swing almost like that one?" Anne asked.

"Good times, weren't they?"

"They were." Anne opened her mouth to tell Alex how much those days meant to her—then and now, then stopped before speaking a single word. Mildred's admonition came back to her again. "*You two have a history, Anne. A past that contains romance and broken hearts.*" Anne was unsure about many things, but the one thing she was positive about was that she didn't want to cause Alex any more pain. So she kept her mouth shut.

"You know, I don't understand why I would have even given Lisabeth the benefit of the doubt," Alex said.

"Stop beating yourself up, Alex. She fooled everyone," Anne said.

"Not you. She didn't fool you."

What could she say?

"I think maybe, if I'm being honest, I let her fool me because I wanted to believe her," Alex said.

"Why's that?" Anne asked.

"Because she was an attractive woman who acted like I was someone special."

Anne's heart nearly tore apart. "You are special, Alex. You have to know that." Her voice cracked.

Alex smiled. "You could be biased, you know."

"Nah."

"Seriously, I think I let my ego get in the way of seeing clearly." Alex rested his forearms on his knees and let his hands dangle in front of him. "What does that say about me as a person? I let my own personal ego put my livelihood at risk."

"You didn't know, Alex. Quit being so hard on yourself," Anne said.

"Hurts to admit that."

"Well, it's over and done with, so let it go," Anne said. "We all make mistakes and have to move on."

"I hope the police find her. I'd like to know why. Why did she play me? How could she have done such damage? I want answers," Alex said.

Anne let a moment pass, then took a deep breath. "You might not like the answers you get, Alex. Maybe you should just let it go." She let out her breath. "Just. Let. It. Go."

"You're right, I suppose," Alex said, then grinned and gently shoved her. "As usual."

Anne grinned back. "See? That wasn't so hard, was it?"

* * *

"Mom, you look awesome," Ben said as Anne came out of her bedroom.

Anne stopped, her heart beating a little faster. "Thank you, Ben." She couldn't remember the last time her son had complimented her appearance. Either she must look really different without glasses and with makeup, or her son was growing up.

"I love your dress, Mommy. I want one just like it," Liddie said, twirling in circles around Anne.

Anne smiled down at her daughter, but she knew Liddie was right. The dress was beautiful. She'd searched for a dress that looked like an antique similar to the one Aunt Edie wore in the pictures Mildred had of them on the debut night. She'd finally found the perfect one at a retro shop in Middle Village.

The beautiful wrap dress by Lea D'Crenza was deep red. Designer Lea D'Crenza always wanted women to be aware of their essential femininity, and the vintage dress was a prime example of the designer's intent with its silk ruffle around the top and down the side. The shoulder straps tied and featured four large rhinestone balls. The ruffle and lining were silk, and the rest of the dress was form fitting and very elegant.

Aunt Edie would have been pleased.

"You smell good too," Ben said as he passed her to get the book he'd been reading off the kitchen counter and put it in his bag.

"Thank you," Anne said. Her confidence took another boost.

"I packed all my dolls and my Barbies," Liddie chimed in. "Becca and Cindy said they were bringing theirs too."

"Okay. Are we ready?" Anne asked, looking around the living room to make sure nothing was left.

"I'm going to the car," Ben announced, leading his sister down the stairs.

Anne grabbed the old stole that had once been her great-grandmother's and laid it around her shoulders. She spared a final appraisal of herself in the full-length mirror.

For the special evening, she'd pulled her hair up into a classic French twist, letting a few tendrils curl around her face. The dress fit her like it'd been custom made for her. Overall, she was pleased with the effect.

And a little nervous.

She couldn't think like that or she'd talk herself into missing the dance. Liddie and Ben were excited to go to the church and play with their friends. Anne grabbed her clutch and headed down the stairs.

Her nerves intensified tenfold as she led the kids into the church's fellowship hall, where the youth would be babysitting all the kids. Most of the people dropping off their children were married couples. Anne swallowed against the lump in her throat as she hugged Ben and Liddie good-bye and headed down the hall.

With each step, her heels tapped against the floor. Off in the distance of the big gym, the beat from the music thumped. Anne grew more and more anxious with every step.

She finally made her way to the Winter Wonderland. Anne took a deep breath and stepped inside.

Remi and Bella had outdone themselves. Up on the stage, with a spotlight shining on it was Aunt Edie's movie poster in the beautiful frame Eli had built. It looked amazing. Old Hollywood memorabilia decorated the walls. The tables along the sides of the dance floor had white and black linen, draped and tied with satin sashes. Even the chairs were adorned with the same fabric.

"What do you think?" Mildred asked as she walked up to greet Anne.

"It's amazing," Anne said, following Mildred to a table. She laid the stole on the back of her chair and set her purse on the table. "I'm very impressed with Remi and Bella's efforts."

"The girls really made it all come together. I hope they raise lots of money for the homeless project," Mildred said.

"Me too." Anne couldn't stop looking around. Everything looked perfect.

"Anne, where did you get that dress?" Wendy asked as a way of greeting. "You look so much like those pictures of your aunt."

Anne smiled. "That was my goal, so thank you."

"You look lovely," Chad, Wendy's husband, said as he leaned over and gave her a brotherly kiss on the cheek.

"Thank you. And you two look stunning," Anne said. It was true. Chad wore a black tuxedo and Wendy wore a most flattering, royal blue party dress. The flaring skirt flirted against her calves as she moved.

"Have you seen Grace?" Wendy asked.

"No. Is she here yet?" Anne automatically scanned the room.

"I saw her and Eli come in a few minutes ago. I think they went to grab something to drink," Wendy said, pointing over to the refreshment area.

"Mrs. Gibson," Patrick Rollings said, coming up behind Anne.

"Hello, Mr. Rollings. How are you?" Anne greeted him.

"I'm wonderful." He nodded toward the movie poster. "I wanted to ask if you would be so kind as to allow me a copy of your aunt's movie poster? Alex said he would be happy to build a special display in the theater for it if you'd allow me a copy."

"Oh, Mr. Rollings, that'd be lovely. Of course. I'll have a copy made for you next week," Anne gushed. Oh, if only Aunt Edie were here for this. She'd be on cloud nine.

"That would be perfect. Thank you," Patrick said, then moved on.

The room began to fill with people. Every person in Blue Hill must have come. That would be wonderful for the fund-raising. Anne spoke to many people. While she'd loved New York, she was glad to be back home in Blue Hill. It'd always been home in her heart.

"Don't you look beautiful!" Grace exclaimed.

Anne turned and hugged her friend. "You look beautiful too."

"Thanks."

"Where's Eli?" Anne asked when she didn't see him behind Grace.

"He ran into someone he needed to talk to, but I saw you." Grace smiled. "I can't get over how different you look without your glasses."

"Do I look bad without them?" Anne asked, suddenly self-conscious.

"Oh no," Grace said, shaking her head. "You look great both ways, just really different."

Anne grinned. "Thanks."

"Grace! Grace!" Jay McCallister, photographer for the *Gazette*, rushed up to them. "I've gotten some amazing photographs, so I'm done until they get to the fund-raising part."

The music shifted to a slower song. A waltz.

"Of course," Grace said, leaning into Jay to be heard over the music. "Enjoy yourself."

Jay held out his arms. "Dance with me, boss?"

Grace hesitated as Eli joined them. "Never leave an employee hanging, my dear," he said.

"You don't mind?" Grace asked.

"Of course not." Eli smiled at Anne. "Maybe I can get Anne to give me the dance she owes me."

"Yes." Grace stepped into Jay's arms and off they danced.

Eli held open his arms to Anne. She was trapped, plain and simple. No excuses. She nodded, then let Eli lead her onto the dance floor.

He was smooth, gliding over the floor. A strong dancer. "You're good," Anne told him.

"You look beautiful, Anne Gibson."

Anne kept in step with the waltz. "Thank you. Everyone looks so elegant tonight, don't they?"

"They do. Especially you."

Was he really hitting on her when he was on a date with one of her best friends? Anne didn't know what to say, so she didn't say anything and concentrated on the steps.

Eli laughed, throwing his head back. "My dear, Anne. You blush so easily. I don't mean to embarrass you, only to give you very true compliments."

She felt the heat on her face and let out a slow breath. "Well, thank you."

"I only speak the truth in how beautiful you are, but before your imagination runs wild, I do believe my date is the loveliest woman at the ball."

Anne grinned. "I think she's quite beautiful myself." So he hadn't been hitting on her, only using that Southern charm of his. "Are you enjoying the dance?"

"I am. I've already made a donation to the young Miller ladies to help the homeless. They tell me that you were the one who suggested the project."

Anne nodded. "I'm so happy the girls selected the homeless to be the recipient of tonight's fund-raising endeavors. I never realized how needed it was."

"Neither did I," Eli said as he turned her.

The song was drawing to an end. "Let's make it look really good," Eli leaned and whispered in her ear just before he twirled her, then ended with a dip.

She found herself out of breath as he pulled her upright and released her. "Thank you for the dance, Anne. Now, I must go find my beautiful date for the next dance."

Anne smiled and headed back toward the table but faltered.

Alex stood as stiff as a statue, his stare boring into her.

Oh. Mercy.

"You are a wonderful dancer, I see," Chad said as he and Wendy came alongside her. "My wife is demanding to sit this one out and rest her tired feet."

"You try wearing two-inch heels, buddy, then you'd understand," Wendy said. She shook her head and said to Anne, "Please save me and dance with my husband so I can rest my feet. Just one dance, please?"

Anne laughed. "Sure."

"Bless you," Wendy said as she pushed past Alex to take a seat.

"Let's show them how it's done," Chad said, leading Anne back to the dance floor.

He led her to the center floor and they began to move with the music. While a good dancer, Chad was nothing compared to Eli's fluid and smooth gliding.

"Everyone seems to be having a great time," Chad said over the music's hum.

"It's a fun night, that's for sure," Anne agreed.

"Except Alex doesn't look too happy." Chad motioned toward the table with his chin. "I heard the police are still looking for Lisabeth. Is he bummed about that?"

She glanced at Alex, who, indeed, looked like he was *not* enjoying himself. "I don't know. Maybe."

"I saw Michael and Jennifer here, so I guess the police haven't found Lisabeth yet."

"I haven't heard that they have," Anne said. She'd talked with Josie earlier today and learned the police had searched Lisabeth's apartment and found nothing useful to their case. She had no next of kin, nor did she seem to have any ties of any sort. Josie had said they were out of leads at the moment.

"It's crazy what she did," Chad said.

It was definitely that. Anne was strongly forming the opinion that Lisabeth herself was just crazy, especially for deliberately doing all that damage to the theater.

After the song ended, Chad escorted Anne back to the table. Alex sat beside Mildred, engrossed in a conversation. Anne snatched up her purse. "I'm running to the ladies' room. I'll be right back," she said to Wendy and no one in particular, then made her way around the throng of people to the bathroom.

The main one off the gym was packed, so Anne turned and went around the back of the gym's kitchen area to the little powder room there and slipped inside.

The music thumped as a fast song filled the air. Anne smiled to herself as she washed her hands and fluffed her hair. She opened her purse and reached for her lipstick just as the door to the powder room creaked.

Somebody else must have had the same idea.

Anne turned and froze as Lisabeth Matthews stepped inside the powder room and blocked the door.

CHAPTER TWENTY-ONE

A nne Gibson, just the person I wanted to speak with." Lisabeth's voice was filled with venom.

Anne's heart pounded harshly against her chest. This had to be what a trapped animal felt like. She'd been right—Lisabeth was definitely unbalanced.

"What do you want, Lisabeth?" Anne asked. She kept her hand in her purse, wrapping her fingers around her cell phone.

"Oh, the list is long, but I'll start with some simple things." Lisabeth crossed her arms over her chest and leaned against the door.

Anne very slowly and with minimal movement hit the button to dial Alex's cell phone, grateful the phone was set to silent. She pressed the button for speaker phone and shoved the phone down deep in the purse.

"What is your problem with me?" Lisabeth growled. "Just what did I ever do to you that made you feel like it was your business to try and ruin my life?"

"Lisabeth," Anne said clearly, praying that Alex could hear her. "I never set out to try and ruin your life. You're the one who vandalized the theater so many times. Why?"

Lisabeth's eyes narrowed and she fisted her hands on her hips. "You know, the first time was a whim. Just a whim. I was trying to pick up a couple of jobs. I saw an opportunity to make a slight mess and prove myself as a site cleaner, so I filled out an application, then waited a couple of days, then made a mess that I could go clean up very easily."

"That's no excuse," Anne said.

"I needed the money, not that you would ever understand that," Lisabeth argued.

"Not understand that? Really? That just shows how much you know about me."

"You don't look like you have it too hard to me," Lisabeth said with a sneer.

"Really? It's so easy to have your husband die suddenly, leaving you alone with two young children. And it's so easy to keep things together and as normal as possible for your children. Especially when your library falls victim to budget cutbacks and you lose your job. Yeah, that's a lot of fun. Oh, and then you lose your closest living relative, but it's a blessing in disguise because you get to move home and start afresh. Only, it's hard to start over with kids who miss their friends and the only home they've ever known." Anne found herself out of breath. "Yeah, Lisabeth, it's *so easy*."

Lisabeth's expression softened just a bit. "I didn't know all that. I'm sorry."

"But just because I had to go through all that didn't give me the right to damage someone else's property to create a job opportunity for myself. And it certainly isn't right for you!"

"Just when I felt a little sorry for you, your self-righteousness has to show up with guns blazing, doesn't it?"

"Following the law and respecting other people's property isn't being self-righteous, it's called being a law-abiding citizen," Anne said. Anger coursed through her veins like she hadn't felt in a long time. "Someone with morals and values."

"You might have had to endure some hard times, but don't pretend to know me," Lisabeth said jabbing a finger through the air toward Anne's face. "And really, no one got hurt and most everything I cleaned up anyway, so what was the harm?"

Anne shook her head. How could anyone be so dense? "So you got your foot in the door. Why'd you keep on? You'd gotten a job at the elementary school. Why keep vandalizing the theater?"

Lisabeth's expression changed into something softer. "It wasn't about the money then. It was about Alex."

Anne's heart pounded in double time. "What about Alex?"

"He's amazing. Handsome, talented, kind. Just being around him made me feel good. Made me want to be a better person," Lisabeth said, but she didn't even look at Anne.

"If you think he's so wonderful, why would you damage his project? How does that pay him back for being nice to you?"

Lisabeth's face morphed into one of jealousy and anger. "Because of you. Every time I thought I was making headway with Alex, there you were. Showing up at the work site, all friendly and such. Going to get coffee together. Going out to lunch together. Getting the kids together." She curled her nose as if she caught wind of something rank. "Always there, always getting Alex's attention."

"Alex and I are friends. We've been friends since we were kids," Anne argued.

"Really, Anne? Friends? *Just* friends?" Lisabeth shook her head. "I don't think so. I've seen the way he looks at you when he thinks you aren't watching. I've noticed the way you stare at him with emotion in your eyes."

Anne lifted her purse to her chest.

"Oh, you don't want to admit that, right? Just friends, huh? Then why do you two move almost like you're the same person? Just friends—really? I don't buy that for a second. Who's the liar now, Anne Gibson, huh?"

"I'm not going to stand here and listen to any more of your ridiculous ranting," Anne said, taking a brave step forward. "Officer Michael Banks is here, and I'm sure he'll be delighted to know you've finally been found."

"You aren't going to tell anybody anything. I'm not done talking with you yet." Lisabeth stood in front of the door. "Lucky for me that you decided to use this bathroom back here. I've been watching you, biding my time until you were alone."

Anne didn't know what she found more unnerving: that Lisabeth had been watching her or that she was trapped in a bathroom with a woman who was clearly insane. "Fine, Lisabeth, get on with it and have your say so I can get away from you."

"Anxious to get back to Alex, are you?" Lisabeth asked, her tone flat, like someone who had checked out emotionally. "I think you need to be taught a lesson, Anne Gibson."

"A lesson? Really? On what, pray tell?" Anne struggled to keep her fear at bay and out of her voice. She couldn't let Lisabeth know she was frightened. She had to keep talking and putting on a brave front, and pray Alex was listening and had figured out where they were.

"On minding your own business. Nobody likes a busybody, Anne."

"No, Lisabeth, nobody likes a coward who tries to get attention by committing crimes. You need help."

Lisabeth's face twisted with rage.

Bam! Bam! Bam!

The knock startled Lisabeth. Anne took the opportunity to shove the woman against the mirror.

"Anne! Open the door!" Alex shouted.

She reached for the knob as Lisabeth screamed and rammed her. She barely got the lock turned before Lisabeth shoved her into the wall. Anne's hair fell from the French twist, cascading down to her shoulders.

"Lisabeth Matthews, you're under arrest," Michael's voice broke through the cloud of confusion as someone helped Anne to her feet.

"Are you okay?" Alex asked, cupping her face in his hands.

"I'm fine."

"Did she hurt you?" He kept running his hands up and down her arms and looking her over.

"I'm fine, Alex. More mad than anything."

He pulled her into a tight bear hug. "Don't scare me like that again," he whispered.

"It wasn't my intention to do that," Anne said with a shaky grin as Alex released her.

"Are you okay?" Grace pushed into the bathroom. "I just heard."

"Yes, I'm fine," Anne assured her friend.

"Michael's taking her to the station. Alex found him while you were talking to her. We heard the whole thing. She's busted for the vandalism but also now for attacking you. She won't be bothering anybody for some time," Josie said. "You sure you're okay?"

Anne nodded. "I promise. I'm fine. I just would like to go sit down and get a soft drink."

"Come on," Alex said, keeping his hand at the small of her back as he led her back to the table and pulled out the chair next to Mildred.

"Dear, are you—"

"I'm fine," Anne cut her off. "I promise, I'm fine."

"I'll go get you a soft drink. I'll be right back," Alex said.

Anne let Grace and Wendy and Mildred and everybody else fuss over her for a few minutes, until she'd had about all the fussing she could handle. "Guys, please. I'm fine. All the attention is really making me uneasy."

Wendy stared at her for a long moment, then nodded. "If you say you're fine, you're fine." She glanced around. "Where's my hubby? I want to dance." She winked at Anne.

"Well, I guess I should find Eli as well," Grace said, "if you're sure..."

"I'm sure. Go dance. You look way too pretty to be sitting here with me. Go."

Grace smiled and hurried off.

"Introverts do hate attention, good or bad," Mildred said.

Anne smiled her appreciation.

"Although, I should tell you that I thought Alex was going to rip the place apart when he got the call and couldn't figure out where you were," Mildred said.

"Really?" She probably shouldn't enjoy hearing this, but, considering what she'd just been through, she'd take the little pleasures.

Mildred nodded. "Oh yes, dear. At first he held the phone close to his ear and just got the strangest look on his face. But then he started asking all of us where you went. Wendy told him you'd gone to the ladies' room, so he had Grace and Wendy go searching for you. When they came out without you, I thought the man would come undone."

Now Anne felt bad. She didn't want anyone to worry about her, least of all Alex. He was already beating himself up.

Mildred squeezed her hand. "Remember what I said, Anne. Especially now, when his emotions are all over the place. Worry can make someone confused about their feelings." She let go of Anne's hand and stood. "So can fear." She turned and left.

Anne started to go after her, then realized why she'd left when Alex set a soft drink with ice on the table in front of her. He dropped into the seat Mildred had just vacated.

She took a sip of the cold drink, mulling over Mildred's wise words of advice.

"Do you feel okay? Would you like me to take you home?" Alex asked.

Anne chuckled. "I drove myself. Why on earth would I need you to take me home?"

Alex stared at her for another minute, then smiled and shook his head. "I'm sorry. I forgot I was talking to Wonder Woman."

"Who's always right, don't forget," Anne said with a smile.

"There is that."

Anne took another sip. Alex just staring at her was beginning to make her extremely uncomfortable. "Okay, you want to know what you can do for me?" she asked.

"What? Just say the word and I'll do it," Alex said.

Oh, he just might regret that. "I want you to dance with me."

Pure terror filled Alex's face. "You know I don't dance."

She laughed. "Come on," she said, standing up and tugging on his hand. "You said anything I wanted."

He sighed and got to his feet as she led him to the dance floor. And, as if on cue, the fast song currently playing faded into a slow song.

Alex pulled her close as the music's beat slowed.

Anne found her heartbeat quickening.

"You look beautiful tonight, in case I forgot to tell you earlier," Alex said, his voice low and husky.

"Thank you. I think you look quite handsome yourself." She kept her tone light. This was what Mildred had been trying to tell her. To warn her to take care.

Back in Alex's arms, moving together to a slow song in the dimly lit gym, it was almost like their senior prom.

Almost, but not quite. They weren't in high school. They were responsible adults, with three children involved. Alex was very special to her. He was part of her past—a great part of her past, and maybe, just maybe, one day would be part of her future. But for right now, in this time and place, he was one of her very best friends.

And that was just the way it should be.

For now.

About the Author

Emily Thomas is the pen name for a team of writers who have come together to create the series Secrets of the Blue Hill Library. *Lights! Camera! Action!* was written by Robin Caroll. Robin's passion has always been to tell stories to entertain others and come alongside them on their faith journey—aspects Robin weaves into each of her twenty-four published novels.

When she isn't writing, Robin spends quality time with her husband of twenty-five years, her three beautiful daughters and two handsome grandsons, and their character-filled pets at home.

Robin gives back to the writing community by serving as Executive Director for American Christian Fiction Writers. Her books have finaled/placed in such contests as the Carol Award, Holt Medallion, Daphne du Maurier, *Romantic Times'* Reviewer's Choice Award, Bookseller's Best, and Book of the Year.

As an avid reader, I love to connect with other readers. Visit me on my Web site robincaroll.com and sign up for my newsletter. You can connect with me on Facebook at facebook.com/robincaroll or write to me at PO Box 242091, Little Rock, Arkansas 72223.

A CONVERSATION WITH THE AUTHOR

Q. *In* Lights! Camera! Action! *we learn that Aunt Edie had a role in a vintage beach movie. If you had been cast in a vintage movie role, what movie would it be? What role would you play?*

A. I would have LOVED to play Katie Scarlett O'Hara in *Gone with the Wind*...just because I loved the character of Scarlett...and who wouldn't want to star opposite Clark Gable? I've watched the movie at least twenty times, even though my kids aren't fans of it...YET!

Q. *Who is your favorite leading man from a 1960s-era movie? Why?*

A. Hands down, Sean Connery. I loved *Dr. No*, and *From Russia With Love*, and *Goldfinger*...okay, I'll admit it, I'm a huge James Bond fan. When my husband and I went to Jamaica back in 1996, I was so thrilled to have seen where Ian Fleming was inspired.

Q. *Name one vintage movie you could watch over and over and over again.*

A. *The Good, the Bad, and the Ugly*...*Psycho*...*Once Upon a Time in the West*...*To Kill a Mockingbird*...*Cool Hand Luke*...*The Birds*...*My Fair Lady*...did I mention I'm a huge movie geek?

Q. *Do you see yourself as a small-town or big-city kind of gal?*

A. I'm definitely a big-city type of gal, mainly because it's easiest to blend in when you're in a big city. I find that I'm very much introverted, so enjoy being on my own a lot.

Q. *Who in Blue Hill is most like you? Why?*

A. I'd have to say Aunt Edie…mainly because she's not what people expect. I'm that way…I love boxing; I love Hallmark movies. I love college football (Go, SEC); I love scrapbooking. I've never really fit into the boxes people wanted to put me in. I've been told I'm quite the contradiction. I think Edie was like that…multifaceted. Yeah, I like that…I'm going to start calling myself multifaceted. LOL

Q. *Tell us one "claim to fame" about you or your family.*

A. Well…I'm related, by marriage, to one of the musicians who taught Elvis Presley to play the guitar on the *Louisiana Hayride*.

RECIPES FROM THE LIBRARY GUILD

Becca's Oooey-Gooey Butter Cake

1 box yellow cake mix
1 egg, slightly beaten
1 stick of butter, melted

Glaze
1 package eight-ounce cream
  cheese
1 sixteen-ounce box
  powdered sugar
2 eggs

Mix cake mix, egg, and butter. Press into nine-by-thirteen-inch ungreased pan. Bake thirty to forty minutes until lightly brown at 350 degrees.

For glaze, cream ingredients together and pour over dough.

From the Guideposts Archives

This article by Robert Osborne originally appeared in
Guideposts magazine.

Viewers of Turner Classic Movies (TCM), where I'm known for my introductions to classic films, often ask me when I became such a film fanatic. It's hard to answer. I honestly don't remember a time when I wasn't thinking about the movies.

Of course, in the time and place I grew up—Colfax, Washington, in the forties and fifties—everyone lived for the movies. It's often hard for people who didn't grow up in a place like Colfax, population 2,700, to understand just how central the town movie house was to the life of the community in those years.

The Rose Theater was Colfax's only movie house, except for a few brief months in summer when the Roxy opened up down the street from it to accommodate the inrush of seasonal farm workers. Whether I stepped through its doors from the blazing heat of a summer Saturday or on a chilly night in autumn with my mom and dad, the Rose wasn't just another building on Main Street. It was a doorway into another dimension.

The Rose was where I first saw Fred Astaire dance; where Clark Gable rescued Vivien Leigh from a burning Atlanta in *Gone with the Wind*; where Humphrey Bogart got the better of the Nazis in *Casablanca*; and where Gary Cooper stared down the bad guys in *High Noon*.

But thanks to the newsreels that played before each feature, the Rose was also where I saw the look in President Roosevelt's eye when he singled out December 7, 1941, as a day that would live in infamy; where I saw the *Queen Mary* steaming into the New York Harbor, and Allied troops marching victorious through the streets of Paris. From the wildest heights of fantasy to the darkest of realities, it all happened on that big white screen at the Rose.

Not that the screen was ever white for long. The lights never came up (that's why ushers always carried flashlights) and the action never stopped. Admission was only twenty-five cents. For that, you got the world.

The summer I turned twelve I landed my dream job — working at the Rose. I changed the posters in the glass cases out front and toted a box of plastic letters up a stepladder to change the titles on the marquee. That was more work than it might sound like because in those days the bill switched three times a week. The big studios cranked out films like hotcakes, and it was the job of small-town movie houses like the Rose to show them all.

After a year in charge of the marquee, I was bumped up to ushering by the Rose's owner, Mr. Weskel. I spent my next two years with a flashlight in hand, escorting people to their seats and cleaning up at the end of the day when the lights finally came on. That second part of the job was a lot easier than it is today because back then there was no concession stand, so no spilled popcorn or soda to worry about. After all, people didn't come to the movies to eat. Or talk! Television hadn't yet ruined people's manners in this regard. And, of course, there were no cell phones going off. The theater was almost a sacred place. No one would have thought of profaning it with food and chitchat.

When I turned fifteen, I made it to the top of the ladder: ticket taker. Ticket takers had it pretty good in a number of ways. There was more responsibility (we had to make sure all of the ushers were doing their jobs) and we got double pay if every seat were filled on a Saturday night.

But more than watching the movies, it was the audience's reaction to them that made me realize how important the movies were for a third reason beyond entertaining and educating, a reason that people sometimes forget about today: they inspired.

Throughout my young years in Colfax, the movie house was second only to church as a place to get your bearings — to find the strength to live, no matter what life threw at you, to set your moral compass. When war broke out in 1941, all across the country we saw the first chilling images of Japanese bombs exploding above Pearl Harbor in newsreels in our hometown movie houses.

But in those same movie houses just a few months later, we watched *Mrs. Miniver*, starring Greer Garson and Walter Pidgeon: a film about a British family coping with the realities of life in wartime. With bombs falling on their country every day, the Minivers somehow carried on. Life, with all its little everyday problems and joys, continued. Franklin D. Roosevelt himself credited the film with showing Americans that the outbreak of war didn't mean that it was the end of the world. Like the Minivers over in England, we too could make it through. The movie even came up in one of our church sermons about how Colfax could face the challenges ahead.

Courage, loyalty, perseverance…it was at the Rose that I learned what all those classic qualities really meant, and more besides. Maybe that's why I love my job at Turner Classic Movies as much as I do. For me, the movies I introduce each night aren't just wonderful entertainment. They're old friends: friends that did more than just show me, as a young boy in Colfax, what the world was like. They showed me how best to live in it.

Read on for a sneak peek of another exciting book
in Secrets of the Blue Hill Library!

Mum's the Word

Anne slathered a piece of wheat toast with strawberry jelly and took a quick bite as she walked toward the open doorway leading to the hall. "Hurry up, kids," she called out, "we don't want to be late for school."

To her chagrin, Anne had overslept this morning after forgetting to set her alarm clock last night. She'd been engrossed in a new mystery novel and had completely lost track of time, falling asleep well after midnight. Now, she, Ben, and Liddie were racing to get ready to head out the door. She'd fixed the kids a quick breakfast of cereal and toast, and then packed their lunches while they finished getting ready for school.

Anne popped the last bite of toast into her mouth as the kids entered the kitchen, each carrying a backpack. "Ready to go?"

"Yep," Ben said, slinging his backpack over one shoulder and heading toward the back door. Lately, her nine-year-old had been eager to get to school every morning so he'd have time to visit with Carter Pratt, a new boy in Ben's class who had moved from Chicago to Blue Hill with his family two weeks ago.

Liddie's brow wrinkled as she stood in the middle of the kitchen. "I think I forgot something, Mommy."

"What did you forget, honey?" Anne grabbed the five-year-old's pink jacket off the back of a kitchen chair and slipped it on her. They'd been enjoying warm weather these first few days of October, but today's forecast warned of thunderstorms this morning and falling temperatures later this afternoon.

"I don't know." A shadow of worry darkened Liddie's chocolate brown eyes. "But I think it's something important."

"It can't be that important if you don't remember," Ben said impatiently, waiting near the door. "Come on, we have to go!"

Anne reached out and placed a hand on Liddie's shoulder, gently steering her toward the door. "Don't worry, Liddie. I'm sure you'll remember eventually."

The kids walked out the door of their private family entrance and made their way to the silver Impala parked in the driveway.

"Wait!" Liddie shouted, coming to a stop. "I remember now!"

"What is it?" Anne asked her.

She spun on her heel and looked up at Anne. "I need a yellow hat, Mommy! A silly, yellow hat. We're learning about the color yellow."

Anne's heart sank. They were already running late for school, and she was due to open the library in an hour. "Are you sure you need a yellow hat today? Usually your teacher sends a note home about things like this."

"Yes," Liddie said with a resolute nod. "My teacher gave me a note, but I must have lost it."

Ben frowned at his sister. "How could you lose it?"

Liddie shrugged. "I don't know. I just did."

"Let's look in your backpack," Anne said, hoping this silly hat day was scheduled for next week. Two weeks ago, the kindergarten students had been asked to dress in all blue when they were learning that color.

Liddie handed over her backpack and Anne quickly sorted through it. At the very bottom, she found a school library book with a piece of paper sticking out of the top. She pulled the note out of the book and saw that it had been written by the school librarian, Francine Delaware.

Dear Parents,

We invite the kindergarten students to bring a yellow hat to school for our Friday afternoon library hour — the sillier the hat, the better! Please contact me if you have any questions.

Mrs. Delaware

Anne breathed a sigh of relief. "You don't need the hat until this afternoon. I'll find one and bring it to the school at lunchtime."

Liddie nodded. "Okay, but it has to be silly. And yellow."

"Got it," Anne said with a smile, wondering if she should try to make a hat out of craft paper or dig around in the attic for one. Aunt Edie had loved wearing hats, and Anne knew there were several stored up there, as well as a few in Liddie's bedroom, since she liked to play dress-up.

"Maybe you have a yellow hat in your toy box," Anne said as the three of them climbed into the car. She waited until the kids belted themselves into the backseat before she started the engine.

"No, I have a red one and a purple one and a pink one," Liddie told her. "No yellow."

Anne glanced at the rearview mirror as she backed out of her driveway onto Bluebell Lane, and saw Ben turn to his sister. "You have that Tweety Bird ski hat that you could wear," Ben suggested. "It's mostly yellow."

"That's right," Anne said, heading into Blue Hill. "You look so cute in that hat."

"That's a winter hat," Liddie said. "And it's not silly enough."

"Oh, it's pretty silly," Ben countered.

"But it has to be very silly," Liddie insisted. "And all yellow."

"Don't worry, I'll figure something out," Anne said, happy that this small crisis could be solved so easily. If Aunt Edie didn't have a yellow hat, Anne could fashion one out of paper. She'd stocked up on construction paper for crafts in the Children's Room of the library and knew she had plenty of yellow among the rainbow of colors.

After she dropped off the kids at Blue Hill Elementary School, Anne returned home and headed up to the attic, one flight above their third-floor family bedrooms. She switched on the attic light, figuring she had just enough time to sort through Aunt Edie's old hats before the library was due to open. If she couldn't find a yellow hat, then she'd grab some yellow paper and craft supplies to take down to the first floor and fashion a hat in between assisting patrons.

Bella Miller was scheduled to come into work at eleven this morning, which would give Anne plenty of time to make a trip to the elementary school to deliver the hat to Liddie.

As she made her way through the maze of boxes, trunks, and crates in the cavernous attic, Anne began to hum the tune for "This Little Light of Mine," which Liddie had sung during her bath last evening. She knew some of Aunt Edie's old dresses and hats were stored in trunks near the northwest corner of the attic. Judging by the cobwebs in her path, Anne hadn't ventured this far into the attic for a while. She waved her hand in front of her as the path grew a little dimmer. Gray clouds filled the sky, leaving little sunlight to shine in through the leaded attic windows.

Someday she'd have to ask Alex to rewire the attic and add a few more lights, Anne told herself as she reached the first trunk. She opened the lid and knelt down to sort through the clothes inside. They were neatly folded and she did her best to keep them that way as she searched through the trunk for some hats. But there were only dresses from the forties and fifties, along with some old boots and shoes.

A boom of thunder sounded directly above the house, shaking the walls in the attic and making Anne jump. She took a deep breath as she closed the lid, her heart pounding. Her gaze moved to the closest window and she saw lightning flicker across the sky. "Looks like the forecast was right," she murmured as she moved to another trunk.

When she opened the lid, she was thrilled to see that it was filled with hatboxes. She took the first one out and opened the lid, finding a chic black hat with lace netting in the front and small red roses on the brim. "Very nice," she murmured, replacing the lid, "but not yellow."

She opened more boxes, finding a dove gray hat in one and a purple hat in the other. Only three boxes remained in the trunk. She pulled them all out and opened the first one in front of her. This one contained a green hat with a jaunty arrangement of yellow and green feathers. Anne smiled, trying to imagine where Aunt Edie would have worn such a hat. She even tried it on as another crack of thunder sounded. This time the lights flickered.

"No time for play," she murmured, quickly removing the hat and moving onto the next box. She lifted the lid and emitted a gasp of delight when she saw the yellow hat inside. She lifted the frilly silk and lace pillbox hat out of the box. A white silk flower adorned one side.

Remembering Liddie's insistence that the hat had to be entirely yellow, she glanced at the yellow feathers on the green hat. She might be able to replace the white silk flower with the yellow feathers. She examined the hat in her hands, determining that the white flower would be easy enough to remove. Then it was simply a matter of adding the feathers and arranging them among the yellow lace.

Raindrops hammered the roof above her and the room grew even dimmer. She looked toward the closest window and saw a misty fog obscuring the view.

Anne set the yellow hat back into the box and replaced the lid, then stacked it on top of the box containing the green hat with the yellow feathers. She'd take them both downstairs with her and begin the alterations after opening the library. She smiled to herself, picturing how silly *and* adorable Liddie would look wearing the yellow pillbox hat.

Her gaze moved to the last hatbox in the trunk and curiosity made her lift the lid, just in case another yellow hat lay inside. But to her surprise, there was no hat in this box. Instead, she found an exotic scarf woven with bright red and orange threads. When she reached out to pick it up, her fingertips felt something solid underneath it. She carefully unwrapped the scarf from the object and found a piece of old pottery in the shape of a clay pot. A *very old* clay pot, judging by the color and shape.

It was reddish brown in color, with some decorative sketching along the upper rim. It stood about a foot tall and four inches wide at the base. The mouth of the pot was a little wider, the top rim slightly curled and smooth.

This clay pot was like nothing Anne had ever seen before. Neither was the scarf, which had a few faded spots on it but was otherwise in good condition. She picked up the now-empty hatbox and tilted it toward the light, noticing for the first time a small piece of ivory paper at the bottom. She picked up the small square of paper and turned it over to see Aunt Edie's familiar handwriting on the other side.

"'Egyptian clay pot'," Anne read out loud, "'that I unearthed at an archaeological site near the palaces of Armana. Crafted during the late eighteenth dynasty (c. 1350 BC) for the Pharaoh Akhenaten. Egyptian scarf purchased at Luxor, crafted in the early twentieth century.'"

"Wow," Anne said out loud, her gaze turning back to the pot. She smoothed one palm over the surface, amazed by how soft and smooth it felt. It wasn't just old, it was an ancient artifact. Her aunt had been something of an adventurer and had traveled all over the world, but Anne didn't remember ever seeing this clay pot before.

She carefully wrapped it in the scarf once more and then placed it, along with Aunt Edie's note, back in the box. She'd take it downstairs as well, eager to examine it more closely.

After closing the trunk, she picked up all three boxes, stacking them carefully on top of each other and then headed for the door. Another boom of thunder rattled the windowpanes, and the lights flickered for a moment before going out. The attic was now blanketed in darkness, with only a sliver of misty gray light coming through the windows.

Anne slowed her step, barely able to see the narrow path in front of her. She hoped the electricity wouldn't be out long, but she had a contingency plan in mind. She'd light some candles and retrieve some of the old lanterns from the basement to illuminate the library so she and the patrons wouldn't be wandering around in the dark.

As she turned another corner, her knee smacked hard into the brass corner of a trunk.

"Ow," Anne cried out loud, her knee throbbing at the sudden impact. The hatboxes teetered in her arms, but she steadied them. Then she took a few deep, gasping breaths until the sharp pain in her knee began to fade into a dull, throbbing ache.

Finally able to walk again, Anne maneuvered her way through the cluttered attic until she reached the door. At that moment, the electricity came on again, lighting the stairway in front of her. She walked down to the second floor and carried the boxes into the family kitchen, setting them on the table.

Then she bent down and gingerly touched her knee with her fingertips. She couldn't see any bruise beneath the khaki slacks she wore, but her knee felt a little tender. A quick glance at the clock told her that she didn't have time to nurse it now.

She grabbed the boxes once more and carried them down to the first floor, trying to ignore the ache in her knee. At least the lights were back on and she'd found a fun yellow hat for Liddie.

Best of all, she'd discovered an ancient Egyptian artifact that would make a wonderful display in the History Room of the library.

It was going to be a good day.

* * *

"There," Anne said, stepping back to admire her handiwork. She'd been working on the Egyptian display in the History Room for the last half hour, ever since Bella had arrived to work the checkout desk.

"That looks wonderful," Betty Bultman said, standing beside her. "I've always wanted to visit Egypt."

"So have I," Anne said. "Ever since I started reading Elizabeth Peters's mysteries set in Egypt." Anne had placed her favorite Peters novel, *Crocodile on the Sandbank*, in the display, along with two travel books about Egypt and a nonfiction book about the Great Pyramids. She'd also arranged the woven scarf around the display before adding the ancient clay pot in the center.

Anne walked over to adjust the scarf, her sore knee making her limp a little.

"Are you all right?" Betty asked, her brow furrowing with concern.

"Oh, I'm fine." Anne smiled. "I bumped my knee earlier while I was in the attic."

"Ouch," Betty commiserated as she began browsing the books on the shelf in front of her. "Maybe you should put some ice on it."

"That's a good idea," Anne agreed, planning to do so after lunch. But first she had an errand to run.

Bella looked up as Anne approached her. "I just saw a great hat in the kitchen. Is it yours?"

Anne smiled. She'd successfully replaced the white silk flower with the yellow feathers, just by using a little glue and adjusting the yellow lace on the hat. She'd left it drying on the old kitchen counter. "It belonged to Aunt Edie, but Liddie needs it for school today."

"It must be silly hat day," Bella said. "Mrs. Delaware always made library hour fun."

"It is," Anne said, her smile widening. "I told Liddie I'd have the hat to her by lunchtime, so I need to run to the school. Do you mind watching the library while I'm gone?"

"Not at all."

The thunderstorm had kept the library empty for most of the morning, but the sun was shining once more so Anne expected a busier afternoon ahead.

"Thanks," Anne told Bella as she headed toward the kitchen door, "I shouldn't be gone long."

Anne walked into the first-floor kitchen and retrieved the hat from the counter. She carefully checked the yellow feathers, pleased to find all of them securely attached. The pair of bobby pins Anne had retrieved from her bedroom earlier would keep the hat from falling off of Liddie's small head. She couldn't wait to see the expression on her daughter's face when she saw the hat.

Turning around, Anne pulled the car keys out of her pocket and headed for the back door.

A high-pitched scream tore through the air, followed by a loud thump.

Anne froze for a moment, startled by the sound. It had come from inside the library. She tossed her keys and the hat onto the kitchen table, ignoring the pain in her knee as she ran toward the door leading into the library. Bella wasn't at the checkout desk anymore, but Anne could hear voices in the adjacent History Room. She raced to the open doorway and then stopped, shocked to see Mildred Farley sprawled on the floor.

The seventy-three-year-old woman lay on her back in her navy blue pantsuit, one foot twisted underneath her. Anne's gaze moved to Mildred's face, which was ghostly pale. But Mildred's eyelids fluttered as Bella and Betty knelt on either side of her, softly calling her name.

Anne hurried over to Mildred's side and knelt beside Bella, who scooted out of the way so that Anne could lean closer and talk to Aunt Edie's oldest and dearest friend. "Mildred, are you all right?"

Mildred didn't say anything, just emitted a slight moan.

Anne looked over at Betty. "What happened?"

"I don't know," Betty replied. "I was in the next room, checking out with Bella, when we both heard the scream and the fall."

Anne turned her attention back to Mildred, wondering if she should call an ambulance. She gently picked up Mildred's thin right wrist and felt for her pulse. It was fast, but strong. "Mildred? Mildred, can you hear me?"

After a moment, Mildred's eyes fluttered open. "Yes, dear, I can hear you."

"What happened?" Anne asked, now holding Mildred's hand in her own. The skin was cold and clammy. "Are you all right?"

"No," Mildred said, her gray eyes wider now and filled with fear. "No, I'm not all right. In fact, we're all in terrible danger!"

A Note from the Editors

We hope you enjoy Secrets of the Blue Hill Library, created by the Books and Inspirational Media Division of Guideposts, a nonprofit organization that touches millions of lives every day through products and services that inspire, encourage, help you grow in your faith, and celebrate God's love in every aspect of your daily life.

Thank you for making a difference with your purchase of this book, which helps fund our many outreach programs to military personnel, prisons, hospitals, nursing homes, and educational institutions. To learn more, visit GuidepostsFoundation.org.

We also maintain many useful and uplifting online resources. Visit Guideposts.org to read true stories of hope and inspiration, access OurPrayer network, sign up for free newsletters, download free e-books, join our Facebook community, and follow our stimulating blogs.

To learn about other Guideposts publications, including the best-selling devotional *Daily Guideposts*, go to ShopGuideposts .org, call (800) 932-2145, or write to Guideposts, PO Box 5815, Harlan, Iowa 51593.